Praise for Ja...

'Janet Evanovich's characters are ecc... an... ...ted, the violence often surreal a... pl... ...y s... ... ...e produces ... many laughs as anyone writing crime today ...e *Times*

'Evanovich's series of New Jersey comedy thrillers are among the great joys of contemporary crime fiction . . . all the easy class and wit that you expect to find in the best American TV comedy, but too rarely find in modern fiction' *GQ*

'Stephanie Plum in ass-kicking form . . . utterly delightful' *Cosmopolitan*

'The pace never flags, the humour is grandly surreal, and the dialogue fairly sizzles off the page' *Irish Times*

'As smart and sassy as high-gloss wet paint' *Time Out*

'A classic screwball comedy that is also a genuinely taut thriller' *Daily Mail*

'Reads like the screen-play for a 1930s screwball comedy: fast, funny and furious . . . The rollicking plot . . . keeps the reader breathless' *Publishers Weekly*

'An engaging mix of slapstick, steam, and suspense' *People*

'Non-stop laughs with plenty of high jinks' *USA Today*

'Undeniably funny' *Scotsman*

'Romantic and gripping, this ... *Housekeeping*

'Janet Evanovich's madcap ... farce' *New York Times Book ...*

# Lean Mean Thirteen

# Janet Evanovich

**headline**
review

First published in Great Britain in 2007
by HEADLINE REVIEW
An imprint of HEADLINE PUBLISHING GROUP

First published in paperback in Great Britain in 2008
by HEADLINE REVIEW

1

ISBN 978 0 7553 3759 0 (B-format)
ISBN 978 0 7553 3758 3 (A-format)

Typeset in New Caledonia by Avon DataSet Ltd,
Bidford on Avon, Warwickshire

Printed and bound in Great Britain by
Mackays of Chatham plc, Chatham, Kent

Headline's policy is to use papers that are natural, renewable and
recyclable products and made from wood grown in sustainable forests.
The logging and manufacturing processes are expected to conform
to the environmental regulations of the country of origin.

HEADLINE PUBLISHING GROUP
An Hachette Livre UK Company
338 Euston Road
London NW1 3BH

www.headline.co.uk
www.hachettelivre.co.uk

Thanks to Sara Parker
for suggesting the title for this book.

Hugs and thank yous to my fabulous editor
– SuperJen Enderlin.

# One

For the last five minutes, I'd been parked outside my cousin Vinnie's bail bonds office in my crapolla car, debating whether to continue on with my day, or return to my apartment and crawl back into bed. My name is Stephanie Plum, and Sensible Stephanie wanted to go back to bed. Loco Stephanie was thinking she should get on with it.

I was about to do something I knew I shouldn't do. The signs were all there in front of me. Sick stomach. Feeling of impending disaster. Knowledge that it was illegal. And yet, I was going to forge ahead with the plan. Not that this was especially unusual. Truth is, I've been dealing with impending doom for as long as I can remember. Heck, when I was six years old I sprinkled sugar on my head, convinced myself it was pixie dust, wished myself invisible, and walked into the boys' bathroom at school. I mean, you don't know the water's over your head until you jump in, right?

The door to the bonds office opened, and Lula stuck her head out. 'Are you gonna sit there all day, or what?' she yelled at me.

Lula is a black woman with a Rubensesque body and a Vegas wardrobe that's four sizes too small. She is a former 'ho, currently working as a file clerk for the office and a wheelman for me . . . when the mood strikes. Today, she was wearing big fake-fur Sasquatch boots, and her ass was packed into poison-green Spandex pants. Her pink sweatshirt had *Love Goddess* spelled out in sequins across her boobs.

My wardrobe runs a lot more casual than Lula's. I was wearing jeans and a long-sleeved knit shirt from the Gap. My feet were stuffed into knock-off Ugg boots, and I was bundled into a big quilted jacket. I have naturally curly brown hair that looks okay when I wear it shoulder length. When it's short, the best you can say is that it has energy. I'd swiped on some extra mascara today, hoping to boost my bravado. I had a favor to perform that I suspected was going to come back to haunt me. I grabbed my bag, wrenched the driver-side door open, and angled myself out of the car.

It was the end of February, and there was gloom as

far as the eye could see. It was almost ten a.m., but the street lights were on, and visibility in the swirling snow was about six inches. A truck chugged past, throwing slush halfway up my leg, soaking my jeans, bringing out my trash mouth. Winter wonderland Jersey-style.

Connie Rosolli looked around her computer at me when I walked into the office. Connie is Vinnie's office manager and his first line of defense against the stream of pissed-off bondees, bookies, hookers, various bill collectors, and stiffed smut peddlers hoping to reach Vinnie's inner sanctum. Connie was a couple years older than me, a couple pounds heavier, a couple inches shorter, a couple cups bigger, and had hair a couple inches higher than mine. Connie was pretty in a kick-ass, central Jersey, third-generation Italian kind of way.

'I have three new skips,' Connie said. 'One of them is Simon Diggery again.'

Skips are people who fail to show for a court appearance after Vinnie has bonded them out of jail. Vinnie loses money when bondees fail to appear, so that's where I come in. I work for Vinnie as a fugitive apprehension agent, better known as bounty hunter, and my job is to find the skips and drag them back into the system.

'Don't look to me to help you out with Simon Diggery,' Lula said, plunking herself down on the brown Naugahyde couch, picking up her copy of *Star* magazine. 'Been there, done that. Not doing it again. No way.'

'He's an easy catch,' I said. 'We know exactly where to find him.'

'There's no "we" gonna happen. You're on your own. I'm not freezing my sweet Jesus, sitting in some bone orchard in the dead of night, waiting for Simon Diggery to show up.'

Diggery was, among other things, a professional grave robber, relieving the recently deceased of rings, watches, and the occasional Brooks Brothers suit if it was Diggery's size. Last time Diggery was in violation of his bond, Lula and I caught him hack-sawing a cocktail ring off Miriam Lukach. We chased him all over the cemetery before I tackled him in front of the crematorium.

I took the three new files from Connie and shoved them into my shoulder bag. 'I'm off.'

'Where you going?' Lula wanted to know. 'It's almost lunchtime. I don't suppose you're gonna be passing by some place I could get a meatball sub. I could use a meatball sub on a nasty day like this.'

4

'I'm going downtown,' I told her. 'I need to talk to Dickie.'

'Say what?' Lula was up on her feet. 'Did I hear you right? Is this the Dickie that called the police on you last time you were in his office? Is this the Dickie you told to go fuck hisself? Is this the Dickie you were married to for fifteen minutes in another life?'

'Yep. That's the Dickie.'

Lula grabbed her coat and scarf from the chair. 'I'll ride with you. I gotta see this. Hell, I don't even care about the meatball sub anymore.'

'Okay, but we're not making a scene,' I said to Lula. 'I need to talk to Dickie about a legal issue. This is going to be non-confrontational.'

'I know that. Non-confrontational. Like two civilized people.'

'Hold on. I'm going too,' Connie said, getting her purse from her bottom desk drawer. 'I don't want to miss this. I'll close the office for a couple hours for this one.'

'I'm not making a scene,' I told her.

'Sure, but I'm packin' just in case it gets ugly,' Connie said.

'Me too,' Lula said. 'It isn't diamonds that's a girl's best friend. It's a .9mm Glock.'

Connie and Lula looked at me.

'What are *you* carrying?' Connie asked.

'A brand-new can of hairspray and this lip gloss I've got on.'

'It's a pretty good lip gloss,' Lula said, 'but it wouldn't hurt to have a piece as a backup.'

Connie stuffed herself into her coat. 'I can't imagine what legal problem you'd want to discuss with Dickie, but it must be a bitch to get you out in this weather.'

'It's sort of personal,' I said, relying on the one really decent bounty hunter skill I possessed . . . the ability to fib. 'It dates back to when we were married. It has to do with . . . taxes.'

We all went head-down into the cold. Connie locked the office door, and we got into Lula's red Firebird. Lula cranked the engine over, hip-hop blasted out of the CD player, and Lula motored off.

'Is Dickie still downtown?' Lula wanted to know.

'Yes, but he's in a new office. 3240 Brian Place. His firm is Petiak, Smullen, Gorvich, and Orr.'

Lula cruised down Hamilton and turned onto North Broad. The wind had cut back, and it was no longer snowing, but there was still a thick cloud cover overhead. At best, the weather could now be described as grim. I was silently rehearsing my fake speech about how I needed information for an audit.

And I was making promises to myself as performance incentive. I was seeing macaroni and cheese in my near future. Butterscotch Tastykakes. Onion rings. Snickers bars. Okay, so this had all the makings of a cluster fuck, but there was a Dairy Queen Oreo Cheese-Quake Blizzard waiting for me somewhere.

Lula took a left at Brian and found a parking place half a block from Dickie's office building.

'I'm gonna smack you on the head if you don't stop cracking your knuckles,' Lula said to me. 'You gotta chill. You need some tax information, and he's gotta give it to you.' Lula cut her eyes to me. 'That's all there is to it, right?'

'Pretty much.'

'Uh oh,' Lula said. 'There's more, isn't there?'

We all got out of the Firebird and stood huddled against the cold.

'Actually, I have to plant a couple bugs on him for Ranger,' I told Lula. There it was, out in the open, swinging in the breeze . . . the favor from hell.

Carlos Manoso goes by the street name Ranger. He's my friend, my bounty hunter mentor, and in this case . . . my partner in crime. He's Cuban American with dark skin and dark eyes and dark brown hair recently cut short. He's half a head taller than I am, and two months older. I've seen him naked, and when I say *every* part of him is perfect you can take it to the bank. He was Special Forces, and while he's no longer military, he's still got the skills and the muscle. He owns a security company named RangeMan now. Plus, he does the high-bond skips for Vinnie. He's a hot guy, and there are strong feelings between us, but I try to keep some distance. Ranger plays by his own set of rules, and I don't have a complete copy.

'I knew it!' Lula said. 'I knew this would be good.'

'You need something better than taxes,' Connie said. 'You're going to need a diversion if you want to plant bugs.'

'Yeah,' Lula said. 'You need us to go along with you. You need some hustle and bustle.'

'How about if we say we want to start a business together,' Connie said. 'And we need advice on permits and partnership agreements.'

'What kind of business we got?' Lula asked. 'I gotta know what I'm getting into with you.'

'It's not a real business,' Connie said. 'We're just pretending.'

'I still gotta know,' Lula said. 'I'm not putting my good name on just any old thing.'

'For crissake,' Connie said, flapping her arms and

stamping her feet to keep warm. 'It could be anything. We could cater parties.'

'Yeah, that's believable,' Lula said. 'On account of we're all such gourmet cooks. The only time I turn my oven on is to heat up my apartment. And Stephanie probably don't even know where her oven is.'

'Okay, how about a dry cleaner, or chauffeured limos, or dog walking – or we could buy a shrimp boat?' Connie offered.

'I like the limo idea,' Lula said. 'We could buy a Lincoln and dress up in bad-ass uniforms. Something with some bling.'

'It's okay with me,' Connie said.

I nodded and pulled my scarf up over my nose. 'Me too. Let's go inside. I'm freezing.'

'Wait,' Lula said. 'We need a name. You can't have a limo company without a name.'

'Lucky Limos,' Connie said.

'The hell,' Lula said. 'I'm not joining up with a limo company's got a lame name like that.'

'Then *you* name it,' Connie said to Lula. 'I don't give a fig what the friggin' company is called. My feet are numb.'

'It should be something that reflects on us,' Lula said. 'Like The Bitches Limos.'

'That's a stupid name. No one's going to hire a limo from a company with a name like that,' Connie said.

'I know some people,' Lula said.

'Lovely Limos, Lonely Limos, Loser Limos, Lumpy Limos, Looney Limos, La De Da Limos, Limos for Liars, Lampshade Limos, Landfill Limos, Leaky Limos, Lemon Limos, Long Limos, Large Limos, Lazy Limos, Loosey Goosey Limos,' I said.

Connie looked at me and grimaced.

'Maybe it should be called Lula's Limos,' I said.

'Yeah, that got a ring to it,' Lula said.

'Then it's a deal. Lula's Limos.'

'Deal,' Connie said. 'Get out of my way, so I can get inside and defrost.'

We all pushed through the front door to Dickie's building and stood in the foyer, sopping up the sudden blast of heat. The foyer opened to a reception area, and I was relieved to see an unfamiliar face behind the desk. If anyone had recognized me from my last visit, they would have immediately called for security.

'Let me do the talking,' I said to Lula.

'Sure,' Lula said. 'I'll be quiet as a mouse. I'll zip my lip.'

I approached the desk and made an attempt

at demure. 'We'd like to see Mr Orr,' I told the woman.

'Do you have an appointment?'

'No,' I said. 'I'm terribly sorry to drop in like this, but we're starting a new business, and we need some legal advice. We were down the street looking at real estate and thought we'd take a chance that Mr Orr might have a moment for us.'

'Of course,' the woman said. 'Let me see if he's available. The name?'

'Capital City Limos.'

'Hunh,' Lula said behind me.

The woman buzzed Dickie and relayed our information. She got off the phone and smiled. 'He has a few minutes between appointments. You can take the elevator to your left. Second floor.'

We all moved into the elevator, and I pushed the button for the second floor.

'What was that?' Lula wanted to know. 'Capital City Limos?'

'It just popped out, but it sounds classy, right?'

'Not as classy as Lula's Limos,' Lula said. 'I'd call Lula's Limos any day of the week over Capital City Limos. Capital City Limos sounds like it got a stick up its ass, but you'd be in for a good time in Lula's Limos.'

The door opened, and we spilled out of the elevator into another reception room with another new face at the desk.

'Mr Orr is expecting you,' the woman said. 'His office is at the end of the corridor.'

I led the parade in a sedate march to Dickie's office. I got to his open door and rapped lightly. I peeked in and smiled. Friendly. Non-threatening.

Dickie looked up and gasped.

He'd put on a few pounds since the last time I saw him. His brown hair was thinning at the top, and he was wearing glasses. He was dressed in a white shirt, red and blue striped tie, and dark blue suit. I'd thought he was handsome when I married him, and he was still a nice-looking guy, in a corporate sort of way. But he felt soft compared to Joe Morelli and Ranger, the two men who were currently in my life. Dickie lacked the heat and raw male energy that surrounded Morelli and Ranger. And of course, I now knew Dickie was an asshole.

'No need for alarm,' I said calmly. 'I'm here as a client. I needed a lawyer, and I thought of you.'

'Lucky me,' Dickie said.

I felt my eyes involuntarily narrow and did some mental deep breathing.

'Lula and Connie and I are thinking about starting a limo service,' I said to Dickie.

'You bet your ass,' Lula said. 'Lula's Limos.'

'And?' Dickie said.

'We don't know anything about starting a business,' I said. 'Do we need some sort of partnership agreement? Do we need a business license? Should we incorporate?'

Dickie slid a piece of paper across his desk. 'Here are the law firm rates for services.'

'Wow,' I said, looking at the rates. 'This is a lot of money. I don't know if we can afford you.'

'Again, lucky me.'

I felt my blood pressure edge up a notch. I planted my hands on my hips and glared down at him. 'Am I to assume you would rather not have us as clients?'

'Let me think about that for a nanosecond,' Dickie said. 'Yes! Last time you were in my office you tried to kill me.'

'That's an exaggeration. Maim you, yes. Kill you, probably not.'

'Let me give you some free advice,' Dickie said. 'Keep your day jobs. The three of you in business will be a disaster, and if you last long enough to go into menopause as business partners, you'll turn into cannibals.'

'Did I just get insulted?' Lula asked.

Okay, so he's a jerk, I said to myself. That doesn't change the mission. You have to keep your eye on the prize. You need to be cordial and find a way to plant the bugs. Hard to do when Dickie was in his chair behind the desk, and I was standing in front of it.

'You're probably right,' I said to Dickie. I looked around and moved to the mahogany shelves that lined one wall. Law books interspersed with personal flotsam. Photographs, awards, a couple carved-wood ducks, some art glass. 'You have a wonderful office,' I told him. I went from photograph to photograph. A picture of Dickie with his brother. A picture of Dickie with his parents. A picture of Dickie with his grandparents. A picture of Dickie graduating from college. A picture of Dickie on some ski slope. No pictures of Dickie's ex-wife.

I'd inched my way along his wall, and I was now slightly behind him. I cleverly turned to admire the handsome desk set . . . and that was when I saw it. A picture of Dickie and Joyce Barnhardt. Dickie had his arm around Joyce, and they were laughing. And I knew it was recent because Dickie's forehead was unusually high in the photograph.

I sucked in some air and told myself to stay calm,

14

but I could feel pressure building in my fingertips, and I worried my scalp might be on fire.

'Uh oh,' Lula said, watching me.

'Is that J-J-Joyce?' I asked Dickie.

'Yeah,' Dickie said. 'We've reconnected. I had a thing with her a bunch of years ago, and I guess I never got over the attraction.'

'I know exactly how many years ago. I caught you porking that pig on *my* dining-room table fifteen minutes before I filed for divorce, you scum-sucking, dog-fucking lump of goose shit.'

Joyce Barnhardt had been a fat, buck-toothed, sneaky little kid who spread rumors, picked at emotional wounds, spit on my dessert at lunchtime, and made my school years a nightmare. By the time she was twenty, the fat had all gone to the right places. She dyed her hair red, had her breasts enlarged and her lips plumped, and she set out on her chosen career of home wrecker and gold digger. Looking back on it all, I had to admit Joyce had done me a favor by being the catalyst to get me out of my marriage to Dickie. That didn't alter the fact that Joyce will never be my favorite person, though.

'That's right,' Dickie said. 'Now I remember. I thought I could finish up before you got home, but you came home early.'

And next thing, Dickie was on the floor, my hands around his neck. He was yelling as best he could, considering I was choking him, and Lula and Connie were in the mix. By the time Lula and Connie wrestled me off him, the room was filled with clerical staff.

Dickie dragged himself up and looked at me wild-eyed. 'You're all witnesses,' he said to the roomful of people. 'She tried to kill me. She's insane. She should be locked up in a looney bin. Call the police. Call animal control. Call my lawyer. I want a restraining order.'

'You deserve Joyce,' I said to Dickie. 'What you *don't* deserve is this desk clock. It was a wedding present from my Aunt Tootsie.' And I took the clock, turned on my heel, tipped my nose up ever so slightly, and flounced out of his office, Connie and Lula at my heels.

Dickie scrambled after me. 'Give me that clock! That's *my* clock!'

Lula whipped out her Glock and pointed it at Dickie's nose. 'Were you paying attention? Her Aunt Tootsie gave her that clock. Now get your little runt ass back in your office and close the door before I put a big hole in your head.'

We took the stairs for fear the elevator might be too

slow, barreled out the front door and speed-walked down the block before the police could show up and haul me off to the clink. I saw the shiny black SUV parked across the street. Tinted windows. Motor running. I paused and gave the car a thumbs-up, and the lights flashed at me. Ranger was listening to the bugs I'd just left in Dickie's pockets.

We rammed ourselves into Lula's Firebird, and Lula rocketed the car away from the curb.

'I swear, I thought you were gonna burst into flames when you saw that picture of Dickhead and Joyce,' Lula said. 'It was like you had those glowing demon eyes you see in horror movies. I thought your head was gonna rotate.'

'Yeah, but then a calm came over me,' I said. 'And I saw I had a chance to plant the bugs in Dickie's pockets.'

'The calm must have come while you were squeezing his neck and banging his head against the floor,' Connie said.

I blew out a sigh. 'Yep. That was about the time.'

We had food spread all over Connie's desk. Meatball subs in wax paper wrappers, a big tub of coleslaw, potato chips, pickles, and diet sodas.

'This was a good idea,' I said to Lula. 'I was starved.'

'Guess going apeshit makes you hungry,' Lula said. 'What's up next?'

'I thought I'd do some phone work on Simon Diggery. Maybe I can get a lead on him that'll take me someplace other than a graveyard.'

Diggery was a wiry little guy in his early fifties. His brown hair was shot with gray and tied back in a ponytail. His skin looked like old leather. And he had arms like Popeye from years of hauling dirt. Most often, he worked alone, but on occasion he could be seen walking the streets at two in the morning with his brother Melvin, shovels on their shoulders like Army rifles.

'You're not going to get anywhere with phone calls,' Lula said. 'Those Diggerys are wily.'

I pulled a previous file on Diggery and copied phone numbers and places of employment. In the past, Diggery had delivered pizzas, bagged groceries, pumped gas, and cleaned kennel cages.

'It's a place to start,' I said to Lula. 'Better than knocking on their doors.'

The Diggerys all lived together in a raggedy double-wide in Bordentown. Simon, Melvin, Melvin's wife, Melvin's six kids, Melvin's pet python, and Uncle Bill

Diggery. If you knocked on the door to the double-wide, you'd only find the python. The Diggerys were like feral cats. They scattered into the woods behind their home the minute a car stopped in the driveway.

When the weather was especially bad and the ground was frozen, grave robbing was slow work and Simon would sometimes take odd jobs. I was hoping to catch him at one of those jobs. Since the jobs were random, the only way to learn of them was to trick a family member or neighbor into giving Simon up.

'What's the charge this time?' Lula asked.

I paged through the file. 'Drunk and disorderly, destruction of private property, attempted assault.'

Everyone knew Diggery was Trenton's premier grave robber, but his arrests were seldom associated with desecration of the dead. He was most often arrested for disorderly conduct and assault. When Simon Diggery got drunk, he swung a mean shovel.

I gathered my information together and stuffed it into my bag along with the clock. 'I'm working at home for the rest of the day.'

'I feel like working at home until July,' Lula said. 'I'm fed up with this weather.'

I'd just gotten into my car when my mom called on my cell.

19

'Where are you?' she wanted to know. 'Are you at the bail bonds office?'

'I was just leaving.'

'I was wondering if you would stop at Giovichinni's for me on your way home. Your father is out in the taxi all day, and my car won't start. I think I need a new battery. I want a half-pound of liverwurst, a half-pound of ham, a half-pound of olive loaf, and a half-pound of turkey. Then you can get me some Swiss cheese and some good rye. And a rump roast. And get an Entenmann's. Your grandmother likes the raspberry coffee cake.'

'Sure,' I said. 'I'm on my way.'

The bail bonds office sits with its back to downtown Trenton and its front to a small ethnic neighborhood known as the Burg. I was born and raised in the Burg, and while I now live outside Burg limits, I'm still tethered to it by family and history. Once a Burgerbit, always a Burgerbit. Giovichinni's is a small family-owned deli a short distance down on Hamilton, and it's the Burg deli of choice. It's also a hotbed of gossip, and I was certain news of my rampage was circulating through every corner of the Burg, including Giovichinni's.

I was currently driving a burgundy Crown Vic that

used to be a cop car. I'd needed a car fast, and this was the only car I could afford at Crazy Iggy's Used Car Emporium. I promised myself the Vic was temporary, put it in gear, and motored to Giovichinni's.

I hurried through the store, head down, all business, hoping no one would mention Dickie. I walked away from the butcher unscathed, rushed past Mrs Landau and Mrs Ruiz without saying hello, and I stood in line at the checkout behind Mrs Martinelli. Thank goodness, she didn't speak English. I looked past Mrs Martinelli and knew my luck had run out. Lucy Giovichinni was at the register.

'I hear you trashed your ex's office this morning,' Lucy said, checking my groceries. 'Is it true you threatened to kill him?'

'No! I was there with Lula and Connie. We had some legal issues we wanted to run by him. Honestly, I don't know how these rumors get started.'

And this was only the beginning. I could see it coming. This was going to turn into a disaster of biblical proportions.

I carried my bags to the Vic, loaded them into the trunk along with Aunt Tootsie's desk clock, and got behind the wheel. By the time I reached my parents' house, sleet was slanting onto the windshield. I parked in the driveway and dragged the bags to the front door, where my Grandma Mazur was waiting.

Grandma Mazur came to live with my parents when my Grandpa Mazur bypassed the FDA and took his transfat needs to a higher authority.

'Did you get the coffee cake?' Grandma asked.

'Yep. I got the coffee cake.' I slid past her and carried everything to the kitchen, where my mother was ironing.

'How long has she been ironing?' I asked Grandma.

'She's been at it for about twenty minutes. Ever since the call came in about you sending Dickie to the hospital and then eluding the police.'

My mother ironed when she was stressed. Sometimes she ironed the same shirt for hours.

'I didn't send Dickie to the hospital. And there were no police involved.' At least none that I ran across. 'Lula and Connie and I went to Dickie for some legal advice and somehow these rumors got started.'

My mother stopped ironing and set the iron on end. 'I never hear rumors about Miriam Zowicki's daughter, or Esther Marchese's daughter, or Elaine Rosenbach's daughter. Why are there always rumors about *my* daughter?'

I cut myself a slice of coffee cake, wolfed it down,

and crammed my hands into my jeans pockets to keep from eating the whole cake.

Grandma was stowing the food in the fridge. 'Stephanie and me are just colorful people, so we get talked about a lot. Look at all the crazy things they say about me. I swear, people will say anything.'

My mother and I exchanged glances because almost everything crazy that was said about Grandma Mazur was true. If a mortuary viewing was closed casket, she pried the lid open to take a peek. She sneaked out to Chippendales performances when the road show hit town. She drove like a maniac until she finally lost her license. And she punched Morelli's Grandma Bella in the nose last year when Bella threatened to put the curse on me.

'Would you like a sandwich?' my mother asked. 'Can you stay for dinner?'

'Nope. Gotta go. I have phone work to do.'

Joe Morelli is my off-again, on-again boyfriend. Patience has never been his strong suit, but he's settled into a waiting game while we both struggle with commitment issues. He's six feet of hard muscle and Italian libido. His hair is currently longer than he would prefer, more out of laziness than fashion choice.

He's a plainclothes Trenton cop who tolerates my job and my association with Ranger, but would prefer I go a safer route . . . like working as a human cannonball. Morelli owns a little fixer-upper house not far from my parents, but he sleeps over when all the planets are lined up correctly. For almost two weeks now, the planets have been misaligned, but it looked like today was about to improve because Morelli's SUV was parked in the lot next to my apartment building.

I pulled up next to Morelli's car and cut the Vic's engine. I looked up at my windows and saw that lights were on. I live on the second floor of a no-frills three-story brick building on the edge of Trenton. My unit overlooks the parking lot, and that's fine by me. I can amuse myself watching the seniors smash into each other trying to park.

I grabbed my shoulder bag with my failure-to-appear files, and hurried into the building. I took the elevator, swung my ass down the second-floor hall, opened the door to my apartment, and stood looking at Morelli. He'd left his boots in my small foyer, and he was at the stove, stirring a pot of spaghetti sauce. He was head-to-toe gorgeous male in thick gray socks and a faded Blue Claws T-shirt that hung loose over his jeans. He had a large spoon in one hand and a glass of

24

red wine in the other. His big, goofy, orange dog, Bob, was at his feet. Morelli smiled and put the spoon and the glass down when he saw me.

'You're home early,' he said. 'I thought I'd surprise you with dinner. This feels like a spaghetti night.'

Who would have thought Joe Morelli, the scourge of the Burg, the bad boy every girl wanted and every mother feared, would grow up and get domesticated.

I went to his side and looked into the pot. 'Smells wonderful. Do I see hot sausages in there?'

'Yep. From Giovichinni's. And fresh basil and green peppers and oregano. Only a little garlic since I have big plans for tonight.'

My hamster, Rex, lives in an aquarium on the kitchen counter. Rex likes to snooze in his soup can during the day, but Morelli had fed Rex some green pepper, and he was out of his can, busy stuffing the pepper pieces into his cheeks.

I tapped on the side of the cage by way of saying hello, and sipped some of Morelli's wine.

'You look good with a spoon in your hand,' I said to Morelli.

'I'm gender secure. I can cook. Especially if it's man food. I draw the line at folding laundry.' He draped an arm across my shoulders, and nuzzled my neck. 'You feel cold, and I'm feeling very warm. I could share some of my heat with you.'

'What about the sauce?'

'Needs to simmer for a couple more hours. I don't have that problem. I've been simmering for days.'

# Two

I rolled out of bed a little after eight a.m. and went to the window. Not snowing or sleeting, but not great weather either. Gray skies, and it looked cold. Morelli was gone. He'd caught a double homicide at ten last night and never returned. Bob had stayed with me, and Bob was now pacing between my bedroom and the front door.

I pulled on some sweats, stuffed my feet into my boots, grabbed my coat, and hooked Bob up to his leash.

'Okay, big guy,' I said to Bob. 'Let's make tracks.'

We walked around a couple blocks until Bob was empty, and then we went back to my apartment for breakfast. I made coffee, and while the coffee brewed, Bob and I ate the cold spaghetti.

I dropped a couple noodles into Rex's food dish, and gave him fresh water. There was some upheaval in the wood chips in front of the soup can, Rex's nose poked through and did some twitching, and Rex emerged. He scurried to his food dish, packed the noodles into his cheeks, and scurried back to his soup can. This is pretty much the extent of my relationship with Rex. Still, he was a heartbeat in the apartment, and I loved him.

I carried my coffee into the bathroom and took a long, hot shower. I blasted my hair with the hair dryer and swiped some mascara on my lashes. I got dressed in a sweater and jeans and boots, and took the phone and my paperwork into the dining room. I was working my way through Diggery's neighbors and a second cup of coffee when I heard the lock tumble on my front door.

Morelli strolled into the kitchen and poured himself a cup of coffee. 'I have news.'

'Good news or bad news?'

'Hard to tell,' Morelli said. 'I guess it depends on your point of view. Dickie Orr is missing.'

'And?'

'Forced entry on his front door. Blood on the floor. Two bullets extracted from his living-room wall. Skid marks on the wood floor in the foyer as if something had been dragged across it.'

'Get out!'

'Police responded when his neighbors called saying they heard shots. Chip Burlew and Barrelhead Baker were the first on the scene. They got there a few minutes before midnight. Front door open. No Dickie. And it gets better. Marty Gobel caught the case, and when he talked to Dickie's office first thing this morning everyone fingered you.'

'Why would they do that?'

'Possibly because you went gonzo on him yesterday?'

'Oh yeah. I forgot.'

'What was that about?'

'Lula and Connie and I wanted to get some legal advice, and I sort of lost it when I saw a picture of Dickie and Joyce Barnhardt. He had it on his desk.'

'I thought you were over Dickie.'

'Turns out there was some hostility left.'

And now Dickie might be dead, and I wasn't sure *what* I felt. It seemed mean-spirited to be happy, but I wasn't experiencing a lot of remorse. The best I could manage on short notice was that there would be a hole in my life where Dickie used to reside. But then, maybe not. Maybe there wasn't even much of a hole.

Morelli sipped his coffee. He was wearing a gray sweatshirt under a navy jacket, and his black hair curled over his ears and fell across his forehead. I had a flashback of him in bed when his hair was damp against the nape of his neck, and his eyes were dilated black and focused on me.

'Good thing I have an alibi,' I said.

'And that would be what?'

'You were here.'

'I left at ten to take the murders in the Berringer Building.'

Uh oh. 'Do you think I killed Dickie?' I asked Morelli.

'No. You were naked and satisfied when I left. I can't see you leaving that mellow state and going off to Dickie's house.'

'Let me analyze this a little,' I said to Morelli. 'Your expertise in bed is my alibi.'

'Pretty much.'

'Do you think that will hold up in a court of law?'

'No, but it'll look good for me in the tabloids.'

'And if it wasn't for all that good sex and spaghetti, you'd think I was capable of killing Dickie?'

'Cupcake, I think you're capable of most anything.'

Morelli was grinning, and I knew he was playing with me, but there was some truth in what he was saying as well.

'I have limits,' I told him.

He slipped an arm around my waist and kissed my neck. 'Fortunately, not too many.'

Okay, so probably I should tell Morelli about Ranger and the bugging, but things were going so well I hated to put a fly in the ointment. If I tell Morelli about the bugging, he'll do his Italian thing, yelling at me and waving his arms and forbidding me to work with Ranger. Then, since I'm of Hungarian descent on my mother's side, I'll have to do my Hungarian thing and glare at him, hands on hips, and tell him I'll work with whoever I damn well want. Then he'll stomp out of my apartment, and I won't see him for a week, during which time we'll both be upset.

'Are you staying for a while?' I asked Morelli.

'No. I need to talk to someone in Hamilton Township about the Berringer murders. I was passing by and thought you'd want to know about Dickie.' Morelli looked over my shoulder at the open file. 'Diggery again? What's he done this time?'

'Got drunk and trashed a bar on Ninth Street with his shovel. Smashed about two thousand dollars' worth of booze and glassware, and chased the bartender down the street.'

'You aren't spending the night in the cemetery, are you?'

'Wasn't planning on it. The ground is frozen. Diggery will wait until someone new is planted and the digging is easier. I checked the obits. No one was buried yesterday, and there aren't any funerals today. Is there a specific reason you're interested, or are you just making conversation?'

'I was thinking about the left-over spaghetti.'

'Bob and I ate it for breakfast.'

'In that case, I'll bring dinner,' Morelli said. 'Do you have a preference? Chinese? Pizza? Fried chicken?'

'Surprise me.'

Morelli set his cup on the dining-room table and kissed the top of my head. 'Gotta go. I'll take Bob with me.'

And Morelli and Bob were gone.

I dialed Lula. 'I'm not having any luck getting information out of Diggery's relatives. I'm going to take a ride over there and look around for myself. Do you want to ride along?'

'Hell no. Last time we were in his shit-hole trailer, you opened a closet door and a twenty-foot snake fell out.'

'You can stay in the car. That way, if the snake gets me, and you don't see me after an hour's gone by, you can call to have someone haul my cold dead body out of the house.'

'As long as I don't have to get out of the car.'

'I'll pick you up in a half hour.'

I gathered my files together, turned my computer off, and called Ranger.

'Yo,' Ranger said.

'Yo yourself. Dickie's disappeared.'

'That's what I hear.'

'I have a few questions.'

'It wouldn't be smart to answer those questions on the phone,' Ranger said.

'I'm going out with Lula this morning to look for Diggery, but maybe we can get together this afternoon.'

'Keep your eyes open for the snake.'

And Ranger disconnected.

I bundled myself up in my big quilted coat, scarf, and gloves, took the elevator to the lobby, and pushed out into the cold. I walked to the burgundy Crown Vic and gave it a kick to the driver's side door with my boot.

'I hate you,' I said to the car.

I got in, cranked the engine over, and drove to the office.

Lula came out when I drove up. She wrenched the passenger side door open and looked in at me. 'What the heck is this?'

'A Crown Vic.'

'I know it's a Crown Vic. Everybody knows a Crown Vic. What are you doing driving one? Three days ago, you were driving an Escape.'

'A tree fell on it. It was totaled.'

'Must have been a big tree.'

'Are you going to get in?'

'I'm weighing the consequences. People see me in this they think I'm arrested . . . again. It's gonna be damaging to my good reputation. Even without that, it'll be humiliating. Hard enough being hot without overcoming a humiliating automotive experience. I got a image to think about.'

'We could use your car.'

'Yeah, but suppose by some miracle you catch Diggery? I'm not putting his moldy ass in my Firebird.'

'Well, I'm not driving to Bordentown in this POS all by myself. I'll buy you lunch if you'll get in the car.'

Lula slid onto the passenger seat and buckled up. 'I got a craving for a Cluck Burger Deluxe today. And a large fries. And maybe one of them Clucky Apple Pies.'

I had sixteen dollars and fifty-seven cents in my purse, and it had to last me until I brought in a skip and got a new infusion of money. Two-fifty for a Cluck Burger Deluxe. A dollar-fifty for fries. Another dollar for the pie. Then she'd need a drink. And I'd get a bargain-meal cheeseburger for ninety-nine cents. That would give me ten dollars left for an emergency. Good thing Morelli was bringing dinner.

I took Hamilton to Broad and headed south. I thought I was hearing a strange grinding sound coming from under the hood, so I turned the radio up.

'You're not gonna guess what Connie picked up on the police band this morning,' Lula said. 'Dickie's missing, and it don't look good. There was blood and bullets all over the place. Hope you got a alibi.'

'I was with Morelli.' Earlier in the evening.

'Don't come much better than that,' Lula said.

'Did you hear if they have any suspects?'

'You mean besides you?'

'Yeah.'

'Nope. You're it, so far as I could tell.' Lula cut her eyes to me. 'I don't suppose it was you.'

'No.'

'Okay, so it wasn't you directly, but it might have had something to do with the bugs you put on him.'

'You didn't just say that. And you're never going to say that again,' I said to Lula. 'In fact, yesterday you didn't see or hear *anything* about bugs.'

'I must have hallucinated it.'

'Exactly.'

'My lips are sealed.'

I turned off South Broad and took Route 206 to Groveville. I crossed the railroad tracks and started looking for the road that led to Diggery's house.

'This don't look familiar,' Lula said.

'That's because we were here in the summer last time.'

'I think it's 'cause we're in the wrong place. You should have MapQuested this,' Lula said. 'I always MapQuest.'

'We're not in the wrong place. We just missed a road.'

'Do you know the name of the road?'

'No.'

'See, you needed to MapQuest.'

A rusted-out pickup blew past us. It had a gun rack across the back window, a Grateful Dead sticker on the bumper, and a rebel flag flying from the antenna. It looked to me like it belonged in Diggery's neighborhood, so I hung a U-turn and kept it in sight, leaving Groveville for a winding two-lane road strewn with potholes.

'This looks more like it,' Lula said, watching the countryside fly by. 'I remember some of these pathetic excuses for a house.'

We passed a shanty constructed of tar paper and

particleboard, eased around a bend in the road, and Diggery's trailer was to the left, set back about fifty feet. I continued driving until I was out of sight of the trailer. I turned around, cruised past Diggery's again, and parked just beyond the bend. If Diggery saw me parking in front of his house, he'd be halfway to Newark by the time I got out of my car.

'I don't think anybody's home,' Lula said. 'I didn't see any cars in the yard.'

'I'm going to snoop around anyway. Are you coming?'

'I suppose, but if I see that snake, I'm outta there. I *hate* snakes. I don't care if that snake wraps itself around your neck, I'm telling you right now, I'm not staying to help.'

Diggery lived on a sad patch of parched and frozen hardscrabble. His double-wide trailer had rust stains running from top to bottom, with cankerous rot eating at the trailer floor. The piece of junk was set a foot off the ground on cinderblocks and was held together with duct tape. Grave robbing obviously didn't pay all that well. There were hardwoods behind the trailer. No leaves at this time of year, just barren, naked stalks of trees. It was late morning, but there was little light filtering through the thick gray cloud cover.

'There's a back door on the other side,' I said to

Lula. 'You take the back door, and I'll take the front door.'

'The hell I will,' Lula said. 'First off, I don't want no Diggery opening that door and knocking me on my ass trying to get to the woods. And second . . . well that's all there is. There's no second. I'm going in behind you, so I can be first out if the snake's there.'

There was no answer when I knocked on the door, but then I hadn't expected an answer. The little Diggerys were in school. The big Diggerys were probably picking through Dumpsters, looking for lunch. I pushed the door open and cautiously looked inside. I flipped a switch by the door and a forty-watt bulb blinked on in what might pass for the living room. I stepped in and listened for rustling, slithering sounds.

Lula stuck her head in and sniffed the air. 'I smell snake,' she said.

I didn't know what a snake smelled like, but I suspected it was a lot like a Diggery.

'Snoop around and see if you can find something that tells us where Simon is working,' I said to Lula. 'A pay stub, a matchbook, a map with a big orange X on it.'

'We should have brought rubber gloves,' Lula said.

'I bet this place is covered with snake spit.'

'The snake stuff is getting old,' I said to her. 'Could you back off from the snake stuff?'

'Just trying to be vigilant. If you don't want me reminding you to be careful, hey, okay by me. You're on your own.'

Lula opened a closet door and a mop fell out at her.

'Snake!' Lula screamed. 'Snake, snake, snake!' And she ran out of the trailer.

I looked out at Lula. 'It was a mop.'

'Are you sure? It looked like a snake to me.'

'It was a mop.'

'I think I wet my pants.'

'Too much information,' I said to her.

Lula crept back into the trailer and looked at the mop lying on the floor. 'Scared the beejeezus out of me,' she said.

We made our way through the living area and the kitchen. We looked through a tiny bedroom that was stacked with bunks. We opened the door to the master bedroom and there it was . . . the snake. It was curled on the bed, and it was looking at us with lazy snake eyes. It had a lump in its throat that was about the size of the family dog, or maybe a small Diggery.

I was paralyzed with fear and horror and

gobstopping fascination. My feet wouldn't move, and I could barely breathe.

'We're disturbing him,' Lula whispered. 'We should leave now and let him finish his breakfast.'

The snake swallowed and the lump moved six inches farther down its throat.

'Oh crap,' Lula whispered.

And next thing I knew, I was in my car.

'How did I get in the car?' I asked Lula.

'You let out a shriek and ran out of the trailer and all the way here. I bet I got footprints on my back where you ran over me.'

I slouched in my seat and concentrated on getting my heart to stop racing. 'That wasn't a snake. Snakes aren't that big, are they?'

'It was the snake from hell. It was a motherfucking mutant reptile.' Lula shook her finger at me. 'I told you we didn't want to go in there. You wouldn't listen.'

I was still shaky enough that I had to two-hand the key to get it in the ignition. 'Took me by surprise,' I said.

'Yeah, me too,' Lula said. 'Do I get my lunch now?'

I dropped Lula at the office and looked at my watch. It was a little after one. I had more skips sitting in my bag, waiting to get found, but I was having a hard time working up enthusiasm for the whole bounty hunter thing. I decided procrastination was the way to go, so I called Morelli.

'Is there anything new on Dickie?' I asked him.

'No. As far as I know, he's still missing. Where are you?'

'I'm in my car in front of the office, and I'm trying to calm myself.'

I could hear Morelli smile over the phone line. 'How's the snake?'

'Big.'

'Did you catch a Diggery?'

'No. Didn't even come close.'

I disconnected Morelli and called Ranger.

'Can we talk?' I asked him.

'Your place or mine?'

'Yours.'

'I'm parked behind you.'

I looked in my rearview mirror and locked eyes with him. He was in the Porsche Cayenne.

'Sometimes you freak me out,' I said to Ranger.

'Babe.'

I got out of my garbage-scow Crown Vic and into Ranger's shiny, immaculate SUV.

'You involved me in a murder,' I said to Ranger.

'And you have no alibi,' Ranger said.

'Is there anything you don't know?'

'I don't know what happened to Dickie.'

'So I guess that means you didn't snatch him?'

'I don't leave bloodstains,' Ranger said.

Ranger was dressed in his usual black. Black Vibram soled boots, black jeans, black shirt, black wool pea coat, and his black Navy SEAL ball cap. Ranger was a shadow. A mystery man. A man who had no time or desire to mix and match colors.

'Those bugs I planted on Dickie . . . what was that about?' I asked him.

'You don't want to know.'

'Yes, I do.'

'You *don't*.'

I stared him down. 'I *do*.'

Ranger did what for him was a sigh. The barest whisper of expelled breath. I was being a pain in the keester.

'I'm looking for a guy named Ziggy Zabar. His brother Zip works for me and came to me for help when Ziggy disappeared last week. Ziggy's a CPA with a firm downtown. They prepare the tax reports for Petiak, Smullen, Gorvich, and Orr. Every Monday, the partners hold a meeting off-site, and Ziggy had the meeting on his calendar. He was seen getting into his car to go to the meeting, and then he disappeared. The four partners swear Zabar never showed up, but I don't believe it. There's something not right about the firm. Dickie has legitimate credentials and has passed the Jersey bar. His partners have law degrees from Panama. Right now, I can't tell if Dickie is dumb or dirty.'

'Did the bugs work?'

'The meeting was cancelled. We listened until a little after ten and packed up when Dickie went to bed.'

'So you weren't listening when shots were fired.'

'No, but I was in his house after the police sealed it, and it looks to me like Dickie left the house wearing the same clothes he had on all day. We've tried scanning to pick up a bug, but haven't had any luck. Either he's out of range, or the bugs have been found and destroyed.'

'Now what?'

Ranger took a little plastic bag from his pocket. It contained another bug. 'Do you think you can plant this on Peter Smullen?'

I felt my jaw drop and my eyebrows shoot up into my forehead. 'You're not serious.'

Ranger took a file off the dashboard and handed it to me. 'Smullen wasn't in the office yesterday. He had a dentist appointment. So he shouldn't recognize you. Here are a couple pictures of Smullen, a short bio, plus our best guess at what his schedule will be like tomorrow. He divides his time between Trenton and Bogota. When he's in town, he's a creature of habit, so running into him won't be a problem. Try to tag him tomorrow morning, so I can listen to him all day.'

'And I'm going to do this, why?'

'I'll let you wrestle with that one,' Ranger said. He looked through the Cayenne windshield at my car. 'Is there a reason you're driving the Vic?'

'It was cheap.'

'Babe, *free* wouldn't be cheap enough.'

'You haven't asked me if I killed Dickie,' I said to Ranger.

'I know you didn't kill Dickie. You never left your apartment.'

There was a time when I considered Ranger's surveillance an invasion of privacy, but that time was long gone. There's not much point to worrying about things you can't control, and I had no control over Ranger.

'Where is it? On my car?' I asked him, doing a pretty

decent job of not sounding completely pissed off.

Ranger's mouth didn't smile, but his eyes crinkled a little at the corners. 'GPS unit in your bag. Please don't remove it.'

I took the file and the bug-in-a-bag and got out of the Cayenne. 'I imagine you'll be watching my every move.'

'Just like always,' Ranger said.

I got into the Crown Vic, cranked the engine over, and turned the heat on full blast. I looked in my rearview mirror. No Ranger.

I studied the pictures of Peter Smullen. He was an average-looking guy with receding brown hair and a beer belly. Heavy five o'clock shadow in all the photos. Lips like a flounder. His file put him at five feet eight inches. Forty-six years old. Married with two kids, ages twenty and twenty-two. Both kids and the wife were in Colombia. Smullen kept a bachelor apartment in Hamilton Township. When Smullen was in town, at precisely eight a.m., he'd roll into a parking garage that was a block from his office at the law firm and get a triple shot Frappuccino at the Starbucks on the corner.

I'd get him at the Starbucks.

I closed the file, turned to lay it on the seat next to me, and the Vic's driver's side door was suddenly wrenched open. Joyce Barnhardt glared in at me and called me the 'c' word.

Joyce was six feet tall in four-inch, spike-heeled black boots. She was wearing a black leather duster lined with fake fur, her eyes were enhanced with rhinestone-studded fake eyelashes, her red enameled nails were long and frightening. The package was topped with a lot of shoulder-length brilliant red hair arranged in curls and waves. Joyce had never moved beyond Farrah Fawcett.

I narrowed my eyes at her. 'Is there a point to this conversation?'

'You killed him. You found out we were a couple, and you couldn't handle it. So you killed him.'

'I didn't kill him.'

'I was inches from marrying the little turd, and you ruined it all. Do you have any idea how much he's worth? A fucking fortune. And you killed him, and now I get nothing. I *hate* you.'

I turned the key in the ignition and put the Vic into drive. 'I have to go now,' I said to Joyce. 'Good talk.'

'I'm not done,' Joyce said. 'I'm just beginning. I'm going to get even. I'm going to make your life a misery.' Joyce pulled a gun out of her coat pocket and aimed it at me. 'I'm going to shoot out your eye. And then I'm going to shoot you in the foot, and the knee, and the ass . . .'

I stomped on the gas pedal and rocketed off with my door still open. Joyce squeezed off two rounds, putting a hole in the rear window. I looked in my mirror and got a glimpse of her standing in the middle of the road, giving me the finger. Joyce Barnhardt was nuts.

I drove one block down Hamilton and turned into the Burg. I was thinking that after the traumatic Joyce experience, I needed something to calm myself . . . like a piece of the raspberry Entenmann's. Plus, my dad had all kinds of things stashed in his cellar, like electrician's tape that I could use to patch my rear window. Wind was whistling through the bullet hole, creating a draft on the back of my neck. It would have been perfectly okay in July, but it was damn cold in February. I wound through the maze of Burg streets to my parents' house and parked in the driveway. I got out and examined the car. Hole in the rear window, and Joyce had taken out a tail light.

I hunched against the sleet and ran to the front door. I let myself in, dropped my bag on the sideboard in the foyer, and went to the kitchen. My mother was at the sink, washing vegetables. Grandma was at the little table with a cup of tea. The Entenmann's box was on the small kitchen table. I held my breath and approached the box. I flipped the lid. Two pieces left. I anxiously looked around. 'Anyone want this Entenmann's?' I asked.

'Not me,' Grandma said.

'Not me either,' my mother said.

I shrugged out of my jacket, hung it on the back of the chair, and sat down.

'Anything new in the world of crime?' Grandma asked.

'Same ol', same ol',' I told her. 'What's new with you?'

'I'm outta that glue stuff for my dentures. I was hoping you could run me out to the drugstore.'

'Sure.' I wolfed down the last of the cake and scraped back in my chair. 'I can take you now, but then I need to get back to work.'

'I'll just go upstairs to get my purse,' Grandma said.

I leaned toward her and lowered my voice. 'No gun.'

Grandma Mazur carried a .45 long barrel named Elsie. It wasn't registered, and she didn't have a permit to carry concealed. Grandma thought being old gave her license to pack. She called it the equalizer. My mother kept taking the gun away, and the gun kept mysteriously returning.

'I don't know what you're talking about,' Grandma said.

'I've got enough problems with the police right now. I can't afford to get pulled over for a broken tail light and have them discover you're armed and dangerous.'

'I never go anywhere without Elsie,' Grandma said.

'What's all the whispering about?' my mother wanted to know.

'We were trying to decide if I needed to put on some fresh lipstick,' Grandma said.

I looked over at her. 'You don't need lipstick.'

'A woman always needs lipstick.'

'Your lipstick is fine.'

'You're getting to be just like your mother,' Grandma said.

There was a time when that statement would have freaked me out, but now I was thinking maybe it wouldn't be so bad to have some of my mother's qualities. She was a stabilizing influence on the family. She was the representative of accepted social behavior. She was the guardian of our health and security. She was the bran muffin that allowed us to be jelly doughnuts.

Grandma and I were at the front door, and I remembered the hole in the windshield. 'Duct tape,' I called to my mother. 'Where would I find it, the garage or the cellar?'

My mother came with a roll. 'I keep some in the kitchen. Are you fixing something?'

'I have a hole in my back window.'

Grandma Mazur squinted at the Vic. 'Looks like a bullet hole.'

'Dear God,' my mother said. 'It's *not* a bullet hole, is it?'

'No,' I told her. 'Absolutely not.'

Grandma Mazur buttoned herself into her long royal blue wool coat. She buckled a little under the weight but managed to right herself and get to the car.

'Isn't this the kind of car the cops use?' she asked.

'Yes.'

'Does it have one of them flashing lights?'

'No.'

'Bummer,' Grandma said.

# Three

I followed Grandma up and down the aisles, past personal products to Metamucil, hemorrhoid remedies, hair spray, Harlequin romances, greeting cards. She got her denture glue and moved to lipsticks.

A gap-toothed, redheaded kid rounded a corner and came to a stop in front of us.

'Hi!' he yelled.

He was followed by Cynthia Hawser. Cynthia and I had been classmates. She was married now to a gap-toothed, redheaded guy who'd fathered three gap-toothed, redheaded kids. They lived a block over from Morelli in a little duplex that had more toys than grass in the front yard.

'This is Jeremy,' Cynthia said to Grandma and me.

Jeremy had trouble written all over him. Jeremy just about vibrated with energy.

'What a cute little boy,' Grandma said. 'I bet you're real smart.'

'I'm too smart for my britches,' Jeremy said. 'That's what most people tell me.'

An old man shuffled up and looked us over. He was wearing a wavy jet-black toupee that sat slightly askew on his bald dome. He had bushy, out-of-control eyebrows, a lot of ear hair, and even more slack skin than Grandma. I thought he looked to be on the far side of eighty.

'What's going on here?' he asked.

'This is Uncle Elmer,' Cynthia said. 'There was a fire in his apartment at assisted living so he came to live with us.'

'It wasn't my fault,' Uncle Elmer said.

'You were smoking in bed,' Jeremy said. 'It's lucky you didn't cream yourself.'

Cynthia grimaced. 'You mean *cremate*.'

Uncle Elmer grinned at Grandma. 'Who's this sexy young thing?'

'Aren't you the one,' Grandma said to Elmer.

Elmer winked at her. 'The boys at the home would love you. You look hot.'

'It's the coat,' Grandma said. 'It's wool.'

Elmer fingered the coat. 'Looks like good quality. I

was in retail, you know. I can tell quality.'

'I've had it for a while,' Grandma said. 'I was taller when I first bought it. I've shrunk up some.'

Elmer gave his head a small shake, and the toupee slid over one ear. He reached up and righted it. 'The golden years are a bitch,' Elmer said.

'You don't look like you shrunk much,' Grandma said. 'You're a pretty big guy.'

'Well, some of me's shrunk and some of me's swollen up,' Elmer said. 'When I was young, I got a lot of tattoos, and now they don't look so good. One time, I got drunk and got Eisenhower tattooed on my balls, but now he looks like Orville Redenbacher.'

'He makes good popcorn,' Grandma said.

'You bet. And don't worry, I still got it where it counts.'

'Where's that?' Grandma asked.

'In the sack. Hangs a little lower than it used to, but the equipment still works, if you know what I mean.'

'Uncle Elmer poops in a bag,' Jeremy said.

'It's temporary,' Elmer said. 'Just 'til the by-pass heals up. They put some pig intestine in me on an experimental basis.'

'Gee,' I said, 'look at the time. We have to be running along now.'

'Yeah, I can't be late for dinner tonight,' Grandma said. 'I want to make the early viewing at the funeral parlor. Milton Buzick is laid out, and I hear you wouldn't even recognize him.'

'You got a good funeral parlor here?' Elmer asked Grandma.

'I go to the one on Hamilton Avenue. It's run by two real nice young men, and they serve homemade cookies.'

'I wouldn't mind some homemade cookies,' Elmer said. 'I could meet you there tonight. I'm looking for a lady friend, you know. Do you put out?'

Cynthia smacked Uncle Elmer on the head. 'Behave yourself.'

'I haven't got time,' Elmer said, readjusting his hair. 'I gotta know these things.'

'Now what?' I asked Grandma Mazur when we'd settled ourselves in the car.

'I gotta go home, so I can get ready for tonight. That Elmer is a frisky one. He'll get snapped up fast. Myra Witkowski would snap him up in an instant if I let her.'

'Remember, I'm looking for Simon Diggery. Check out Milton's jewelry for me, and let me know if he's going in the ground with anything pricey enough to get Diggery out to the cemetery on a cold night.'

＊

Morelli and Bob strolled in a little after six. Morelli shucked his boots and jacket in the foyer and dumped a grocery bag and a six-pack onto the kitchen counter. He grabbed me, and kissed me, and cracked open a beer from the six-pack.

'I'm starving,' he said. 'I didn't have time for lunch.'

I pulled a bunch of chili dogs and a bucket of cheese fries out of the grocery bag. I put two dogs and some fries in a bowl for Bob and unwrapped a dog for myself.

'This is what I love about you,' I said to Morelli. 'No vegetables.'

Morelli ate some hotdog and drank some more beer. 'Is that all you love about me?'

'No, but it's high on the list.'

'The Berringer murders are going into the toilet. The security company didn't have film in any of the surveillance cameras. Everyone hated the two people who were killed. It was cold and overcast and there was no exterior lighting in the back of the building. No one saw anything. No one heard anything. Forced entry. Nothing stolen.'

'Maybe you should hire a psychic.'

'I know you're being a wise-ass, but I'm about at that point.'

'What's happening with Dickie? Am I still a suspect?'

'Right now, Dickie is just a missing person who disappeared under suspicious circumstances. If his body floats in on the tide, you could be in trouble. Marty Gobel is still the primary investigator, and he wants to talk to you first thing tomorrow. I gave him your cell number.'

'Do you think I should use the orgasm defense?'

'Yeah, my reputation could use a boost.' Morelli finished off his second hotdog and ate some fries. 'I'm not on the case, but I've been poking around on my own, and I don't like Dickie's partners. I'm probably going to regret saying this, but maybe you should bring Ranger in. He can do things I can't. Ranger doesn't mind bending the law to get information. Have him take a look at the partners.'

'You're worried about me.'

Morelli wiped his hands on his jeans and pulled me to him, wrapping his arms around me. 'Dickie was a respected lawyer. And Joyce is making a lot of noise. This is going to go high profile, and the politicians will have to point a finger at someone. When the media gets hold of this case, unless new evidence is found, you're going to be in the spotlight.' He rested his cheek on the top of my head. 'I can manage the media attention. I couldn't manage having you taken away from me.'

I tipped my head back and looked at him. He was serious. 'Do you think I might be arrested and convicted?'

'I think the possibility is slim, but I'm not willing to take a chance on it. Ask Ranger for help and keep your head down. Don't do anything to bring more attention to yourself.'

I was dragged awake by something ringing in the dark room. Morelli swore softly, and his arm reached across me to the nightstand, where he'd left his cell phone.

'What?' Morelli said into the phone.

Someone was talking on the other end, and I could feel Morelli coming awake.

'You're fucking kidding me,' he said to the caller. 'Why does this shit always happen in the middle of the night?'

I squinted at my bedside clock and grimaced. Three a.m.

Morelli was up and moving around the room, looking for his clothes. He still had the phone to his ear. 'Give me an address,' he said, and a moment later he snapped his phone closed. He slipped his watch onto his wrist and pulled his jeans on. He sat on the edge of the bed and tugged on socks. He leaned over and kissed me. 'I have to go, and I probably won't get back tonight. I'll take Bob with me.'

'Is this about the Berringer murders?'

'Someone else was just found dead in the building.'

He clipped his gun onto his belt and pulled a sweater over a T-shirt. 'I'll call when I can.'

I had a third of a jar of peanut butter in my pantry, no milk, no bread, no juice. Half a box of Cheerios. I dropped some Cheerios into Rex's food dish and mixed some up with the peanut butter for myself. I washed the Cheerios and peanut butter down with black coffee and grabbed my coat.

Marty Gobel, the cop who was in charge of Dickie's disappearance, was supposed to call to talk. If I wasn't Morelli's girlfriend, I'd probably be getting finger-printed. Good thing I had something solid in my stomach because otherwise I might be inclined to throw up. I really didn't want to go to jail.

Peter Smullen was first on my list of hideous jobs. According to Ranger's research, Smullen would be rolling into Starbucks a little after eight. I arrived fifteen minutes in front of the hour and tried to look inconspicuous by studying the shelves of coffee mugs for sale. Not that inconspicuous was much of a problem. The place was packed, and anyone under seven feet tall wasn't going to stand out.

I saw Smullen push through the door at five of eight and realized I might have a problem. He was buttoned into a black cashmere overcoat. There was no way to drop a bug into his suit pocket. Fortunately, the store was warm and the line was long. If the line went slowly enough, he'd un-button his coat. I watched from my spot at the front of the store. I had a plan. I was going to wait until he had his coffee, and then I'd approach him. My coat was open, and I was wearing a low-cut V-necked sweater with a push-up bra. I looked pretty good considering my boobs were real, but it was hard to compete with all the double-D silicon jobs.

Smullen finally got to the counter and put in his order. He unbuttoned his coat to get his wallet, and I almost collapsed with relief. I had access to his pockets. He shuffled to the pick-up counter, got his triple Frappuccino, and when he turned toward the door, he was flat against me. I had my boobs pressed into his chest and my leg between his.

'Whoops,' I said, sliding my hand under his coat,

dropping the bug into his pocket. 'Sorry!'

Smullen didn't blink. He just hung on to his Frappuccino as if this happened every morning. And maybe it did. There were a *lot* of people in the store. I took one step back and one step to the side to let Smullen get past me, and he inched his way toward the door and disappeared.

I felt someone lean in to me from behind, and a coffee was placed in my hand.

'Nice,' Ranger said, guiding me out to the sidewalk. 'I couldn't have gotten that close. And he wouldn't have been distracted by my chest.'

'I don't think he even noticed.'

'A man would have to be dead not to notice,' Ranger said.

'Morelli's worried I'll be involved in Dickie's disappearance. He said I should ask you for help.'

'He's a good man,' Ranger said.

'And you?'

'I'm better.'

Lula was filing when I walked into the bonds office.

'What's with this?' I asked.

'Hunh,' Lula said. 'You act like I never do nothing. It's just I'm so efficient I get my work done before anyone notices. My name should be Flash. You ever see any files laying around?'

'I assumed you were throwing them away.'

'Your ass,' Lula said.

For a short time, we had a guy named Melvin Pickle doing our filing. Pickle was a filing dynamo. Unfortunately, he was so good he was able to get a better job. Les Sebring hired him to work in his bonds office, and Connie had to coerce Lula to take back filing responsibilities.

Connie was carefully adding a topcoat to her nails. 'Having any luck with the new batch of FTAs?'

'No, but Milton Buzick is getting buried today. I'm waiting to get a jewelry report from Grandma.'

'If he got a Rolex on, I don't want to know,' Lula said. 'Two things I'm not doing. I'm not going back to that trailer, and I'm not sitting in no cemetery. Dead people creep me out.'

'What about Carl Coglin?' Connie asked. 'He looks pretty straightforward. He has a small shop attached to his home.'

'Who's Carl Coglin?' Lula wanted to know.

I pulled Carl's file out of my bag and flipped it open. 'Sixty-four years old. Never married. Lives alone. His sister put up the bond. Accused of destruction of personal property. Doesn't go into detail. Lists his occupation as taxidermist.'

'Taxidermist,' Lula said. 'We never busted a taxidermist before. It could be fun.'

A half hour later, we were in North Trenton, standing in front of Coglin's house. This was a working-class neighborhood filled with people stretched too thin to plant flowers in the spring. Houses were neat but shabby. Cars were tired.

Coglin lived in a redbrick single-family house with mustard trim. The paint was blistered and the wood around the windows had some rot. The front porch had been enclosed as an afterthought, and a small sign on the door advertised Coglin's taxidermy business.

'Don't look to me like taxidermy pays real well,' Lula said.

A scrawny little guy answered my knock, and I knew from the picture on file that it was Coglin. Hair the color and texture of steel wool. Wire-rimmed glasses.

'Carl Coglin?' I asked.

'Yes.'

'I represent Vincent Plum Bail Bonds. You missed your court date last week, and I'd like to help you reschedule.'

'That's nice of you,' Coglin said, 'but I don't want to inconvenience you.'

'It's my job.'

'Oh,' Coglin said. 'Well, what does this rescheduling involve?'

'You need to go to the courthouse and get rebonded.'

We were standing in Coglin's front-porch show-room, and it was hard not to notice the animals lining his walls.

'Where's the mooseheads?' Lula asked Coglin. 'I thought you taxidermy guys stuffed lions and tigers and shit. All I see is cats and dogs and pigeons.'

'This is *urban* taxidermy,' Coglin said. 'I restore pets and found objects.'

'What's a found object?' Lula wanted to know.

'Treasure found in nature. For instance, if you were walking through the park and you found a deceased pigeon, that would be a found object. And sometimes I make performance pieces. The performance pieces are mechanicals. There's a growing market for the mechanicals.'

Lula looked at a woodchuck posed on a piece of Astro-turf. Some of its fur had been worn away, and it had what appeared to be part of a tire track imprinted on its back. 'You're a sick man,' Lula said.

'It's *art*,' Coglin said. 'You don't understand art.'

'I understand roadkill,' Lula said.

'About that rescheduling,' I said to Coglin.

'Maybe I could reschedule next week,' Coglin said. 'I can't leave now. I have to stay at the house. I have a fresh opossum on the table.'

'Oh boy,' Lula said.

'It's hard to get an opossum at this time of year,' Coglin said. 'I was lucky to find it. And it won't be good when it defrosts.'

'This won't take long,' I told him.

'You're not going to leave without me, are you?' he asked.

'No.'

Coglin looked at his watch. 'I suppose I could go with you if this doesn't take long. Let me get my coat and lock the back door. In the meantime, feel free to browse my showroom. All these items are for sale.'

'I'm glad to hear that,' Lula said. 'I always wanted a stuffed dead dog.'

Coglin disappeared into the house, and I tried not to look too hard at the critters. 'These animals are creeping me out,' I said to Lula. 'It's like being in a whacked-out pet cemetery.'

'Yeah,' Lula said. 'They've seen better days.' She picked up a stuffed squirrel. 'This guy's got three eyes. He must have lived next to the nuclear power plant.'

I heard the back door slam and then a motor crank over.

'Car!' I said to Lula.

We ran to the back of the house and saw Coglin pull away in a green Isuzu SUV. We turned and sprinted through the house, out the door to the Vic.

'There he goes,' Lula said, pointing to the corner. 'South on Centerline.'

I had the Vic in gear and moving. I took the corner on two wheels and put my foot to the floor. Coglin was a block ahead of me.

'He's turning,' Lula said.

'I'm on it.'

'He's got a light,' Lula said. 'He has to stop for the light.'

I jumped on the brake, but Coglin ran it. He sailed through the light and was lost in traffic.

'Guess he didn't feel like going to jail,' Lula said.

The light changed and I slowly moved forward. I looked over at Lula and saw she still had the squirrel.

'We were in such a rush to get out of the house, I

forgot I was holding this here mutant rodent,' Lula said.

'It doesn't look like a third eye,' I said to her. 'It looks like a switch. Maybe this is a mechanical rodent.'

Lula pushed the switch and studied it. 'It's making a noise. It's sort of ticking. It's . . .'

*BANG*. The squirrel exploded.

We both shrieked. I jumped the curb and sideswiped a streetlight.

'What the fuck?' Lula said.

'Are you okay?'

'No, I'm not okay. That squirrel just friggin' blew hisself apart on me. I got squirrel guts on me.'

'Doesn't look like guts,' I said, examining the hair and skin plastered to the dashboard. 'Looks like he was stuffed with some kind of foam that melted when it exploded.'

'This guy's building rodent bombs,' Lula said. 'We should report him to someone. You can't just go around building rodent bombs, can you?'

I backed up and tried to open my door, but it wouldn't open. I rolled the window down, climbed out *Dukes of Hazzard* style, and examined the damage. Some of the door was bashed in where I'd hit the light. I climbed back into the car and drove off the sidewalk.

'I got foam and squirrel hair stuck to me,' Lula said. 'I probably need a rabies shot or something.'

'Yeah,' I said. 'Problem is, I don't know whether to take you to a veterinarian or an upholsterer.'

'Smells funky,' Lula said, sniffing her finger. 'What's it smell like?'

'Squirrel.'

'I didn't know squirrels had a smell.'

'This one does,' I told her.

'I'm gonna need to take this coat to the dry cleaner, and I'm gonna send the bill to that Coglin freak. He got some nerve exploding a squirrel on me.'

'You *took* the squirrel.'

'Yeah, but it was entrapment. I think I got a case.'

'Maybe we should go to lunch,' I said to Lula. 'Take your mind off the squirrel.'

'I could use some lunch.'

'Do you have any money?'

'No,' Lula said. 'Do you?'

'No.'

'There's only one thing to do then. Senior buffet.'

Ten minutes later, I pulled into the Costco parking lot.

'Where we gonna start?' Lula wanted to know, taking a shopping cart.

67

'I like to start in produce and then go to the deli and then frozen.'

Costco is the all-American free lunch. If you can't afford to buy food, you can buy a minimum membership at Costco and get freebies from the give-away ladies. You just have to kick your way through the seniors who stand ten deep around them.

'Look over there,' Lula said. 'They got a give-away lady frying up them little bitty sausages. I love those little sausages.'

We had some apple slices dipped in caramel, some carrots and raw broccoli dipped in ranch dressing, some goat cheese, some frozen pizza pieces, some tofu stir-fry, some brownie pieces from the bakery, and some of the sausages. We did a test-drive on Guatemalan coffee and sparkling apple cider. We used the ladies room, and we left.

'Whoever invented Costco knew what they were doing,' Lula said. 'I don't know what I'd do without my Costco membership. Sometimes, I even buy shit there. Costco's got everything. You can buy a casket at Costco.'

We got into the Vic, and I drove us back to Coglin's house. I idled at the curb for a couple minutes, watching to see if anything was going on, then I motored around the block and took the alley that led to Coglin's backyard. No car in his parking place, so I parked there.

'Gonna see if he's hiding in a closet?' Lula asked.

'Yep.'

I knocked on Coglin's back door and yelled, 'Bond enforcement!'

No answer.

I opened the door and yelled again. Still no answer. I stepped into the kitchen and looked around. It was just as we'd left it over an hour ago, except for the opossum on the kitchen table. The opossum looked like a balloon with feet. And it smelled worse than squirrel. A lot worse.

'Whoa,' Lula said. 'He wasn't kidding about this sucker defrosting.'

'Maybe we should put it in the freezer for him.'

Lula had her scarf over her nose. 'I'm not touching it. Bad enough I got squirrel on me. I don't need no 'possum cooties. Anyways, it's not gonna fit in his freezer with the way it's all swelled up.'

'Coglin isn't here,' I said to Lula. 'He would have done something with this animal if he'd returned.'

'Fuckin' A,' Lula said. 'I'm outta here.'

I parked in front of the office, behind Lula's

Firebird, and Lula and I got out of the Vic and gaped at the telephone pole at the corner. It was plastered with posters of me. It was a candid photo, and the caption read WANTED FOR MURDER.

'What the heck?' I said. My first reaction was panic deep in my chest. The police were looking for me. That only lasted a moment. This wasn't any sort of official 'wanted' poster. This was made on someone's home scanner and printer.

I tore the posters off the pole and looked down the street. I could see posters on a pole half a block away.

'There's posters all over the place,' Lula said. 'They're stuck to store windows, and they're stuck on parked cars.' She unlocked her Firebird. 'I'm going home. I gotta get this squirrel funk off me.'

I went into the office and showed Connie the posters.

'It's Joyce,' Connie said. 'I saw her putting them up, but I didn't realize what they were.'

'They're probably all over town. I should probably ride around and take them down, but I have better things to do with my time . . . like find out who killed Dickie.'

'Anything I can do to help?'

'Yes. I need a background search. Joyce says he's worth lots of money.'

Connie punched his name into one of the search programs and the screen filled with information. 'He leased a $42,000 Audi a year ago. His house is appraised at $350,000. And it's mortgaged to the rafters. No litigation pending against him. Nothing derogatory in his file. He's part owner of the building housing his law firm. His partners are also listed as owners. Looks like the building was bought outright. No mortgage there.'

Connie printed the report and passed it over to me.

'Any calls for me?' I asked her.

'No. Were you expecting calls?'

'I was supposed to talk to Marty Gobel this morning. I expected him to call my cell.' Not that I wanted to talk to Marty Gobel, but it was better than having a warrant issued for my arrest.

I dialed Morelli. No answer.

Ranger was next up.

'Babe,' Ranger said.

'Anything new on Dickie?'

'No, but the natives are restless. I can feel Smullen sweating on the bug.'

I left the bonds office, climbed into the Vic, and drove to Dickie's house. It was easy to find since it was the only house on his block draped in yellow crime scene tape. It was a large cape with black shutters and a red door. Probably thirty years old but recently painted. Two-car garage. Nicely landscaped. Medium-size lot. Very respectable, if you overlooked the tape. I wasn't sure what I'd expected to find, but I'd felt compelled to do a drive-by. Morbid curiosity, I suppose, since Joyce had been impressed with his wealth. As it was, he seemed comfortable but not excessively rich.

I did a mental reenactment of the crime. I imagined the door to Dickie's house open, and Dickie getting dragged out by whoever shot him. There would have been a car in the driveway. Shots were fired a little before midnight, so it was dark. Overcast sky. No moonlight. Still, you'd think someone would have at least seen the car leave. If you hear shots fired, and you care enough to call the police, you care enough to look out the window.

I parked the Vic, crossed the street, and knocked on the door of the house across from Dickie's. The knock was answered by a woman in her fifties.

'I'm investigating the Orr incident,' I told her. 'I'd appreciate it if you could just answer a few questions for me.'

'I suppose, but I've already spoken to the police. I don't have much more to say.'

'You reported the shots?'

'Yes. I was getting ready for bed. I heard the shots, and I thought it was kids. They ride through and shoot at mailboxes. But then when I looked out the window, I saw the car pull out of the Orr driveway. And I saw that the front door to the house was left open.'

'What did the car look like?'

'It looked a little like your police car. It was dark out, so I can't be certain, but I think it was that burgundy color. And the shape was similar. I'm not much of a car person. My husband would have known exactly, but he was already in bed. He didn't get to the window in time.'

'Did you see any people in the car? Did you see the license plate?'

'No. I just saw the car. It pulled out of the driveway and went north, toward 18th Street.'

I thanked her and went back to the Vic.

I had two means of exit from the Vic. I could crawl across the consul and go out the passenger side door, or I could crawl out the driver's side window. It was easier to crawl out the window, but that meant the window stayed open, and it was freezing cold when I returned to the car. Although, since I had half a rotting squirrel stuck to my dashboard, there was some advantage to the open window.

I'd chosen to do the crawl over the consul thing this time so as not to tip off the neighbors I wasn't really a cop. I returned to the Vic, got some heat going, and reviewed my choices. I could take a shot at finding one of the remaining skips. I could go on a poster hunt. I could head over to my parents' house and talk to Grandma about Milton Buzick. Or I could go home and take a nap.

I was leaning toward the nap when my phone buzzed.

'I need help,' Grandma said. 'I got a hot date tonight with Elmer. We're going to the Rozinski viewing, and I'm thinking I might have to show some skin to keep Elmer away from Loretta Flick. I figure I can open a couple buttons on my blue dress, but I can't get my boobs to stay up. I thought you might be able to get me one of them push-up bras.'

Forty-five minutes later, I had Grandma in the Victoria's Secret dressing room, trying on push-up bras.

'Okay,' Grandma said from the other side of the door. 'I got them all lifted up, and they look pretty good except for the wrinkles.'

'I wouldn't worry about the wrinkles,' I told her. 'It looked to me like Elmer has cataracts.'

'Maybe I need one of them thongs to go with this bra,' she said.

I didn't want to think about Grandma in a thong. 'Some pretty panties might be better.'

'As long as they're sexy. I might get lucky tonight.'

If she got lucky, Elmer would drop dead before dinner. 'I'll pick out something that will match while you're getting dressed,' I told Grandma.

We were at the register with the bra and panties, and I heard something sizzle in my head, and the next thing I knew I was on the floor and my lips were tingling.

'Wha . . .' I said.

Grandma was bending over me. 'You got zapped by Joyce Barnhardt. I heard you go over, and I turned around and saw Joyce standing there with a stun gun. We called the police, but she ran off. Dirty rotten coward.'

I looked past Grandma and saw a mall rent-a-cop nervously looking down at me.

'Are you okay?' he asked. 'We got a doctor coming.'

'Get me up on my feet,' I said.

'I don't know if I should,' he said. 'Maybe you should just lay there until help gets here.'

'Get me up!' I yelled at him. 'I don't need a doctor. I need a new car and a new job and ten minutes alone with Ranger. This is all his fault.'

The rent-a-cop got me under my armpits and hoisted me up. I went down to my knees, grabbed hold of his shirt, and pulled myself up again.

'Jeez, lady,' he said.

'Don't worry,' I told him. 'This happens to me a lot. I'm good at it.'

Grandma led me through the mall, and we managed to get to the parking lot and the Vic without the doctor finding me. I was supposed to be keeping a low profile. I didn't want to find myself on the evening news. Local bounty hunter stun-gunned in mall. Details at eight.

Grandma stood back and looked at my car. 'Was your car decorated like this when we left it? I don't remember all this writing on it.'

Someone had spray painted PIG CAR in black and white on the passenger side door and trunk lid.

'It's new,' I said.

'I would have used brighter colors,' Grandma said. 'Gold would have looked good. You can't go wrong with gold.'

'The black and white goes better with the squirrel hair stuck to the dash,' I told her.

'I was wondering what that was,' Grandma said. 'I figured it was one of them new animal print decorator schemes.'

'Lula helped me with it.'

'Isn't she the one,' Grandma said.

I got behind the wheel and motored out of the lot and onto the highway.

'Do you hear a grinding sound?' Grandma asked.

'All cars sound like that,' I said. 'You're just noticing it because I don't have the radio on loud enough. What about Milton? Did you notice if he was wearing jewelry?'

'Nothing worth anything. His lodge lapel pin. That was about it. I know you're looking for Simon Diggery. It'll take something good to get him out in this weather. I'll check out Harry Rozinski, but he probably won't have anything worth taking, and he's not Diggery's size.'

'Do you need a ride tonight?'

'No. Elmer has a car. He's picking me up.'

It was a little after four when I dropped Grandma off. Lights were on in Burg houses and tables were being set for dinner. This was a community where families still sat together for meals. I turned right onto Hamilton and ten minutes later, I was in my apartment building. I let myself in, and Bob rushed over to me.

'Where's Joe?' I asked him.

Not in the kitchen. Not in the dining room. Not in the living room. I went to the bedroom and found him asleep in my bed.

'Hey Goldilocks,' I said.

Morelli came awake and rolled onto his back. 'What time is it?'

'Four-thirty. Have you been here long?'

'Couple hours.'

'I heard a news report on the Berringer murders while I was in the car. They said the police were baffled.'

'Baffled and tired. I need some sleep. I'm too old for this middle-of-the-night murder shit.'

'There was a time when you did all sorts of things in the middle of the night.'

'Come here and you can tell me about them.'

'I thought you were tired.'

'I just want to talk,' Morelli said.

'That's a big fib. I *know* what you want to do.'

Morelli smiled. 'Hard for a man to keep a secret.'

# *Four*

Morelli was at my kitchen counter, drinking coffee, eating cereal. His hair was still damp from the shower, and he was clean-shaven. In ten minutes, he'd have a five o'clock shadow. He was wearing worn-out black jeans, a pale gray cable-knit sweater, and black motorcycle boots.

'You don't look like a cop,' I told him. 'All the other guys wear suits.'

'I've been asked by the chief not to wear a suit. I look like a casino pit boss when I wear a suit. I don't inspire trust.'

I poured myself a bowl of cereal and added milk. 'It was nice of you to bring all this food.'

'Your cupboards were empty. And your refrigerator. I'm guessing the bounty hunter business is slow.'

'It comes and goes. Problem is, I only make enough

money to live day by day. I can't make enough to get ahead.'

'It would be easier if you moved in with me.'

'We've tried that. It's always a disaster. Eventually, we drive each other nuts.'

'It's your job,' Morelli said.

'It's your expectations.'

He put his cereal bowl in the sink and buckled his gun onto his belt. 'Yeah, my expectations are that you'll give up your job.'

'Are we fighting?'

'Am I yelling and waving my arms?'

'No.'

'Then we aren't fighting.' He crooked an arm around my neck and kissed me. 'I have to go. I'm working with Phil Panchek. He hates being baffled without me.'

'Marty Gobel never called to talk to me. Does that mean I'm off the hook?'

'No. It means he's dreading talking to you for fear you don't have an alibi, and he's procrastinating as long as possible.'

Bob was leaning against me. 'Are you taking Bob?'

'Yeah, I'll drop him off at my house. He has a routine. He eats the couch. He takes a nap. He gnaws on a dining-room table leg. He takes a nap. He spreads the garbage all over the kitchen floor. He takes a nap.'

I fondled Bob's ear. 'You're lucky you have a dog who can amuse himself while you're gone.'

Morelli shrugged into his jacket and clipped Bob's leash on him. 'Later.'

I finished my coffee and cereal and hand-washed the dishes. I took a shower and put in the minimum effort on my hair. Truth is, the minimum effort isn't that far removed from the maximum effort, and my hair pretty much looks the same no matter what I do with it. I applied some mascara and looked myself in the eye in the mirror.

'Today is the day,' I said to myself. 'Time to get serious. If you don't catch someone soon, you'll get kicked out of your apartment.'

I got dressed in my lucky jeans and my lucky black sweater. It was still cold, but it wasn't snowing or sleeting, so I traded my fake Uggs for running shoes . . . just in case I had to chase down Diggery. I had cuffs in my back jeans pocket. Pepper spray in my jacket pocket. A stun gun clipped to my belt. I went to the kitchen and took my gun out of my cookie jar. It was a little five-shot Smith & Wesson. I spun the barrel. No bullets. I looked in the jar. No bullets. I rummaged through kitchen drawers. No bullets. I put the gun back into the cookie jar. I didn't really want to shoot anyone today anyway.

I got bundled up in my parka and scarf and gloves, and went out to the Vic. I crawled in and plugged the key into the ignition. It took a while, but the engine finally caught. All right, so I didn't have a great car. No big deal, I told myself. At least it was running. And today was the day it was all going to turn around. I was going after Diggery first and then Coglin. And then I was going to plow through the rest of the cases.

I took Broad and headed for Bordentown. It was just past rush hour, and traffic was heavy but moving. The cloud cover had finally lifted and the sky was as blue as it gets in Jersey. I was on Route 206, cruising along, listening to the radio, when the grinding sound coming from under the hood turned into BANG, BANG, BANG and the car coasted to a stop at the side of the road. It wasn't entirely unexpected, but it left me breathless all the same. Another example that sugar isn't pixie dust, and wish as hard as you might, it won't make you invisible.

I was sitting there trying to keep from crying, running through my options, and Ranger called.

'Babe, you're stopped on Route 206. What's up?'

I remembered the gizmo in my bag. RangeMan was monitoring me. 'My car died.'

Fifteen minutes later, I looked in my rearview mirror and saw Ranger pull in behind me. He got out of his car and into mine. Ranger didn't smile a lot, but clearly he was amused.

'I don't know how you do it,' Ranger said. 'In a matter of days, you've managed to turn a perfectly good piece-of-shit car into something so fucked up it's a work of art.'

'It's a gift.'

'The bullet hole in the rear window?'

'Joyce Barnhardt,' I told him. 'She's unhappy with me because she thinks I killed Dickie.'

'And the crud on the dash?'

'Squirrel bomb.'

He looked incredulous for a moment and then burst out laughing. In all the time I'd known Ranger, this was maybe the third time I'd seen him actually laugh out loud, so it turned out to be worth getting squirrel-bombed.

Ranger dropped back to a smile and tugged me out of the car. He kicked the door closed, slung an arm around my shoulders, and walked me back to his Porsche Cayenne. 'Where were you going?' he asked.

'I'm looking for Simon Diggery,' I said. 'I stopped by his double-wide on Tuesday, but no one was home. I thought I'd try again.'

Ranger opened the Cayenne door for me. 'I'll go with you. If we're lucky, we might get to see his snake eat a cow.'

I looked back at the Vic. 'What about my car?'

'I'll have it picked up.'

Ranger didn't bother parking out of sight of Diggery's trailer. He drove the Cayenne onto the blighted grass and pulled up between the trailer and the stand of hardwoods. We got out of the Porsche, and he gave me his gun.

'Stay here and shoot anyone who makes a run for it, including the snake.'

'How do you know I don't have my own gun?'

'Do you?'

'No.'

Ranger did another one of those almost sighing things and jogged around to Diggery's front door. I heard him rap on the door and call out. There was the sound of the rusted door opening and closing and then silence. I held my ground.

After a couple minutes, Ranger reappeared and motioned for me to join him.

'Simon is off somewhere, but the uncle is here. And stay away from the sink,' Ranger said.

I gave him his gun back, followed him into the trailer, and immediately checked out the kitchen area. The snake was sprawled on the counter, its head in the sink. I guess it was thirsty. The uncle was at the small built-in table.

The uncle wasn't much older than Simon Diggery, and the family resemblance was there, blurred over a little by hard drinking and an extra fifty pounds. He was wearing black socks and ratty bedroom slippers and huge boxer shorts.

'Give you a quarter if you pull your shirt up,' Bill Diggery said to me.

'I'll give *you* a quarter if you put your shirt on,' I told him.

Ranger was against the wall, watching Diggery. 'Where's Simon?' Ranger asked.

'Don't know,' Bill said.

'Think about it,' Ranger told him.

'He might be at work.'

'Where is he working?'

'Don't know.'

Ranger's eyes flicked to the snake and back to Bill. 'Has he been fed today?'

'He don't eat every day,' Bill said. 'He probably ain't hungry.'

'Steph,' Ranger said. 'Wait outside so I can talk to Bill.'

'You aren't going to feed him to the snake, are you?'

'Not all of him.'

'As long as it's not all of him,' I said. And I let myself out.

I closed the door and waited for a couple minutes. I didn't hear any screams of pain or terror. No gunshots. I hunkered down in my jacket and shoved my hands into my pockets to keep warm. A couple more minutes passed, and Ranger came out, closing the door behind him.

'Well?' I asked.

'Simon is working in the food court at Quakerbridge Mall. Bill didn't know more than that.'

'Did you feed Uncle Bill to the snake?'

'No. He was right . . . the snake wasn't hungry.'

'Then how did you get him to talk?'

Ranger slid an arm around me, and I felt his lips brush my ear when he spoke. 'I can be very persuasive.'

No kidding.

Quakerbridge is on Route One, northeast of

Trenton. It seemed like a long way for Diggery to drive for an odd job in a food court, but what the heck, maybe Diggery was lucky to get it. And maybe he had a better car than I did. That thought brought me up to a sobering reality. Diggery for sure had a better car than I did because I had no car at all.

Ranger drove out of Diggery's neighborhood and headed north. We were on Route 206, and I was dreading the section of highway where I'd left the Vic. I didn't want to see the poor, sad, broken-down car. It was a reminder of what was wrong with my life. Crappy job, hand-to-mouth existence, no future I was willing to commit to. If it was June and the sun was shining, I might feel different, but it was cold and the clouds had returned and a mist had started to fall.

'I need macaroni and cheese,' I said to Ranger, clapping my hands over my eyes. 'I promised myself French fries, jelly doughnuts, birthday cake . . . and I never got them.'

'I have a better way to make you happy,' Ranger said. 'Less fattening but more addicting.'

'Pharmaceuticals?'

'Sex. And you can open your eyes. The Vic's gone.'

'Gone where?'

'Car heaven.'

Twenty minutes later, Ranger stopped at a light on Broad, and his cell buzzed. He answered on a Bluetooth earpiece and listened for a couple minutes, his mood somber, his expression not showing anything. He thanked the caller and disconnected.

'They found the accountant, Ziggy Zabar,' Ranger said. 'He washed ashore about a quarter mile south of the Ferry Street Bridge. He was identified by a credit card and a medic alert bracelet for a heart condition.'

Ranger parked behind the medical examiners' truck, and we walked the distance to the crime scene. It was turning into a miserable day and the weather was holding the crowd down. Only a few hardy photographers and reporters. No gawkers. A handful of uniforms, a couple plainclothes guys. An EMS team that looked like they wanted to be somewhere else. No one I recognized. We ducked under the yellow tape and found Tank.

Tank is Ranger's next in command and his shadow. No need to describe him. His name says it all. He was dressed in RangeMan black, and he looked impervious to the weather.

Tank was with Ziggy Zabar's brother Zip, also in RangeMan black, his face stoic, his posture rigid.

'We picked the call up from police dispatch,' Tank said, stepping away from Zip. 'He's been in the water awhile, and he's not in great shape, but I've looked at him, and even in his condition it's obvious it was an execution. Single bullet nice and clean in the forehead. He's wearing an ankle shackle, so I'm guessing he was attached to something heavy, and the tide broke him loose.'

I sucked in some air. I didn't know Ziggy Zabar, but it was horrible all the same.

We stayed for a while, keeping Zip company while he watched over his dead brother. The police photographer left and the EMS guys came in with a body bag. I could hear the motor running on the ME truck at the top of the hill. The uniforms had their collars turned up and were shuffling their feet. The mist had turned into a drizzle.

Ranger was wearing his SEAL ball cap. He tucked my hair behind my ears and put his hat on my head to keep me dry. 'You look like you need that birthday cake.'

'I'd settle for a peanut butter sandwich and some dry socks.'

'I want to talk to the ME, and then I have some things to do.' He handed me the keys to the Cayenne.

'Use my car. I can ride with Tank and Zip. I don't care if you destroy the car, but take care of the hat. I want it back.'

I scrambled up the hill, hoisted myself into the Porsche, and turned the heat on full blast. As I pulled off the service road onto Broad, my cell phone buzzed. It was Marty Gobel.

'I need you to come in and make a statement,' Marty said. 'I know this isn't anything you want to do, but I can't put it off any longer.'

'That's okay,' I told him. 'I understand. I'll be there in ten minutes.'

The cop shop is on Perry Street. Half the building is the courthouse and half the police station. It's redbrick, and the architecture could best be categorized as utilitarian municipal. Money wasn't wasted on fancy columns or art. This is strictly a 60-watt building. Still, it serves its purpose, and it's in a neighborhood where it's convenient for the police to find crime.

I parked in the public lot across the street and stowed the pepper spray, handcuffs, and stun gun in the console. I applied fresh lip gloss and went to talk to Marty.

I crossed the lobby to the cop-in-a-cage and gave him my name. Court was in session across the hall and people were milling around, waiting to pass through security.

Marty met me in the lobby. We got coffee and found an empty room where he could take my statement.

'So,' Marty said when we were seated, 'why did you kill Dickie Orr?'

I felt my mouth drop open and my eyes go wide.

Marty gave a bark of laughter. 'I'm just fucking with you,' he said. 'The guys made me do it.'

'Should I have an attorney present?' I asked him.

'Do you have one?'

'My brother-in-law.'

'Oh jeez, are you talking about Albert Kloughn? He chases ambulances. He paid for his law degree with chickens. Got it somewhere in the islands, right?'

I did some mental knuckle cracking. 'What do you want to know?'

'Do you have an alibi?'

Oh boy.

An hour later, I pushed my chair back. 'I'm done,' I told Gobel. 'If you want any more you'll have to feed me.'

'The best I could do is a Snickers bar.'

'How many?'

Gobel closed his notepad. 'I'm done anyway. You

and Morelli aren't planning on going out of the country any time soon, are you?'

I slanted my eyes at him. 'What are you saying?'

'Well, you know, you're kind of a suspect. Actually, you're our *only* suspect.'

'What's my motive?'

'You hated him.'

'Everybody hated him.'

'Not true. Not *everybody*. And you stand to inherit a lot of money. He had a will drawn up when you were married, and it never got changed. You get everything.'

'What?' I said it on a whoosh of air because it literally knocked the wind out of me.

'You didn't know?'

'I don't believe it.' This was the most contentious divorce in the history of the Burg. The shouting was heard for miles. We called each other names that didn't even exist.

'Believe it,' Marty Gobel said.

'How do you know about the will? Aren't wills secret?'

'Not this one. His girlfriend has a copy. Joyce Barnhardt. He was in the process of changing it, so she would be his sole heir, but he never signed it.'

'You're kidding again, right? This is another joke.'

'Swear to God. If they ever find his body you'll be rich. Of course, you might not be in a good position to enjoy it.'

I left Gobel, locked myself in the Cayenne, and called Morelli. 'Did you know I was Dickie's sole heir?' I asked him.

'No. How did you find that out?'

'Gobel. Joyce told him. Apparently she has a copy of Dickie's will.'

'So you talked to Marty. How'd it go?'

'By the time we were done, I was sort of feeling I might have killed Dickie.'

There was a moment of silence. 'You didn't, did you?'

'No! Yeesh. I'm going home. I'm all discombobulated.'

'Look in the freezer when you get home. I got you happy food.'

'How happy?'

'Stouffer's macaroni and cheese. The family size.'

'I love you!'

I could feel Morelli smile at the other end. 'I own you now. I know where all the buttons are.'

I rushed home and went straight to the freezer. I yanked the door open and there it was – the family size. I almost fainted from joy. I popped it into the microwave and ran into the bedroom to get dry clothes. I was changing out of my socks, and I realized the room didn't feel exactly right. I'd left the bed unmade and rumpled, and now it was less rumpled, and the pillows were all lined up on the headboard. And my T-shirt drawer was partially open.

I moved to the chest beside the bed and got the cylinder of pepper spray from the top drawer. I looked under the bed and in every closet. Didn't find anyone. Whoever had been here was now gone.

I called Morelli.

'I've got it in the microwave,' I told him. 'When did you bring it over?'

'Yesterday. When I brought all the rest of the stuff. Why?'

'I think someone was in my apartment while I was gone this morning.'

'Probably Ranger fingering your underwear.'

'No. I was with Ranger. And if Ranger was here, I'd never know.' And if Ranger wanted to finger my underwear, he'd do it while I was wearing it.

'If you're worried, you can move yourself over to my house. Bob loves company.'

'How about you?'

'I'd like it too. Just kick the beer cans and pizza boxes out of your way and make yourself at home.'

'Could it have been the police looking for evidence?'

'No. We couldn't use evidence obtained that way. And besides, no one's that smart here. Only television cops do that sort of thing.'

'Good to know. Gotta run. My mac and cheese just dinged.'

'I've got some paperwork to finish, and then I'm heading out. Where will I find you?'

'I'm going to stay here. There weren't any death threats spray-painted on the walls, so maybe I'm just imagining things. I'm a little spooked, what with being accused of murder.'

'You're not accused yet,' Morelli said. 'You're only under suspicion.'

I hung up, stuffed my feet into the shearling boots, and pulled a hooded fleece sweatshirt over my head. I liked Morelli's house better than my apartment, but all my clothes and makeup and hair things were here. When Morelli spent the night with me, he borrowed my razor, used whatever soap was in the bathroom, and re-dressed in the clothes that hit the floor the night before. He kept some underwear and socks here, and that was it. When I stayed with Morelli, it was a whole production.

I polished off the mac and cheese and washed it down with a beer. I was now warm inside and out, and no longer cared so much about the Dickie issue.

I'd dropped a cheesy macaroni into Rex's food cup, and he was busy stuffing it into his cheeks. His whiskers were whirring and his tiny black eyes were bright.

'Time to go get a Diggery,' I said to Rex. 'Now that I'm full of mac and cheese, I can do *anything* – leap tall buildings in a single bound, stop a speeding locomotive, get a bikini wax.'

Rex flicked a glance at me and scurried into his soup can.

# *Five*

It was mid-afternoon and still gray and drizzly, but the drizzle wasn't freezing on the roads. I thought that was a good sign. I was on my way to the mall in Ranger's car and hat, and I was feeling very kick-ass. I was armed with the pepper spray and the stun gun. I had my cuffs. I had my paperwork. I was ready to do a takedown.

I parked at the food court entrance and made a tour of the concessions. Pizza, burgers, ice cream, smoothies, Chinese, cookies, subs, Mexican, sandwiches. I didn't see Diggery. Then I did a fast scan of the tables and spotted him on the far side, against a wall. He was talking to someone, and there were papers spread across the table.

I got a diet soda and found an empty table just behind Diggery. He was busy talking and didn't notice me. He seemed to be filling out some sort of form. He finished the form, gave it to the woman across from him, and she gave him some money and left. A new person immediately sat down and gave Diggery a large yellow envelope.

I wasn't taking any chances with this. I wasn't going to give Diggery an opportunity to bolt and run. I quietly moved to Diggery and clapped a bracelet on his right wrist.

Diggery looked down at the cuff and then up at me. 'Fuck,' Diggery said.

'You need to get rebonded,' I told him. 'You missed your court date.'

'I'm conducting business now,' Diggery said. 'A little respect, okay? I don't come barging into your office, do I?'

'This isn't an office. It's a food court. What the heck are you doing?'

'He's doing my taxes,' the woman across from him said. 'He does them every year.'

I looked at the woman. 'You let *him* do your taxes?'

'He's certifiable.'

Couldn't argue with that. 'He's also under arrest,' I told her. 'You're going to have to make other arrangements.'

'What arrangements? I can't do these forms. I can't figure them out.'

Four more people came forward. Three men and a woman.

'What's going on?' one of the men asked. 'What's the holdup?'

'Simon has to leave now,' I told him.

'No way. I've been waiting for an hour, and I'm next in line. You want a piece of Simon, take a number.'

'Get up,' I said to Diggery.

'It's gonna get ugly,' he said. 'You don't want to piss off Oscar over there. He don't got a lot of patience, and he's missing his afternoon TV shows to do this.'

'I can't believe you're doing taxes.'

'It was just one of them things that mushroomed. Not that it should be so surprising since I have a very strong entrepreneurial side to me.'

I looked at my watch. 'If we hustle, I can get you bonded out today, and you can be back here in a couple hours.'

'I'm not waiting no more couple hours,' Oscar said, giving me a shot to the shoulder that knocked me into the woman behind me.

I took the stun gun out of my coat pocket. 'Back off,' I said to Oscar. 'Simon is in violation of his bond, and he needs to go with me.'

Janet Evanovich

'I've got one of those too,' the woman behind me said. And ZINNNNG.

When I came around, I was on my back on the floor, and I was looking at the rent-a-cop from the lingerie trip with Grandma.

'Are you okay?' he said. 'Did you have a spell? Can you get a flashback from a stun gun?'

'It's my life,' I said to him. 'It's complicated.'

He dragged me up and set me in a chair. 'Do you want water or something?'

'Yeah, water would be good.'

By the time he came with the water, the clanging in my head had almost completely stopped. I sipped the water and looked around. No Diggery. His clients were gone too. No doubt moved on to a taco stand or gas station. I was missing my cuffs and stun gun. I was probably lucky they hadn't taken my shoes and my watch.

I retreated to the parking lot, and carefully maneuvered the car onto the highway. I drove on autopilot and suddenly realized I was stopped in front of my parents' house. I checked to make sure I was no longer drooling, then went into the house. My dad was in front of the television, sound asleep with the paper draped over his stomach. My mother and grandmother were in the kitchen cooking.

Grandma was wearing tight black Spandex yoga pants and a pink T-shirt that said *I'm Sassy*, and she'd dyed her hair red. My mother was at the stove, but the ironing board was up, and the iron was plugged in. I suspected it was the red hair that got the iron out.

Since the iron was already out, I decided I'd just jump in. 'So,' I said to Grandma, 'how'd the date go?'

'It was pretty good,' Grandma said. 'The funeral parlor had a new cookie. Chocolate with white chocolate chips. And they did a real good job with Harry Rozinski. You couldn't hardly tell half his nose was eaten away with the skin cancer.'

'Was he wearing jewelry?'

'No. But Lorraine Birnbaum was next door in viewing room Number Four, and she was all decked out. She was wearing a real nice-looking watch, and they left her wedding band and diamond on her. The diamond was real big too. You probably don't remember Lorraine. She moved away when you were little. She came back to live with her daughter after her husband died last year, but she didn't last too long. Her memorial said she was being buried on Friday.'

'Did Elmer behave himself?'

'Yeah. That was the only disappointment. I was

ready to put out, but he got some acid reflux from the cookies and had to go home.'

My mother was at the stove sautéing ground beef for stuffed peppers. She reached for the cupboard where she kept her liquor stash, paused, then pulled herself together and went on with the sautéing.

'Sissy Cramp and I went shopping today,' Grandma said, 'and I got these new clothes and went to the beauty parlor. I thought I should spruce up since Elmer has all that nice black hair. It's a marvel that at his age he hasn't got a gray hair on his head.'

'He hasn't got *any* hair on his head,' I told Grandma. 'He wears a wig.'

'That would explain a lot of things,' Grandma said.

My mother and I looked at each other and shared a grimace.

'I read where red is the hot color for hair this year,' Grandma said. 'So I had Dolly do me red this time. What do you think?'

'I think it's fun,' I told Grandma. 'It brings out the color in your eyes.'

I could see my mother bite into her lower lip, and I knew she was eyeing the liquor cabinet again.

'It makes me feel like a whole new person,' Grandma said. 'Sissy says I look just like Shirley MacLaine.'

I zipped my jacket. 'I just stopped in to say hello. I have to get back to the office.'

I checked myself out in the hall mirror on my way to the door to make sure there were no leftover effects from the stun gun . . . like my tongue hanging out or my eyes rolling around in my head. I didn't notice anything, so I left my parents' house, buckled myself into the Cayenne, and called Lula.

'Un hunh,' Lula said.

'I'm going to check on Carl Coglin. Want to ride along with me?'

'Sure. Maybe I can explode another squirrel on myself.'

Five minutes later, I picked her up in front of the bonds office.

'Now this is what I call a car,' Lula said, getting into the Cayenne. 'Only one place you get a car like this.'

'It's Ranger's.'

'Don't I know it. I get a rush just sitting in it. I swear, that man is so hot and so fine it's like he isn't even human.'

'Mmm,' I said.

'Mmm. What's that supposed to mean? You think he isn't fine?'

'He involved me in a murder.'

'He told you to choke Dickie in front of the whole law office staff?'

'Well, no. Not exactly.'

'Not that Dickie don't deserve getting choked.'

'Dickie's scum.'

'Fuckin' A,' Lula said.

'Although it would appear I'm the sole beneficiary in his will.'

'Say what?'

'Apparently, he had a will drawn up when we were married, making me heir, and he never got around to changing it.'

'How do you know that?'

'Joyce has a copy. She told the police about it, and they brought me in for questioning.'

'Then it's Joyce that involved you in this murder.'

'Yes!'

'Bitch,' Lula said.

I drove up Hamilton and pointed the Porsche toward North Trenton. It was four o'clock, and another day was slipping by without a capture. If this continued, I'd have to scrounge around for another job. At least something part-time.

'What's the plan here?' Lula wanted to know.

'If he's home, we grab him and cuff him and drag

him to the car. You have cuffs, right?'

'Not with me. You're the big-deal bounty hunter. You're supposed to have the cuffs.'

'I lost my cuffs.'

'Again? Honest to goodness, I've never seen anybody lose things like you.'

'You usually have cuffs,' I said to Lula.

'They're sort of attached to my bed. Tank was over, and we got playful.'

Eeek. Either one of them in handcuffs attached to a bed wasn't a good picture. 'I didn't realize you were a couple.'

'We're one of them couples who don't see each other all the time. We just see each other some of the time. And sometimes it goes to once in a while.'

'Okay, then we can grab Coglin and stun-gun him. Do you have your stun gun?'

'Sure I got my stun gun.' Lula pulled her stun gun out of her big purse. 'Uh-oh, low battery.'

I knew she had her Glock. And I knew it was loaded. But I didn't especially want her to shoot Coglin.

'How about I grab him and sit on him until he gives up?' Lula said.

'I guess that would work.'

I cruised down Coglin's street and idled in front of

his house. Lights were off inside. I drove around the block and scoped out the back of the house. No car parked in the alley. I cut the engine and Lula and I got out and walked to Coglin's back door. I rapped on the door and announced myself. No answer.

Lula had her hand on the doorknob. 'It's unlocked,' she said, pushing the door open, stepping inside. 'This guy's real trusting.'

'Maybe he never came back.'

We went room by room, flipping lights on, looking around. The stuffed animals were everywhere. He had an entire bedroom filled with pigeons.

'Who would want a stuffed pigeon?' Lula asked. 'I mean, what sort of a market do you suppose there is for a dead pigeon?'

We went back downstairs, made our way out to the porch showroom, and Lula stopped in front of a beaver.

'Look at this bad boy,' Lula said. 'Now, this is what I'm talking about. This here's the biggest fuckin' rodent ever lived. This is practically prehistoric.'

I'd never seen a beaver up close and personal, and I was surprised at the size. 'Do you suppose they're always this big?'

'Maybe Crazy Coglin overstuffed it.'

Lula picked up a remote that had been placed beside the beaver. The remote had two buttons. One of the buttons was labeled EYES and the other BANG!

Lula pressed the EYES button and the beaver's eyes glowed. She pressed it again and the eyes shut off.

'Probably I don't want to press the BANG! button,' Lula said. 'This here looks to me like a exploding beaver. And it's not like it's some second-rate squirrel. This mother's gonna make a mess. This is atomic. This is something you only give to the enemy.'

I looked over at Lula and smiled.

'I know what you're thinking,' Lula said. 'You're thinking of Joyce and how she deserves this beaver. You're thinking we have a obligation to give this beaver to Joyce.'

'She likes animals.'

'Yeah, especially big trained dogs and ponies.'

'Maybe the second button doesn't explode it. Maybe the beaver sings a song or something.'

'The button says BANG!'

'It could be mislabeled.'

'I see where you're going,' Lula said. 'You're thinking we have to say a lot of Hail Marys if we send this to Joyce and explode it on her. But it wouldn't be our fault if it exploded accidental. Or if there was a misunderstanding on our part.'

'I wouldn't want to maim her.'

'Of course not.'

'Just because she shot at me, zapped me with a stun gun, and ratted me out to the police isn't any reason to do her bodily harm.'

'Whatever.'

'Still, it would be fun to send her a singing beaver.'

Lula looked at her watch. 'How long we gonna stand here doing this rationalizing shit? I got stuff to do.'

I scrounged around in my purse and came up with eight dollars and forty cents. I left it on the table and pocketed the remote.

'What's that?' Lula wanted to know.

'It's for the beaver. I'm in enough trouble. I don't want to be accused of stealing a . . . singing beaver.'

'And you think it's worth eight dollars and forty cents?'

'It's all I've got.' I wrapped my arms around the beaver and hefted it off the table. 'This weighs a ton!'

Lula got her hands under his butt and helped me to the door. We loaded the beaver into the Cayenne cargo area and drove it across town to Joyce's house.

Joyce lives in a big white colonial with fancy columns and a large yard. The house is the result of her last divorce. Joyce got the house, and her husband got a new lease on life. There was a red Jeep in the driveway, and lights were shining in the downstairs windows.

Lula and I dragged the beaver out of the back of the Cayenne and lugged it to Joyce's front porch. We set the beaver down, I rang the bell, and Lula and I ran for cover. We hunkered down behind the red Jeep and gulped air.

The front door opened, and Joyce said, 'What on earth?'

I pushed the button to make the eyes glow, and I peeked around the car. Joyce was bent over looking at the beaver.

A man came up behind her. Not Dickie. A younger, chunkier guy in jeans and a thermal T-shirt. 'What is it?' he asked.

'It's a beaver.'

'Well, bring it inside,' he said. 'I like beaver.'

Joyce pushed and pulled the beaver inside and closed the door. Lula and I scurried to a window on the side of the house where curtains hadn't been drawn and looked in at Joyce and the Jeep guy. The two of them were examining the beaver, patting it on the head, smiling at it.

'Think they've had a few drinkipoos,' Lula said. 'Anyone in their right mind wouldn't bring the beaver from hell into their house.'

After a minute or two, Joyce and the Jeep guy got tired of the beaver and walked away. I waited until they were a safe distance, and then I pushed the BANG! button. There was a moment's lag, and then BLAM! Beaver fur and beaver stuffing as far as the eye could see.

The fur and glop hung from couches, chairs, tables, and table lamps. It was in Joyce's hair and was stuck to the back of her shirt. Joyce froze for a beat, turned, and looked around with her eyes bugged out.

'Fuck!' Joyce shrieked. 'Fuck, fuck, fuck!'

'Holy crap,' Lula said.

We sprang from the window and ran through the neighbor's yard to where we'd parked the car. We jumped in, and I laid rubber out of there.

'Guess it wasn't a singing beaver after all,' I said.

'Yeah, darn,' Lula said. 'I was looking forward to hearing some singing.'

I was smiling so wide my cheeks ached. 'It was worth my last eight dollars.'

'That was awesome,' Lula said. 'That Coglin is a freakin' genius.'

Lula had her Firebird parked in the small lot behind the office. I dropped her off at her car and motored home to my apartment.

Morelli was watching television when I came in.

'You look happy,' he said. 'You must have had a productive day.'

'It started off slow, but it ended okay.'

'There's a casserole in the refrigerator. It's from my mom. It has vegetables in it and everything. And I could use another beer. The game's coming on.'

Hours later, we were still in front of the television when Morelli's cell phone rang.

'I'm not answering it,' Morelli said. 'The guy who invented the cell phone should rot in hell.'

The ringing stopped and a minute later, it started again.

Morelli shut the phone off.

We had three minutes of silence, and my phone rang in the kitchen.

'Persistent bastard,' Morelli said.

The ringing didn't stop, and finally Morelli went to the kitchen and answered the phone. He was smiling when he came back.

'Good news?' I asked.

'Yes, but I'm going to have to go to work.'

'The Berringer case?'

'No. Something else.'

He went to the bedroom, rousted Bob off the bed, and snapped the leash on him. 'I might have to go under for a while, but I'll call,' Morelli said. 'And don't worry about Dickie. I'm sure it'll work out okay.' He grabbed his jacket and kissed me. 'Later.'

I closed and locked the door after him and stood for a moment taking the pulse of the apartment. It felt empty without Morelli. On the other hand, I could watch something sappy on television, wear my ratty, comfy flannel jammies, and hog the bed.

# Six

I got up late because there was no real good reason to get up early. I made coffee and ate junky cereal out of the box and pushed it down with a banana. My files were spread across the dining-room table. Coglin, Diggery, and a third file I hadn't yet opened. Today was the day for the third file. I had the file in my hand when my phone rang.

'Are you all right?' my mother asked.

'Couldn't be better.'

'Have you seen the paper this morning?'

'No.'

'Don't look,' she said.

'Now what?'

'It's all over the news that you killed Dickie.'

'Tell her I'll visit her in the big house,' Grandma yelled at my mother. 'Tell her I'll bring cigarettes so she can pay off the butch guards.'

113

'I'll call you back,' I said to my mother.

I disconnected and looked out my peephole. Good deal. Mr Molinowski's morning paper was still lying in front of his door. I tiptoed out, snatched it up, and scurried back into my apartment.

The headline read LOCAL BOUNTY HUNTER PRIME SUSPECT IN ORR DISAPPEARANCE. Front page. And the article was accompanied by an unflattering picture of me taken while I was waiting for Gobel in the municipal building lobby. They'd interviewed Joyce, and Joyce was quoted as saying I'd always been jealous of her and had fits of violent behavior even as a child. There was a mention of the time Grandma and I accidentally burned down the funeral home. There was a second file photo of me with no eyebrows, the result of my car exploding into a fireball a while back. And then there were several statements by secretaries who'd witnessed me going postal on Dickie. One of the secretaries stated that I pointed a gun at Dickie and threatened to 'put a big hole in his head.'

'That was Lula,' I said to the empty hall.

I put the paper back on Mr Molinowski's welcome mat, returned to my apartment, threw the bolt on the door, and called my mother.

'All a pack of lies,' I said to my mother. 'Ignore it. Everything's fine. I went downtown to have coffee with Marty Gobel and someone got the wrong idea.'

There was a pause while my mother talked herself into halfway believing the story. 'I'm having a roast chicken tonight. Are you and Joseph coming to dinner?'

It was Friday. Morelli and I always had dinner at my parents' house on Friday night.

'Sure,' I said. 'I'll be there. I don't know about Joe. He's on a case.'

I drank coffee and read the third file. Stewart Hansen was charged with running a light and possession of a controlled substance. He was twenty-two years old, unemployed, and he lived in a house on Myrtle Street at the back end of the Burg. The house had been posted as collateral on the bond. It was owned by Stewart's cousin Trevor.

I heard a sharp rap on my door and went to look out the security peephole. It was Joyce.

'Open this door,' she yelled. 'I know you're in there.' She tried to rattle the door, but it held tight.

'What do you want?' I called through the door.

'I want to talk to you.'

'About what?'

'About Dickie, you moron. I want to know where he is. You found out about the money and you somehow managed to snatch him, didn't you?'

'Why do you want to know where he is?'

'None of your business. I just need to know,' Joyce said.

'What's with the knit hat on your head?' I asked her. 'I almost didn't recognize you. You never wear a hat.'

Joyce fidgeted with the hat. 'It's cold out. Everyone wears a hat in this weather.'

Especially everyone who has beaver fur stuck to their hair.

'So where the frig is he?' Joyce asked.

'I told you, I don't know. I didn't kill him. I didn't kidnap him. I have no clue where he is.'

'Great,' Joyce said. 'That's how you want to play it? Okay by me.'

And she stomped away.

'What's wrong with this picture?' I asked Rex. 'How did this happen?'

Rex was asleep in his soup can. Hard to have a meaningful conversation with a hamster in a can.

I thought that with the way my morning was running, it wouldn't hurt to have Lula along when I went to see Stewart. Lula wasn't much good as an apprehension agent, but she understood the need for a doughnut when a takedown went into the toilet.

'So what did this guy do?'

Lula was in the passenger seat of Ranger's Cayenne, looking through Stewart Hansen's file. 'It just says controlled substance here. Who wrote this? It don't tell you anything.'

I turned onto Myrtle and drove by the house. It looked benign. Small cottage. Small plot of land. Indistinguishable from every other house on the street. Christmas lights still up outlining the front door. Not lit. I circled the block and parked one house down. Lula and I got out and walked up to Stewart Hansen's house.

'This house is closed up tight,' Lula said. 'It got blackout drapes on all the windows. Either they're trying to conserve energy, or else they're running around naked in there.'

I had new cuffs and a stun gun from Connie. 'Easier to stun-gun someone when he's naked.'

'Yeah, you got a lot to choose from. You ready to do this?'

I gave her a thumbs-up, and she hauled out her gun and jogged around the house to secure the back door. I felt comfortable she wouldn't have to shoot anyone because Lula, holding her big Glock, dressed in her Sasquatch boots, poison-green tights, and matching Spandex mini skirt, topped off with shocking-pink rabbit fur jacket, was enough to make a strong man faint.

I had my cell phone on speaker, clipped to my jacket, the line open. 'Are you in place?' I asked Lula.

'Yep,' Lula said from the back of the house.

I rapped on the front door with my two-pound Maglite. No one answered, so I rapped again, and yelled, *'Bond enforcement!'*

'Shit,' Lula said on speakerphone. 'Turn your head when you do that. You just about busted my eardrum.'

'I'm going in,' I told her.

'Don't exert yourself breaking the door down. The back is open.'

I heard a gunshot and had a moment of panic.

'Oops,' Lula said. 'Ignore that.'

The front was locked, so I waited for Lula to open the door for me. She was smiling wide when she let me in.

'You're not gonna believe this,' she said. 'We hit the jackpot on this one. We must have died and gone to heaven, and no one told us.'

I stepped into a small foyer constructed of raw wallboard. A door opened off the foyer, and beyond the door was cannabis. The house was a pot farm. Grow lights, silver reflective walls, fans and vents, and racks and more racks of shelves filled with plants in various stages of growth.

'Wait until you see the dining room,' Lula said. 'They got primo shit growing in the dining room.'

I gave her a raised eyebrow.

'Not that I would know,' Lula said.

'There's weed sticking out of the pockets of your jacket.'

'I gathered some evidence on my way through the house.'

'I assume you didn't see any Hansens?'

'No, but there's a car back there. And the back door to the house was open. I wouldn't be surprised there's someone hiding in here.'

'Do we have to worry about them getting away in the car?'

'No. Someone shot a hole in the right front tire.'

I locked and bolted the front door, and Lula and I began working our way through the house.

'You go first and open the doors, and I'll be behind you with my gun,' Lula said. 'I'd go first, but it's hard to hold a gun and open a door. I want to be able to concentrate on the gun. It's not like I'm afraid or anything.'

'Just don't shoot me in the back.'

'Have I ever shot you? Honest to goodness, you'd think I didn't know what I was doing.'

We searched the living room, dining room, and kitchen.

'At least these boys are neat,' Lula said. 'They got their empty beer bottles all lined up. Guess that's so they have room in here for planting the little seedlings and weighing and bagging. And they got a nice digital scale here. You could see they put some thought to this.'

I poked around in the collection of pots and pans and bottles and jars by the stove. 'Looks like they have a science experiment going on. Alcohol, coffee filters, ether.'

'These guys are nuts,' Lula said. 'They're making hash oil. You could turn yourself into a barbecue making that stuff.'

We moved down the hall to the bedrooms. No need to search under beds because there weren't any. Two sleeping bags were thrown against a wall in one of the bedrooms. A television sat on the floor. The closet was filled with clothes. The rest of the room was cannabis.

'This is kind of cozy,' Lula said. 'I bet it's like sleeping in the jungle.'

We checked out the bathroom and the second bedroom. Lots of weed drying out in the second bedroom, but no Hansens.

'We're missing something,' I said to Lula, going back to the kitchen.

'We opened every door,' Lula said. 'We looked around all the racks. We looked behind the shower curtain, and we moved the clothes all around in the closet. There's no cellar and no garage and no attic.'

'There's a cup of coffee sitting on the counter, and the coffee is still warm. Someone was in here, and I don't think they had time to leave. You were at the back door, and I was at the front door. We checked the windows. No one went out through a window.'

Lula cut her eyes to the cupboard over the counter. 'Maybe he left just before we got here. You know, lucky coincidence for him.'

'Yeah,' I said, cuffs in one hand, stun gun in the other, attention focused on the cupboard. 'That could be it.'

Lula stepped back and two-handed the Glock,

aiming it at the cupboard. I reached up and opened one of the doors. And Stewart Hansen tumbled out, crashing onto the counter, sending the science experiment flying. He flopped off the counter onto the floor and scrambled like a cat on black ice – legs moving but no intelligent forward motion.

In the excitement of the moment, Lula squeezed off a shot that went wide of Hansen but knocked out the ether bottle. The liquid splashed onto the gas stove, and we were all paralyzed for a moment.

'Pilot light,' Hansen said.

We all dove for the back door, and I think I was in the air when the explosion occurred. Or maybe it was the explosion that threw me out of the house.

'Holy crap,' Hansen said.

He was on the ground next to me, and Lula was on her back, skirt up to her neck, next to him.

'Who shot that bottle?' Lula said. 'It wasn't me, was it?' I clapped the cuffs on Hansen, and we all took a bunch of steps backward.

'Anyone else in the house?' I asked Hansen.

'No. I was alone.'

We watched the fire rush through the house. It was like a brush fire, and almost instantly the whole house was burning, and clouds of pot smoke were billowing out over the Burg. Sirens were screaming in the distance, and the three of us leaned against Hansen's car and sucked it all in while tiny pieces of cannabis ash sifted down around us.

'This is good shit,' Hansen said, taking a deep breath.

'Smells like you had some Hawaii 5-O,' Lula said. 'Not that I'd know.'

I looked down to make sure my toes weren't smoking. 'Maybe we should move back a little.'

We all scurried to Hansen's rear boundary.

'This is pretty funny,' Lula said. 'We burned down a house.' And Lula started laughing.

Hansen was laughing too. 'Probably a million dollars' worth of grass in that house,' Hansen said. 'Up in smoke.'

I was laughing so hard I tipped over and found myself on the ground. 'Look at me,' I said. 'I can make snow angels.'

'I'm getting wet,' Lula said. 'Is it raining?'

Sounds carried from the front of the house. The rumble of the fire truck engines and the crackle and squawk of police band radios.

'I am so fucking hungry,' Lula said. 'I need chips. I'd fucking kill for chips.'

A black SUV slid to a stop behind Hansen's car. Tank

left the car and walked toward us. 'I've got her,' he said into his walkie. 'She's in the back with Lula.'

Ranger's Cayenne pulled in behind the SUV. Ranger got out, scooped me up off the ground, and held me close.

'I was afraid you were in the house,' Ranger said. 'Are you all right?'

'I got blown out of it,' I told him. 'And then it started raining.'

'It's not rain. It's from the fire hoses on the other side of the house.' He pulled back a little and looked at me. 'Babe, you're high as a kite.'

'*Yes!* And you are *so cute*.'

Ranger put me in the Cayenne and handed Hansen and Lula over to Tank. We drove the length of the alley and turned onto Chambersburg Street.

'You're always so *quiet*,' I said to Ranger. 'What's with that?'

Ranger didn't move, but I suspected he was rolling his eyes.

'Well?' I said.

'I like quiet.'

'Quiet, quiet, quiet,' I said. And I gave Ranger a shot to the arm.

'Don't do that,' Ranger said.

I gave him another shot.

Ranger pulled to the curb and cuffed me to the sissy bar over the passenger side window.

'Are you going to have your way with me now that I'm handcuffed?' I asked.

'Would you like that?'

'Absolutely not.'

Ranger smiled, put the Cayenne in gear, and pulled away from the curb.

'I saw that smile,' I said.

On the one hand, I was feeling very flirty and clever. On the other hand, in a dark, back corner of my mind I suspected I was one of those people who gets obnoxious on wacky tobacky. No matter which was right, I couldn't seem to stop.

'So,' I said, knowing I was pressing the issue. 'Don't you want to have your way with me?'

'More than you could possibly imagine, but right now you're wet, and you smell like pot. You're lucky I let you in my car.'

'Where are we going?'

'I'm taking you home, so you can take a hot shower and get dressed in dry clothes.'

'And then?'

'We'll see.'

Oh boy.

❖

Ranger was in the kitchen making a sandwich when I straggled in. I'd steamed myself in the shower until the water ran cold, and then I'd slipped into jeans and a T-shirt, letting my hair dry on its own.

He looked over at me. 'How are you feeling?'

'Hungry and tired.'

'You had a full morning. You burned a house down to the ground.'

I took two slices of bread, slathered them with mustard, and added ham and cheese.

'Technically, Lula started the fire. It was an accident. She winged a bottle of ether, and it spilled onto the gas stove.'

'We're holding the kid in the cuffs. What do you want to do with him?'

'He's FTA. I need to turn him in.'

'If you turn him in, you're going to be implicated in the fire. It's going to get you more publicity.'

'I need the money.'

Ranger got a bottle of water from the fridge. 'I can give you a job if you need money.'

'What would I do?'

'Fill my minority quota, for one thing. I only employ one woman, and she's my housekeeper.'

'Besides that?'

'Odd jobs,' Ranger said. 'You can work part-time on an *as needed* basis.'

'Do you need me now?'

Ranger smiled.

'You missed your chance,' I told him.

'I'll get another one. You got a phone call while you were in the shower, and he left a message. You should listen to it.'

The message was from Peter Smullen. He wanted to speak to me. Would I please call him back.

Ranger was leaning against the counter, arms crossed, watching me.

'Hard to believe my day could get any worse,' I said to him.

'You underestimate yourself.'

I dialed Smullen's number and waded through layers of secretaries. Finally, Smullen came on.

'I appreciate the callback,' he said. 'I imagine your days are complicated since Dickie's disappearance.'

'It's been interesting.'

'I was hoping we could get together for a chat.'

'What do you want to chat about?' I asked him.

'Things.'

'That narrows it down.'

'I prefer not to discuss sensitive issues on the phone. I have a full schedule this afternoon, but I was hoping we might meet for a drink after hours. Perhaps the bar at the Marriott at eight?'

'Sure. See you at eight.'

'I have a date,' I said to Ranger. 'It turns out I'm very in demand. Everyone wants to talk to me. The police, Joyce, Peter Smullen.'

'Did Smullen say why he wanted to meet with you?'

'He said he wanted to talk about *things*.' Like, maybe the fact that I planted a bug on him.

'And Joyce?'

'She was here this morning, demanding to know where I stashed Dickie.'

'As in chopped-up body parts you fed to your neighbor's cat? Or alive and living in your closet?'

'I don't know.'

'You should find out. Maybe she knows something we don't.'

'Maybe *you* should talk to her,' I said to Ranger. 'She likes you.'

'You'd throw me into the shark tank?'

That got me smiling. 'Is big, bad Ranger afraid of Joyce Barnhardt?'

'I'd rather face the python.'

'Joyce doesn't have a long attention span. I'm surprised she's still involved in this.'

Ranger's phone buzzed, and he answered it on speaker mode.

'You have a meeting on the calendar for one o'clock,' Tank said. 'Do you need a ride?'

'Yes.'

'I'm in the lot.'

'I'll be right down.'

Ranger took the Cayenne keys from his pocket and placed them on the counter. He counted out four hundred dollars and placed that on the counter as well. 'Caesar is designing a system for a new client tomorrow morning, and a female point of view would be helpful. He'll pick you up at nine. I'll send a uniform with him. The money is an advance on salary for services you'll provide.'

He backed me against the wall, leaned into me, and kissed me. His tongue touched mine, and I felt my fingers involuntarily curl into his shirt as heat rushed through my stomach and headed south. He broke from the kiss and looked down at me with a suggestion of a smile. Just a slight curve to the corners of his mouth.

'That's an advance on services *I* provide,' he said.

He grabbed his jacket and left.

# Seven

Since I was no longer desperate for money, I decided to spend the afternoon on activities designed to keep me out of jail. I heard what Morelli was saying . . . that Dickie was just a missing person and I shouldn't worry. But people had been sent to jail for less. I knew this for a fact. I helped put them there.

First up was the conversation with Joyce. I drove to her house and parked in her driveway behind a Pro Serve van and hatchback. Joyce's front door was open, and I could see a cleaning crew working inside. A couch and chair had been set curbside. Terminal victims of the beaver explosion.

I picked out a guy who looked like he might speak English and asked for Joyce.

'Not here,' he said. 'She let us in and split.'

'That's okay, I'll just look around until she gets back.

I'm her interior decorator. We had an appointment, but I'm early.'

'Sure,' he said. 'Knock yourself out.'

The house was elaborately decorated with a lot of velvet upholstery and gilt-framed mirrors. Rugs were plush. Marble in the kitchen and bathroom. Satin in the bedroom. Flat-screen televisions everywhere. Joyce had married well this last time around. She'd chosen more velvet and gilt than I could manage, but it looked expensive.

There was a designated office/library, the shelves filled with hardcover books that had probably belonged to her ex. A large carved mahogany desk floated in the middle of the room. The desktop was clean. Telephone but no scribble pad. No computer. I checked all the drawers. Telephone book. Nothing else.

I returned to the kitchen and sat at the little built-in workstation. The phone was attached to an answering machine. A Starbucks coffee mug held pens and markers. A couple sticky pads were stacked next to the phone.

I opened the top drawer and found a piece of paper with two nine-digit numbers and a phone number scrawled on it. I recognized one as Dickie's social security number. Odd how you remember things like that. I didn't recognize the second number or the phone number.

I dialed the phone number, and a programmed voice introduced itself as the Smith Barney automated Reserved Client Service Center and asked for an account number. That was as far as I was going to get, so I copied the three numbers on a sticky pad and put the paper in my pocket.

I didn't see anything else of interest on Joyce's desk. I scrolled through calls made and calls received on her phone and copied the list, going back four days.

I packed up and ran into Joyce as I was leaving the kitchen.

'What the fuck?' Joyce said.

'I was looking for you,' I told her.

'Well, you found me. What do you want?'

'I thought if we put our heads together we might be able to figure out what happened to Dickie.'

'I know what happened to him. I just don't know where he is *now*.'

'Why do you care?' I asked Joyce.

'I love him.'

I burst out laughing, and Joyce cracked a smile.

'Okay, even *I* couldn't keep a straight face on that one,' Joyce said.

'Do you think he's dead?'

'Hard to say one way or another until a body turns up. What I can tell you is this – stay out of my way. I've got an investment here, and I intend to collect. And I'll run over anyone who tries to stop me.'

'Hard to believe Dickie had that much money. From what I could see, he wasn't that smart.'

'You have no idea what's involved here. And I'm warning you again. Stay out of it.'

Joyce was really starting to annoy me. Bad enough from time to time Morelli and Ranger tried to push me around, now Joyce was telling me to butt out.

'Looks like you're doing some redecorating,' I said to Joyce. 'Is that animal fur on your chandelier?'

We locked eyes, and I knew the thought was fluttering in her head . . . did Stephanie Plum mastermind the beaver bombing? And then the moment passed, and we both stepped back from it.

I walked to the Cayenne, got in, and powered out of the driveway. I drove to Coglin's house just for the heck of it and saw that the green SUV was parked in the alley, two tires on Coglin's property line. I angle-parked behind the SUV, blocking its exit, and approached Coglin's back door with stun gun in hand.

Coglin answered the door with a sawed-off shotgun in his. 'Now what?' he asked.

'Same ol', same ol',' I told him.

'I'm not going with you. I can't. I gotta stay here. I'll go as soon as I can.'

I looked down the barrel of the sawed-off. 'All right, then,' I said. 'Good conversation. Call me when you're ready to, uh, you know.'

I got into the Cayenne and took off for the bonds office.

'If you're looking for Lula, she isn't here,' Connie said when I walked in. 'She went home to get dry clothes and never came back. Sounds like you had a busy morning. I hear people are driving from all over the state to breathe Burg air.'

'I swear, I didn't have anything to do with that fire. I wasn't anywhere near that house.'

'Sure,' Connie said. 'Did you get Hansen?'

'Yes and no. I came here to use the by–phone number program.'

'Is this for Hansen?'

'No. I'm trying to make sense of the Dickie mess. Joyce is tied up in it. I don't exactly know how or why, but I got some numbers off her phone, and I want to run them down. One of them is for the Smith Barney automated Reserved Client Service Center.'

'That's heavy,' Connie said. 'Reserve clients are those with at least 10 million in assets. What else do you have on that list?'

I pulled a chair up to Connie's desk and gave her the list. 'The three numbers on the sticky page came from a piece of paper in Joyce's desk. The rest came from her phone.'

'Doing some breaking and entering?'

'Only entering. Her door was open. I'd like to get into that account, but it asks for an account number.'

Connie looked at the sticky page. 'Joyce isn't smart. If she had to write the phone number down, I'm guessing the rest of the information is there too.'

'The top number is the phone number. The second number I don't recognize, and the last number is Dickie's social security number.'

'And they were written in this order on her pad?'

'Yep.'

Connie punched the Smith Barney phone number in. The automated voice asked for the account number and Connie gave it the second nine-digit number. The voice asked for the access code and Connie punched in the social security number. Access denied. Connie went through the routine again and gave it just the last four digits of the social security number.

'I'm in,' Connie said. 'There's a zero balance. And the last transaction was a forty-million-dollar withdrawal. That was two weeks ago.' Connie hung up and looked at me. 'That's a shitload of money. Whose account is this?'

'I don't know.'

'It can't be Joyce's,' Connie said. 'She'd be in the Bahamas buying men and goats. The access code is from Dickie's social security number, so the logical assumption would be that it's Dickie's account. But I don't know how Dickie would get that kind of money. That's a lot of billable hours.'

No kidding. When Joyce said Dickie was worth money, I wasn't thinking *this* kind of money. 'Maybe he stole it from the guys who snatched him, and they got cranky.'

Connie took the list of numbers I'd lifted from the phone, typed them into her computer, and plugged them into the by–phone number program.

'After we get rid of the dupes, there are sixteen numbers,' Connie said. 'I'll run them and print them out for you.'

I watched the information come in. Five calls from the law firm in the last two days. And Joyce got an incoming call at one in the morning from Peter Smullen right after Dickie disappeared.

'Isn't Smullen a partner?' Connie asked.

'Yes. That's kind of weird that he called Joyce at one in the morning.'

'Maybe there's something going on with them.'

Yuk. What would that mean for my meeting? I thought Smullen wanted to talk to me about kidnapping and murder. It would be horrible if it turned out he wanted to talk about sex. Maybe he didn't notice the bug. Maybe he noticed the cleavage.

The rest of the list looked benign. I took the printed copy from Connie and shoved it into my bag.

'Gotta go,' I said to Connie.

Connie reached into her top drawer, took out a box of rounds for my Smith & Wesson, and tossed them to me. 'Just in case.'

I left the bonds office, settled myself in the Cayenne, and called Ranger.

'Yo,' Ranger said.

'I took your advice and went to talk to Joyce, and I learned there's a Smith Barney account that has Dickie's social security number as an access code. It has a zero balance and the last withdrawal was forty million dollars.'

'Joyce shared that with you?'

'More or less. When you went through Dickie's house, did you search his home office?'

'No. I wanted to see the crime scene, and I didn't have time for much else. I slid in between police investigations.'

'Maybe it would be a good idea to poke around in Dickie's office and see what turns up. I'd like to prowl through his law office too, but that feels more complicated.'

'Where are you now?'

'I'm at the bonds office.'

'Pick me up at RangeMan.'

RangeMan is located on a quiet side street in downtown Trenton. It's a relatively small, unobtrusive seven-story building sandwiched between other commercial properties. There's a number on the front door and a small brass plaque, but no sign announcing RangeMan. Parking is underground in a gated garage. Ranger's private apartment is located on the top floor. The whole operation is very high-tech and secure.

Ranger was waiting outside for me. I pulled to the curb and placed his hat on the console. He got in and put the hat on.

'Do you feel better now?' I asked him.

'A friend gave this hat to me just before he died. It's a reminder to stay alert.'

I glanced over at him. 'I thought you wore it because it looked hot.'

That got a smile from him. 'Do you think I look hot in this hat?'

I thought he looked hot in *everything*. 'It's a pretty good hat,' I told him.

When I reached Dickie's house, I did a slow drive-by. The crime scene tape had been taken down, and the house no longer felt ominous. No cars in the driveway. No lights shining from windows.

'Park in front of the house,' Ranger said. 'We're going in like we belong here.'

We walked to the door, and Ranger tried the handle. Locked. He took a small tool from his jacket pocket, and in twenty seconds the door was open. I suspected the tool was for show, and if I hadn't been watching he'd say *abracadabra* and the door would unlock.

I followed Ranger in and the ominous feeling returned. There were still bloodstains on the floor, and the house had been tossed.

'Did it look like this when you were here?' I asked.

'No. Someone's been here looking for something, and they weren't subtle.'

We went room by room, not disturbing the mess that had been made. Drawers were open, contents thrown onto the floor. Cushions were on the floor too, and some of them were slashed. Mattresses ditto. His office was more orderly only because it had clearly been carefully picked over. His computer was missing. His files were also missing. No way to know if they'd been taken by the police or by whoever ransacked the house. All messages on the answering machine were from Joyce.

'Time's up,' Ranger said. 'We need to get out of here.'

We left the same way we came in. Ranger slid behind the wheel of the Cayenne, and we drove away. I checked my watch and realized I was due for dinner at my parents'.

I reached Morelli on his cell. 'It's Friday,' I said.

'And?'

'Dinner?'

'Oh crap,' Morelli said. 'I forgot. I can't make it. I'm tied up here.'

I didn't say anything. I just sat on the phone.

'It's my job,' Morelli said. 'You can't get mad at me for doing my job.'

And that was true, but I didn't want to go to dinner

without Morelli. I was afraid I'd get relentlessly grilled about Dickie if I didn't have Morelli on board to distract my mother and grandmother.

'Is that Bob barking?'

'Yeah, Bob's with me.'

'So what kind of job is this?'

'It's a secret job.'

'And when is this secret job going to be done?'

'I don't know. Hopefully soon.'

'I could swear I hear television.'

'Bob's watching a movie.'

I hung up and looked at Ranger.

'No,' Ranger said.

'You don't even know what I was going to ask.'

'You were going to ask me to fill in for Morelli at dinner.'

'Roast chicken.'

'You'll have to come up with something better than roast chicken.'

'Do you have dinner plans?'

'Are you going to nag me on this?'

'Yes.'

'What happened to the Stephanie who thought I was mysterious and scary?'

'Gone.'

Actually, that wasn't entirely true. Ranger was still mysterious and scary at times – just not today, just not compared to my mother and grandmother.

Ranger parked in the driveway behind my father's Buick. 'We need to be out of here at seven-thirty. If you tell Tank I did this, I'll chain you naked to the traffic light on Hamilton and Broad. And I'll shoot your grandmother if she grabs me.'

I was pretty sure he was kidding about the traffic light.

'Isn't this something,' Grandma said when she saw Ranger. 'What a nice surprise. Is Joe coming too?'

'Nope,' I said. 'Just Ranger.'

'Look here, Helen,' Grandma called to my mother. 'Stephanie's swapped out Joseph tonight.'

My mother stuck her head out the kitchen door. 'Where's Joseph?'

'Working,' I told her.

'I'm just spooning out the gravy,' my mother said. 'Everyone sit down.'

The doorbell rang and Grandma ran to get it. 'It's him,' she said to me. 'It's my honey.'

My father got out of his chair in the living room and took his seat at the table. 'I don't care if he craps in a bag,' he said to Ranger. 'I'll give you a hundred bucks

143

if you can scare him into marrying her and moving her into his room at the old people's home.'

'They won't take him back,' I said to my father. 'He started a fire, and they kicked him out.'

'Guess I look like I could still scare *somebody*,' Ranger said to me.

'You look like you could scare *anybody*,' my father said to him. 'Don't you ever wear anything but black?'

'Sometimes white socks,' Ranger said.

Ranger was smiling a little, and I was thinking he was getting into it, starting to enjoy himself.

'This is my honey, Elmer,' Grandma said to everyone.

Elmer was dressed for the occasion in red plaid slacks and a white turtleneck that shoved his loose neck skin up so that it spilled over the top and looked like a turkey wattle.

'Howdy doody,' Elmer said. 'You have a peach of a home here. And just look at all these hot women I'm gonna get to have dinner with.'

'Cripes,' my father said.

My mother put the gravy boat on the table and poured herself a glass of wine.

'Elmer's taking me to the Benchley viewing tonight,' Grandma said, taking her seat. 'It's gonna be a beaut.'

Elmer sat next to Grandma. 'I read it was the pancreatic cancer that got him. He was a young guy too. Seventy-eight.' Elmer reached for the potatoes and his toupee slid over his ear.

The small smile hovered at the corners of Ranger's mouth.

We were passing the chicken, gravy, mashed potatoes, green beans, cranberry sauce, dinner rolls, and pickled vegetable dish when the doorbell chimed. Before anyone could get out of their chair, the door opened and closed and Joyce Barnhardt swept into the house. Her red hair was cut super short and spiked out punk style. Her eyes were lined in black, shadowed in metallic gray. Her lips were inflated to maximum capacity, and her lips and nails were the color of my mother's wine. Joyce removed her leather duster, revealing a black leather bustier that showed a lot of cleavage and black leather pants that displayed what had to be a painful camel toe. She draped the duster over my father's television chair on her way to the dining room.

'Hey, how's it going,' Joyce said. 'I saw the car parked in the driveway, and I said to myself, I bet that's Stephanie's car. So I thought I'd come in and see how she was doing.' Her eyes flicked to Ranger for a split second, and I was pretty sure I saw her nipples get hard behind the black leather.

My father was frozen in his chair with his fork halfway to his mouth. And Elmer looked like he'd just filled his bag.

'Give me your gun,' I whispered to Ranger.

Ranger slid his arm across the back of my chair and leaned close. 'Stay calm.'

'Nice house you've got here, Mrs P.,' Joyce said. 'You obviously have a talent for decorating. I could tell that by the fabric choice on the slipcovers in the living room.'

Grandma beamed at Joyce. 'I've always said that. She's got a real eye for picking out just the right thing.'

'And you set an excellent table too.'

'The secret is you gotta take the olives out of the jar and put them in a little bowl,' Grandma said. 'If you notice, we put everything in a bowl. That's what makes the difference.'

'I'll try to remember that,' Joyce said. 'Put everything in a bowl.'

Grandma turned to my mom. 'Isn't it nice to see such a polite young person? Almost no one appreciates things today.'

My mother tried to refill her wineglass, but the

bottle was empty. 'Darn,' my mother said.

'We cooked up two big chickens,' Grandma said to Joyce. 'You could stay for dinner if you want. We have plenty.'

Joyce wedged a chair between Grandma and Elmer so she could look across the table at Ranger. 'I wouldn't want to impose.'

'I'll get you a place setting,' Grandma said, scraping back in her chair.

'Eddie Haskell,' Ranger whispered against my ear, leaning in to me.

'What?'

'Joyce is doing Eddie Haskell from *Leave It To Beaver*. Eddie Haskell was the obnoxious kid who was always sucking up to the Cleavers.'

'You watched *Leave It To Beaver*?'

'Hard to believe, but I didn't start out at age thirty. I actually had a childhood.'

'Mind-boggling.'

'Sometimes it boggles even *my* mind,' Ranger said.

'What are you two whispering about?' Joyce asked. 'And where's Morelli? I thought this was his gig.'

'Joe's working,' I told her. 'Ranger volunteered to stand in.'

Joyce opened her mouth to say something, thought

better of it, and forked up some chicken.

'I'm going to the kitchen to get some hot gravy,' I told everyone. 'Joyce, why don't you help me?'

I closed the kitchen door behind us, nuked the gravy boat, and turned to Joyce. 'What's going on?'

'I realized I was going about this wrong. We're both looking for Dickie, right? But you have Studman out there working with you. That gives you a real advantage over me. So instead of forcing you to butt out, I'm going to stick to you like glue. You and Studman will find Dickie for me.'

'Ranger won't turn Dickie over to you.'

'I'll worry about that when he finds him. Ranger's a man, and I know what to do with a man. You get them undressed, and they're all basically the same. Scrotum and ego. If you stroke them, they're happy. And I don't see you doing much stroking with Ranger. Looks to me like he's open season.'

I took the gravy boat out of the microwave and carried it back to the table. Ranger's chair was empty.

'Where's Ranger?' I asked Grandma.

'He said he had business to take care of, but he left you the keys to the car. They're by your plate. He said he'd catch up with you later.'

I put the keys in my pocket and wondered about

Ranger's needs. It wasn't as if I was fulfilling them. And it wasn't as if he was a low-testosterone kind of guy.

'That's some outfit you got on,' Elmer said to Joyce. 'I bet you put out.'

'Behave yourself,' Joyce said.

'And you got a nice pair of melons there. Are they real?'

Joyce smacked Elmer on the head and his toupee flew off and landed on the table in front of my mother. She jumped in her seat and beat the toupee to death with the empty wine bottle.

'Omigod,' my mother said, looking at the mangled hair. 'It startled me. I thought it was a giant spider.'

Elmer reached over, retrieved his hair, and settled it back onto his head. 'This used to happen all the time at the home too.'

I made it through the chicken and the chocolate cake. I helped my mom clear the table and do the dishes, and that brought me up to seven-thirty.

'Gotta go,' I said to my mom. 'Things to do.'

'Me too,' Joyce said, following me to the door.

I couldn't have Joyce tail me to my meeting at the Marriott, so as I saw it I had two options. The first option would be to handcuff her at gunpoint to a dining-room chair. The second would be to lose her on the road. I decided to go with option two. Mostly because I had the box of bullets in my purse, but no gun.

Joyce was driving a black Mercedes sedan, which I was pretty sure represented husband number two. She got behind the wheel and gave me a thumbs-up. I got into Ranger's Porsche and responded with a stiff middle finger.

I drove off, and after a block I realized Joyce wasn't following. I checked her out in my rearview mirror and saw that she was out of the car, looking under the hood. I turned around and pulled alongside her.

'What's up?' I asked.

'I don't know much about cars,' Joyce said, 'but I think someone took my engine.'

# *Eight*

I parked in the hotel garage and walked through the garage to the hotel. It was a few minutes before eight, and there was a corporate party going on in the ballroom. Lots of women in cocktail dresses and men in suits congregating in the public areas. Lots of drinking and laughing and flirting. I suspected some of it would get nasty in a couple of hours.

The bar was packed, but Smullen wasn't there. I found a chair in the lobby and waited. After half an hour, I did a tour of the bar and restaurant. Still no Smullen. I called Ranger at nine.

'I've been stood up,' I told him.

'Lucky you,' Ranger said.

'Did you take Joyce's engine?'

'My instructions were to disable the car, but one of my men bet Hal a burger he couldn't get the engine out. So Hal removed the engine.'

I knew Hal. He'd been with RangeMan for a couple of years, and he was one of my favorite people. He looked like a stegosaurus, and he fainted at the sight of blood.

I left the hotel and walked past a few desperate souls hunkered in a corner by the entrance, trying to smoke without freezing their asses off. No one coming or going to the parking garage. Just me, my steps echoing on the cement floor. I approached the Cayenne, and Ranger moved out of a shadow.

'I'll drive,' he said. 'I want to make sure no one's waiting for you in your apartment.'

'I appreciate the thought, but I wasn't going home. I was going to hang out in the cemetery and see if Diggery relieves Lorraine Birnbaum of her diamond.'

'It's seventeen degrees,' Ranger said. 'If Diggery is desperate enough to rob graves in this weather, the least you can do is let him have the diamond.'

Ranger crossed Broad and turned onto Hamilton. A dark figure scuttled from between parked cars, and quick as a flash it scooped something off the road with a shovel. The figure was momentarily caught wide-eyed in Ranger's headlights. And then the figure was gone, sucked back between the parked cars, lost in the night.

I gasped and did a whole body shiver.

'Someone you know?' Ranger asked.

'Crazy Carl Coglin. He's on my FTA list.'

'Babe.'

If I was any kind of bounty hunter, I would have chased Coglin down, but I really didn't want to see what was on the shovel. So I decided to go with Ranger's philosophy. If Coglin needed roadkill that badly, the least I could do was let him keep it.

Three traffic lights later, Ranger cut off Hamilton and parked in my lot. He looked up at my dark apartment windows, shut the Cayenne off, and turned to face me. 'Tell me about your kitchen discussion with Joyce.'

'She realized you would be helping me find Dickie and decided it was smarter to follow me around than to go off on her own. So she's my new best friend. I told her I didn't think it was likely you'd turn Dickie over to her, and she said she had a way with men. She said men were basically scrotum and ego, and they were happy when they got stroked.'

Ranger reached across the console and traced a line down the side of my face. His fingertip was warm and his touch was gentle. 'I'd like to think I'm more than just scrotum and ego, but she was right about the stroking.'

An SUV crept into the lot and parked behind us.

Ranger looked back at it. 'That's Tank. He's giving me a ride back to RangeMan after I check your apartment. I'll leave the Cayenne with you.'

Caesar rang my bell precisely at nine a.m. He was dressed in RangeMan black, and he was slimmer than most of Ranger's men. Caesar wouldn't single-handedly haul an engine out of a Mercedes. I placed him in his late twenties. He handed a tote bag plus winter jacket over to me and politely stepped into my apartment.

'I'll just be a minute,' I told him. 'Make yourself at home.'

He nodded, but he remained standing just inside the door, hands folded in front of him. Parade rest.

I'd worked for RangeMan once before, and Ranger's housekeeper, Ella, knew my size. She'd sent black leather cross-trainers, black cargo pants, a long-sleeved black T-shirt with the RangeMan logo in magenta, and a black webbed canvas belt. The black winter jacket was identical to the one Ranger wore with the logo in black.

I got dressed and looked at myself in the mirror. I was mini-Ranger. I said good-bye to Rex, locked the apartment, and followed Caesar to an immaculate black Ford Explorer. No logo.

Caesar drove to a large rambling colonial north of town. The grounds were perfectly landscaped even in winter, and the house had a sweeping view of the river. We parked in the circular drive, Caesar took a clipboard from the back-seat, and we went to work.

'The owners are off-site,' Caesar said, keying us into the house. 'A vacation in Naples. We're installing a new security system while they're away. The husband does a lot of travel, and the wife stays home with two school-age children. So we need to make the system meet the wife's needs. Ranger thought you would be helpful since you see things from a woman's perspective.'

We did a fast tour of the house and then went through a second time more slowly, making notes. I didn't know anything about living in a house like this, and I didn't have experience as a mother, but I knew something about fear. And I've broken into enough houses to know what serves as a deterrent. In a house this size, I'd want to know if a door was opened. I'd want closed-circuit television on entrances. I'd want exterior security lighting. I'd want some mobile touchpads to give myself flexibility. I'd want to make sure the children's rooms were protected against intrusion. That would mean the screens should be wired into the alarm system.

It was almost noon when Caesar dropped me at my apartment building. I ran upstairs, made myself a peanut butter and olive sandwich, and pawed through my junk drawer while I ate. My job as a bounty hunter heavily relies on my ability to stretch the truth and go into sneaky mode. I have patches and hats for almost any occasion, from pizza delivery to plumbing to security specialist.

I found a patch that advertised Richter Security and used double-sided sticky tape to plaster the patch over the RangeMan logo on the black jacket. I dropped a travel flash drive into my pocket so I could record computer data, and I grabbed a clipboard and pad.

It was Saturday, and I was guessing there would be a single security guard on front-desk duty at Petiak, Smullen, Gorvich, and Orr. I hadn't learned anything from Dickie's house. I was hoping his files were still intact at his office.

I parked the Cayenne in the small lot adjacent to the building, and sat there for a moment, gathering my courage. Truth is, I'm not all that brave. And I'm not all that good at what I do. And I was pretty close to getting nervous bowels. I was going to break into Dickie's office, and I was doing it because it wasn't nearly as frightening as the prospect of going to jail for a murder I didn't commit. Still, it was pretty damn frightening.

I talked myself into getting out of the Cayenne, walked to the front of the building and let myself into the foyer. The large glass door leading to the law offices was locked and, just as I'd suspected, a security guard was behind the desk. I showed him my clipboard and pointed to my watch, and he came to the door.

'Richter Security,' I told him, handing him a business card that went with the Richter Security logo on my jacket. 'I'm scheduled to come in and work up an estimate on a new system.'

'I don't know anything about that,' he said. 'The offices are closed.'

'You were supposed to be notified. There must be someone you can call.'

'I've only got emergency numbers.'

'They specifically requested a Saturday so business wouldn't be disturbed. I moved a lot of jobs around so I could do this and if I can't get in today, I don't have another Saturday opening until October.'

Now, here's the good part. Men trust women. Even if I looked like a five-dollar hand-job hooker, this guy would think I was the real deal. Women grow up wary, and men grow up thinking they're immortal. Maybe that's overstated, but I'm in the ballpark.

'Just exactly what are you supposed to do?' he asked.

'I guess everyone got a little freaked over the disappearance of one of the partners, and they decided to upgrade the security system. My specialty is video surveillance. I'll be designing an enhanced video system for use throughout the building. Obviously, this isn't something that can be done during business hours. No one wants to think their every action is being monitored.'

'Yeah, I guess I can see that. How long will this take?'

'An hour, tops. I just need to draw some room diagrams. Are the partners' offices open?'

'Yeah. No point locking them. They're hardly used. Only Mr Orr came in every day. And sometimes Mr Smullen when he's in town.'

'That's weird. What kind of lawyer doesn't use his office?'

'Don't ask me. I'm just part-time. Maybe they're all a bunch of rich guys who don't need to work. They just like to have their name on the door – you know what I mean?'

'Yeah. Well, I'm not rich like that, so I'd better get to work.'

'Holler if you need anything.'

I started in Dickie's office. My original intent had been to get into his computer and search for a client list, but his computer was gone. That brought me to Plan B. Raid his file cabinet. I went through three drawers of files and understood nothing. Why can't lawyers write in English?

I gave up on the files and sat at his desk. I opened the top drawer and found two file folders. One was labeled NUTS AND STALKERS and the other was labeled CURRENT. Hooray! Now I was getting somewhere. I shoved the folders into my pants, under the waistband, and buttoned my coat over them.

Smullen's office was similar in design to Dickie's. Same furniture, but Smullen's desk drawers were filled with candy bars. Mounds, Baby Ruths, M&Ms, Snickers, Reese's Peanut Butter Cups, Twizzlers. His computer was fresh out of the box. Software installed. Nothing else. No Rolodex. A pen and a pad, but nothing written. Coffee cup stains on his leather desktop. Nothing of interest in his file drawers.

I snitched a couple of Snickers and a Reese's and moved on to Gorvich. His office was also unused. No candy bars in the drawers. Gorvich's drawers were empty.

Ditto Petiak.

C. J. SLOAN had been printed in small block letters on the door to the office next to Petiak's. I had no idea what Sloan did for the firm, but he obviously did it in his office because there were stacks of files on every flat surface. There were four in/out baskets on his desk, and they were all filled with papers. His computer monitor was extra wide. And while there was a lot of clutter in the office, it was all perfectly aligned. Sloan was a totally anal neat freak.

I went into Sloan's computer and struck gold. Sloan had client lists with billable hours, current and past. I plugged my flash drive into a USB port and downloaded a bunch of files.

In a last-ditch effort, when I left Sloan's office, I tried the secretary's desk. She had all the hardware but not much content. Multiline phone, super-duper computer, and a drawer filled with take-out menus. There was a small wooden crate, two cardboard boxes and an industrial staple gun by the desk. Someone was packing.

The elevator binged and before I had time to react, a huge guy stepped out. He was dressed in shirt and tie and a badly fitting dark blue suit. He was late twenties, early thirties, and he lifted. Probably did some roids. His hair was buzzed short and bleached blond. L.A. muscleman.

Muscleman approached the desk and looked down at me. 'Whatchadoin'?'

I had the Pizza Hut menu in my hand. 'Ordering out. Do you like pepperoni?'

'The loser downstairs said he let you up here to install televisions.'

I was on my feet behind the desk. 'I'm doing the prelim on some security monitors.'

'No, you're not. I know who you are. I saw your picture in the paper. You're the nut who tried to choke Mr Orr.'

'You're mistaken. I work for Richter Security. I guess I have a double out there somewhere, eh?'

'I don't make mistakes like that, lady. I got an eye for the girls. I even remember your name. Stephanie Plum. I remember it 'cause it's a 'ho name. Stephanie Juicy. Stephanie Good-to-Eat. Stephanie I'm-Gonna-Sink-My-Teeth-into-You.'

Yikes. 'Sorry,' I told him. 'I'm not on the menu.'

'I think you are. I think I'm gonna have some fun with you before I turn you over to Mr Petiak.'

'Is he your boss?'

'Yeah. And he don't like intruders. He's got things he does to them so they don't intrude anymore, but sometimes he lets me have fun with them first.'

I had pepper spray and a stun gun in my bag. 'Let me show you my identification—'

'The only identification I care about is between your legs, Stephanie Juicy.'

He was around the desk in two strides, reaching out for me. I knocked his hand away, grabbed the staple gun, pressed it into his crotch, and *bam, bam, bam, bam* . . . I stapled his nuts. At least, I thought it felt like nuts, but hell, what do I know. There's other equipment down there, and I guess it could have been most anything.

Muscleman's mouth dropped open and his face turned red. He froze for a moment, sucking air, and then he doubled over and crashed to the floor.

I was in love with the genius who'd invented the electric stapler.

I wasted no time getting out of there. I ran out of the office and flew down the stairs. I crossed the lobby and was out the front door before the guard at the desk was on his feet. I bolted for the lot and ran flat-out into Ranger when I turned the corner. He absorbed the impact without moving and wrapped his arms around me to keep me from falling.

'We need to get out of here,' I told him.

Tank was idling behind the Cayenne. Ranger signaled that he could leave, and Ranger and I got into the Porsche. Ranger drove out of the lot, made a U-turn half a block away, and parked.

'What were you doing in the lot?' I asked him.

'Hal was working the remote monitors and suspected you were in the law office building. He was worried about you.'

'How about you? Were you worried about me?'

'I always worry about you.'

'We didn't get anything out of Dickie's house,' I told Ranger, 'so I decided to look at his office. Didn't think there'd be much activity on a Saturday. Figured I could fly under the radar.'

Ranger peeled the Richter Security label off my jacket. 'And?'

'Dickie's office is a normal, working office. It looked like everything was still intact . . . at least until I got there.' I unbuttoned my jacket, removed the files, and handed them to Ranger.

We were sitting there watching the building when the big blond goon stumbled out the front door. He was doubled over, holding himself. He inched his way to the lot, crawled into a silver Camry, and slowly drove down the street.

Ranger looked over at me, eyebrows raised in question.

'It turned out I wasn't entirely under the radar,' I told Ranger. 'And I had to staple his nuts.'

'Babe.'

'He said he worked for Petiak. I'm not sure what he was doing there on a Saturday because the desk guard said Petiak never comes into the office. And Petiak's office looked unused. For that matter, all the partners' offices looked unused, excluding Dickie's.'

Ranger skimmed the CURRENT folder. 'These are all one-page summaries for quick reference, and at first glance they all look like normal low-grade cases. A couple property damage cases. A criminal case against Norman Wolecky for assault. Litigation against a landscaper. More property damage. I could be missing something, but it doesn't look to me like any of these cases would bring in big money.'

'So we have three partners with empty file cabinets, a fourth partner who chased ambulances, forty million dollars withdrawn from a Smith Barney account, a dead accountant, and a missing Dickie.'

'I talked to Zip about his brother. He said Ziggy did high-volume accounts. He was under the impression Petiak, Smullen, Gorvich, and Orr represented power.'

'Apparently not Dickie. Dickie represented Norman Wolecky.'

Ranger looked at the second folder. 'Nuts and Stalkers.' He flipped it open. 'There are only two summaries in here.'

'Am I one of them?'

'No. I imagine you would be filed under BITCH EX-WIFE. The first summary is for Harry Slesnik. According to this, Slesnik is a self-described separatist who seceded from the United States and declared his town house a sovereign country. He was arrested when he tried to annex his neighbor's garage. Dickie quit the case after being paid in Slesnik dollars. The last piece of paper attached to this is a formal declaration of war against Dickie.

'The second nut is Bernard Gross.'

'I know him,' I told Ranger. 'He's a World's Strongest Man wannabe. Vinnie bonded him out on a domestic violence charge, and he went FTA. I found him in a gym, and when I got him outside he freaked and wrecked my car. He got his hands under the frame and flipped it over like a turtle.'

'Dickie represented him in his divorce . . . at least initially,' Ranger said. 'While deposing Gross, the subject of gynecomastia came up. Dickie made the fatal mistake of referring to them as man boobs, and Gross destroyed the conference room in a fit of steroid-induced rage. Apparently, Gross is sensitive about his . . . gynecomastia.'

'Something to remember. Do you think either of these guys is crazy enough to steal Dickie?'

Ranger handed the file back to me. 'I can see them stealing him. I can't see them keeping him.'

'The office next to Petiak was occupied by someone who actually did work there. Probably the firm's finance officer. I downloaded a bunch of files onto a flash drive, but I'm not sure I have the software on my computer to read them. Spreadsheets and things. I was hoping you could open it.'

Ranger turned the key in the ignition and gave the Cayenne some gas. 'What should we do with your hitchhiker? Do you want to let her tag along, or do you want me to get rid of her?'

I turned and looked out the rear window. Joyce was behind us in a white Taurus. No doubt a rental.

'She must have picked me up when I left my apartment. You can let her follow. It'll kill her when we drive into the RangeMan garage.'

We were in Ranger's office, which was attached to the RangeMan control room. Ranger was relaxed in his chair with a stack of reports in front of him.

'When Ziggy Zabar went missing, I ran Dickie and his partners through the system,' Ranger said. 'Credit reports, real estate, personal history, litigation. They look clean on the surface, but you put them together and it feels off. Smullen spends a lot of time out of the country. Gorvich is a Russian immigrant. Petiak was military. Did a couple tours and got out. Smullen, Gorvich, and Petiak all look like they bought their law degrees a couple years ago. And they all lived in Sheepshead Bay before moving here.'

'So maybe they were getting together for *Monday Night Football* and decided they'd become lawyers and move to Trenton.'

'Yeah,' Ranger said. 'That would work.'

'Here's something weird. It's been four days since Dickie was dragged out of his house, leaving a trail of blood. Ordinarily, the chances of death increase with length of disappearance, but for some reason, the longer this goes on, the more I believe Dickie is alive. Probably just wishful thinking since I'm the prime murder suspect.'

'I think Dickie and his partners were involved in bad business and something happened that made the deal start to unravel. Ziggy Zabar seems to be the first victim. Dickie appears to be the second. And now houses are getting tossed, and Smullen has contacted you and Joyce. We don't really know what happened at Dickie's house. We have gunshots fired and evidence indicating someone was dragged out of the house. DNA testing on the blood hasn't come back yet, so we aren't sure who got shot. It's possible Dickie is in the wind, and someone is scrambling to find him. It's also possible he's dead, and he had something that wasn't recovered before he died.'

'Like the forty million,' I said.

'Yes.'

'What else do we know about the partners?'

'All three partners are in their early fifties. Petiak moved into the area five years ago, and Gorvich and Smullen followed. Petiak owns a modest house in Mercerville. Gorvich and Smullen are renting in a large apartment complex off Klockner Boulevard. Before moving to Trenton, Smullen owned a car wash in Sheepshead, Gorvich had part ownership in a restaurant, and Petiak owned a limo service consisting of one car. Somehow, the three men found Dickie, and between them they managed to buy an office building downtown, an apartment building that sits on the edge of public housing, and a warehouse on Stark Street. No litigation against any of them. Smullen is married, with a wife and children in South America. Gorvich is currently unmarried and has been divorced three times. And Petiak has never married.'

Ranger plugged the flash drive into his computer, opened a spreadsheet, and broke into a smile. 'You downloaded the firm's financial records. Clients. Fees for service. Services provided. There's a separate spreadsheet for each partner.'

I dragged my chair next to his so I could see the screen as he scrolled down.

'Dickie has normal clients and is pulling in around two hundred thousand,' Ranger said after a half hour of reading. 'Smullen, Petiak, and Gorvich have client lists that read like Who's Who in Hell. South American drug lords, gunrunners, mercenaries, and some local thugs. And they're billing big money.'

I'd been taking notes and doing a tally in my head as we moved from one partner to the next, and I had a grip on how much money we were talking about.

'Forty million and change,' I said.

'Now we know who owned the Smith Barney money. We just don't know where it went.' Ranger gathered the reports together, slid them into a large envelope, and handed them over to me. 'This is your copy. I'll have my financial guy go over the material on the flash drive and summarize it for us.' He looked at his watch. 'I have to get to the airport. I'm flying to Miami to escort a high-bond FTA back to Jersey. I should be home tomorrow night. I'll call when I get in. Tank will be available if you have problems.'

# Nine

'Okay, so run this by me again,' Lula said. 'We're all dressed up like Handy Andy for why?'

'Dickie is part owner of an apartment building. On the odd chance that he isn't dead, I thought it might be a place he'd hole up. Or maybe a place someone would hold him hostage. It's on Jewel Street, right on the edge of public housing. I did a drive-by, and it looks like a candidate for urban renewal. There are ten units, and I'm sure they all have leaky faucets and broken toilets. I figure we go in looking like maintenance, and we won't have a problem poking around.'

'I hope you realize I could be shopping right now. There's a big shoe sale at Macy's.'

'Yes, but since you're with me, going on a crime-solving adventure, you get to wear this neat tool belt.

It's got a hammer and a tape measure and a screw-driver.'

'Where'd you get this thing anyway? It don't hardly fit a full-figure woman like me.'

'Borrowed it from my building super, Dillon Rudick.'

I parked the Cayenne next to a Dumpster in the alley behind the building. Joyce was still following me, but I didn't care a whole lot as long as she stayed in her rental car and didn't interfere.

'We'll start at the bottom and work our way to the top,' I told Lula. 'It shouldn't take long.'

'Just suppose we find this dickhead, then what? It's not like he committed a crime. It's not like he's FTA and we can haul his bony ass off to jail.'

'I guess we sit on him and call the *Trenton Times* to come over with a photographer.'

'I would have worn something different if I'd known that. I got a sweatshirt and baggy-ass jeans on so I look handy. This isn't gonna show me off in a photograph. And look at my hair. Do I have time to change my hair color? I photograph much better when I'm blond.'

I opened the back door to the building and peered into the dark interior. It was a three-story walk-up with a central stairway. Four apartments on the first floor, four on the second, and two on the third. It was late afternoon. Coming up to dinnertime. Most tenants would be at home.

I knocked on 1A and a Hispanic woman answered. I told her we were checking toilet seals.

'Toilet don't work,' the woman said. 'No toilet.'

'What do you mean it don't work? You gotta have a toilet,' Lula said.

'Don't work.'

Lula elbowed her way in. 'Maybe we could fix it. Let me have a look at this toilet. Sometimes you just gotta jiggle the handle.'

The apartment consisted of one large room opening off a galley kitchen, plus a single bedroom and bathroom. Seven kids and six adults were watching a small television in the living room. A big pot of something vaguely smelling like chili bubbled on the stove.

Lula wedged herself into the little bathroom and stood in front of the toilet. 'This toilet looks okay to me,' Lula said. 'What's wrong with it?'

'Don't work.'

Lula flushed the toilet. Nothing. She picked the lid up and looked inside. 'There's no water in this toilet,' she said. 'That's your problem.' Lula reached around and turned the valve on the pipe leading to the toilet.

'It's gonna work just fine now,' she said. She flushed the toilet again and the bowl began to fill with water.

The Hispanic woman was waving her arms and talking rapid-fire Spanish.

'What's she saying?' Lula asked me.

I shrugged. 'I don't speak Spanish.'

'You're with Ranger all the time. Don't he ever speak Spanish?'

'Yes, but I don't know what he says.'

The toilet bowl was now entirely filled with water and the water was still running.

'Uh-oh,' Lula said. 'Maybe I should shut the water off.' She reached behind the toilet, turned the valve, and it came off in her hand. 'Hunh,' she said. 'This ain't good.'

'Don't work,' the Hispanic woman said. 'Don't work. Don't work.'

The water was running over the side of the toilet bowl, splashing onto the floor.

'We gotta go now,' Lula said to the woman, giving her the handle to the valve. 'And don't worry, we're gonna put this on our report. You'll be hearing from someone.' Lula closed the apartment door behind us and we headed for the stairs. 'Maybe we should skip right to the second floor,' she said.

'Don't offer to fix anything this time,' I said. 'And let me do the talking.'

'I was just trying to be helpful is all. I saw right off her problem was she didn't have the water turned on.'

'She didn't have it turned on because the valve was *broken.*'

'She didn't communicate that to me,' Lula said.

I knocked on the door to 2A and my knock was answered by a little black woman with short gray hair.

'We're checking to see if there are any maintenance issues with this building,' I told her.

'I don't have any problems,' the woman said. 'Thank you for asking.'

'How about your toilet?' Lula said. 'Does your toilet work okay?'

'Yes. My toilet is fine.'

I thanked the woman and pushed Lula away from the door, over to 2B.

'I know something's wrong here,' Lula said, sniffing the air. 'Smells like a gas leak. Good thing we're going around checking on these things.'

'We're not checking on anything. We're looking for Dickie.'

'Sure, I know that,' Lula said. 'That don't mean we can't detect a gas leak.'

The door was answered by a fat guy wearing boxer shorts. 'Waddaya want?' he asked.

'We been sent by the gas company,' Lula said. 'We smelled a leak.' She stuck her head into his apartment. 'Yeah, it's coming from in here all right.'

'There's no gas in here,' he said. 'Everything's electric.'

'I guess I know gas when I smell it,' Lula said. 'My partner and me are from the gas company. We know these things. How about the oven? Are you sure the oven isn't gas?'

'Waddaya think this is, the Hotel Ritz? The oven don't even work. The oven never worked. I gotta cook everything in the microwave.'

Lula pushed past him. 'Stephanie, you go walk around and make sure there's no gas leakin' out of anything.'

I stepped in and gasped at the stench. I looked at the fat guy and I was pretty sure I knew what was leaking gas, but I held my breath and did a fast run through the apartment to make sure Dickie's corpse wasn't rotting in the bathtub.

'This place reeks,' Lula said to the fat guy. 'What are you cooking in that microwave?'

'Bean burritos. It's all it cooks. It explodes everything else.'

'Guess we found the gas source,' Lula said. 'And you should put a shirt on. It should be illegal for you to go without a shirt.'

'What about my microwave? Are you gonna fix it? It explodes everything.'

'We're from the gas company,' Lula said. 'We don't do microwaves.'

'You got a tool belt on,' the guy said. 'You're supposed to fix things, and I want my microwave fixed.'

'Okay, okay,' Lula said. 'Let me take a look here.'

'Careful of the door,' he said. 'It sticks.'

'That's probably your problem. It takes you too long to get the door open, and then you cook everything too long, and it explodes.' Lula gave the door a good hard yank, a couple screws flew off into space, the hinges snapped, and the door came off in her hand. 'Oops,' Lula said.

I didn't waste any time getting out of there. I was halfway up the stairs to the third floor when I heard Lula slam the door on 2B and come pounding after me.

'Least he won't be stinking things up eating more of them microwave burritos,' Lula said.

My cell phone rang. It was Tank.

'Are you okay?' he asked.

'Yep.'

Tank disconnected.

'Who was that?' Lula wanted to know.

'Ranger's out of town, and Tank's in charge of my safety.'

'I thought I was in charge of your safety.'

I rapped on 3A. 'I'll tell him next time he calls.'

A tall black guy with red dreads answered the door.

'Holy cow,' Lula said. 'It's Uncle Mickey.'

'Your uncle?'

'No. Uncle Mickey's Gently Used Cars! He's famous. He does those commercials on television. "Come to Uncle Mickey's Gently Used Cars and we'll treat you right." Everybody knows Uncle Mickey.'

'What can I do for you girls?' Uncle Mickey asked. 'Are you looking for a deal on a car?'

'No, we're the Fix-It Sisters,' Lula said. 'We're going around fixing things.'

I did a mental eye roll. We were more like the Break-It Sisters.

'What are you doing in a dump like this?' Lula asked Uncle Mickey.

'Not as much profit margin as you'd expect in used cars,' Mickey said. 'Uncle Mickey's fallen on some hard times. Got a lot of overhead. Had a bad run with the ponies.' He peeked out into the hall. 'You aren't going to tell anyone Uncle Mickey lives here, are you?'

'You living here by yourself?'

'Yeah, just Uncle Mickey all by himself in the penthouse. I don't suppose you girls would like to come in and entertain Uncle Mickey?'

'We got work to do,' Lula said. 'You're gonna have to entertain yourself.'

Uncle Mickey disappeared behind his door, and we moved to 3B.

'That was sort of depressing,' Lula said. 'He looks so sincere in those commercials. You just want to rush out and buy one of his cars.'

A voluptuous, dark-haired, dark-eyed woman answered my knock at 3B. She was wearing a red sweater and jeans and had an expensive watch on her wrist and a diamond cocktail ring that went knuckle to knuckle. I put her age at forty with very good genes.

'Yes?' she said.

'We're working our way through college fixing things,' Lula said. 'You got anything broken?'

'I know who you are,' the woman said to me. 'I saw your picture in the paper. You're the woman who murdered Dickie Orr.'

179

'I didn't murder him,' I said. 'I have an alibi.'

'Yeah, right. Everyone's always got an alibi. You're in big trouble. Orr embezzled a shitload of money from the firm, and you killed the little worm before anybody could figure out where he put it.'

'How do you know that?'

'The guy I'm living with is a partner. Peter Smullen. He tells me everything. We're getting married as soon as he gets a divorce from his bitch wife. Then we can buy a house and get out of this dump.'

'Peter Smullen lives here?'

'Usually. When he's not traveling. Or screwing around. He didn't come home last night, and it's going to cost him big. I've had my eye on a bracelet at Tiffany's. I've been waiting for him to pull something like this.'

'A woman's gotta plan ahead,' Lula said. 'Gotta take advantage of those opportunities.'

'Fuckin' A,' Smullen's girlfriend said.

'Okay then,' I said. 'Have a nice day. We'll be moving along.'

Lula and I stopped on the second-floor landing to regroup.

'That was interesting,' Lula said. 'Do you want to try the other tenants? We missed a bunch on the first and second floors.'

'I don't think Dickie is here, but we might as well finish the job we started. And for God's sake, don't offer to fix anything.'

Joyce followed me to my apartment building and parked two rows back. I could be a good person and tell her I was done for the night, or I could be mean and let her sit there for a while before she figured it out. I decided to go with mean. She wouldn't believe me anyway. I took the elevator to the second floor and found a guy in RangeMan black waiting in front of my door.

'I'm supposed to make sure your apartment is safe before you go in,' he said.

Good grief. I guess I appreciated the concern, but this was feeling a little over the top.

I unlocked the door and waited while he did his thing, looking under beds and checking out closets.

'Sorry,' he said when he was done. 'Tank made me do it. If something happens to you while Ranger's away, we're all out of a job.'

'Ranger should get a grip.'

'Yes, ma'am.'

I closed the door and looked at him through the peephole. He was still standing there. I opened the door.

181

'Now what?' I said.

'I'm not allowed to leave until I hear you lock and bolt the door.'

I closed the door, locked and bolted it. I looked through the peephole again. No RangeMan. I hung my coat and bag on the hook in the hall and gave Rex a cracker.

'I have a very strange life,' I said to Rex.

I got a beer out of the fridge and called Morelli's cell phone.

'What?' Morelli said.

'I just wanted to say hello.'

'I can't talk now. I'll call you later.'

'Sure.'

'He won't call,' I said to Rex. 'Men are like that.'

I tried Ranger's cell and got his answering service. 'You're a nut,' I told him.

I took the envelope filled with reports into the living room and began reading through the material. There was nothing in any of the reports to link Smullen, Gorvich, and Petiak together, other than their previous addresses. And that connection was vague. They were all from different neighborhoods in Sheepshead. Ranger had checked not just Smullen, Gorvich, and Petiak, but their parents as well. All families seemed to be hardworking and clean. No criminal records anywhere. No indication of mob connections. Gorvich was Russian-born but immigrated with his parents when he was twelve. There was also nothing to link Smullen, Gorvich, and Petiak to Dickie prior to their entering into business together.

# Ten

I woke up on the couch with Petiak's credit report clutched in my hand and sun streaming in through the two living-room windows. The bad part was I had a crick in my neck from sleeping on the couch all night. The good part was I was already dressed.

I went to the kitchen and started brewing coffee. I poured out a bowl of cereal and added milk, saying a silent thank-you to Morelli. It had been thoughtful of him to bring food, and I was sure he would have called back last night if it had been at all possible. I felt my eyes narrow and my blood pressure rise a little thinking about the phone call I never got and made an effort at composure. He was busy. He was working. He was Italian. Yada yada yada.

I finished the cereal, poured myself a cup of coffee, and took it to the living-room window. I looked down into the parking lot. No white Taurus.

Mr Warnick walked out of the building and got into his vintage Cadillac. He was wearing a sports jacket and tie. All dressed up for church. He didn't look cold. The sky was blue. The sun was shining. Birds were chirping. Spring had sneaked in while I was asleep on the couch.

My head was filled with miscellaneous facts about Smullen, Gorvich, and Petiak. They were all mediocre students in high school. Petiak went to a state college on a military scholarship. Smullen and Gorvich went to colleges that were unfamiliar to me. None of the men had been involved in varsity sports. Smullen had a sweet tooth. Gorvich collected wives but didn't keep them. Smullen had a wife in South America and a girlfriend in a slum in Trenton.

Smullen had arranged a meeting with me but didn't show. He'd also done a no-show on his girlfriend. I had bad vibes about Smullen. I was afraid something had gone down, and it hadn't been good for Smullen.

Next up was a visit to Grandma.

Unfortunately, all RangeMan vehicles are equipped with a tracking device. Between the bug in my purse and the transmitter in the Porsche, RangeMan knew my every move. And the guys were on high Stephanie alert until Ranger returned. I wanted to take a look at the warehouse this morning, and I didn't want to attract a lot of attention. I didn't want five guys in RangeMan black hovering around the structure, wondering if they should break in SWAT-style. So I was going to leave my purse and Ranger's Porsche at my parents' house and take Uncle Sandor's Buick.

Uncle Sandor gave Grandma his '53 powder blue and white Roadmaster Buick when he went into the nursing home. It's a classic car in cherry condition, and it's eerily indestructible. Men think it's a very cool car, but if I had my choice, I'd go with a red Ferrari.

I drove the Cayenne to my parents' house and popped inside.

'I'm going to borrow the Buick,' I told Grandma. 'I'll bring it back in a couple of hours.'

'You could drive it all you want. It almost never gets used.'

I got behind the wheel of the monstrous Buick and cranked the V-eight over. I put it into reverse and backed it out of the garage and onto the street. The car rumbled under me, sucking gas and spewing toxins. I shoved it into drive and muscled it out of the Burg, I took Hamilton to Broad and cut through the center of town.

The warehouse Dickie partly owns is on Stark Street. Stark Street starts bad and gets worse. The early blocks are marginal businesses mixed with slum housing. Shady entrepreneurial private enterprise flourishes on this part of Stark. You can buy everything from shoplifted Banana Republic T-shirts to the drug of your choice to a backseat BJ. It's a long street, and the farther you travel, the more the street gives over to anger and despair. Squatters live in the graffiti-riddled, condemned buildings of middle Stark. And finally, Stark turns to scrub fields and the skeletal remains of factories that are too wasted to draw even gang interest. Beyond this moonscape of scorched brick rubble, at the very end of Stark, just past the salvage graveyard, is a light industrial park. The rent is cheap and the access to Route One is excellent. Dickie's warehouse was in this industrial park.

I turned onto Stark and had the road to myself. Sunday morning and everyone was sleeping off Saturday night. Good thing too, because I would have attracted attention in the Buick. I drove past the junkyard and into the small industrial park. It was dead quiet.

The warehouse was next to an automotive paint and body shop. No cars parked in the warehouse lot, but there were a couple cars in the body shop lot. I docked the Buick next to one of the cars in the body shop. Just in case someone happened by, I didn't want to make it obvious I was in the warehouse.

The body shop was closed up tight, but I could hear a power tool being used inside. The diode on a security camera over a door blinked from red to green. I was being filmed. Probably worked on a motion sensor.

I was debating moving the Buick when the door opened and a huge tattooed, wild-haired guy stepped out.

'Now what?' he said. 'I'm clean.'

It was Randy Sklar. He'd gotten busted for possession about six months ago. Vinnie had bonded him out, and he'd failed to appear. I'd found him in a bar drunk off his ass, and Lula and I had literally dragged him back to the police station.

Only one reason for Randy Sklar to be up and working on a Sunday morning. This was a chop shop and Randy was taking a car apart. You don't let a hot car sit. You take a torch to it and in a couple of hours, the evidence is gone.

I smiled at Randy because before he passed out and I slapped the cuffs on him, he'd been fun at the bar. And I was also smiling because this was a stroke of luck. Randy wasn't going to call the police if I broke into the warehouse. He was going to keep his bay doors down and locked and hope no one wanted to talk to him.

'I'm not looking for you,' I told him. 'I heard you managed to wiggle out of the possession charge.'

'Yeah, there were some problems with police procedure. Are you looking to get rid of the Buick?'

'No. I just want to park here while I go next door.'

'Not much over there,' Randy said. 'Looked to me like they cleaned house.'

'I'm looking for the guy who owns it.'

'Don't know nothing about that. Just know trucks come in and out at night while we're working. Figured it was mob running a hijacking op, so we stayed away. Like to keep a low profile anyway. Then, a couple days ago, there's nonstop activity, and from what I could see through the open bays, the place got emptied out. And no one's been there since. At least no trucks.'

'Cars?'

'Haven't seen any, but they could park on the side. There's a door over there. Looks like there are offices on the second floor.'

'So how's life?'

'Life's okay. You should come back to the bar. I'll buy you a drink.'

'That's a deal.'

I crossed a small patch of blighted grass and circled the warehouse. Four loading docks in the back. Windows at the upper level. A locked front door. And a locked side door. If I were with Ranger this wouldn't be a problem. There was a frosted window and vent on a back corner. Bathroom. I could break the window and climb in. Probably set off a security alarm, but I'd have at least twenty minutes before anyone would respond to this location. And chances were decent no one would come at all.

I went back to the Buick and got a tire iron out of the trunk. I whacked the window with the tire iron and cleaned out the glass as best I could. I carefully crawled through the window with minimum damage. A scrape on my arm and a tear in my jeans.

I was in a bathroom that was best used in the dark. I held my breath and tiptoed out. I'd soak my shoes in Clorox when I got home. I flipped a switch, and overhead fluorescents blinked on.

Randy was right. The warehouse had been swept clean. Not a scrap of garbage anywhere . . . other than in the bathroom. Lots of empty shelves. A couple long folding tables. Some folding chairs neatly stacked against a wall. No hint as to the use other than a lingering odor of something chemical. Gasoline or kerosene.

There was a freight elevator and an enclosed stairwell servicing the second floor. I very quietly took the stairs.

The door at the top was closed. I opened the door and found another empty storage area. An office with a large, smudged, frosted window looked out at the storeroom. I looked more closely and realized the window was dark with soot. This got my heart to flop around a little in my chest. I tried the door. Locked. I took a deep breath and used the tire iron on the office window.

I looked inside the office, and it took a moment to figure it out. Sometimes things are so ghastly it takes time for your mind to catch up with your eye. I was looking at a cadaver sitting in a chair behind a desk. The desk, the chair, the body, and the wall behind it were scorched black. All burned to a crisp. It was so terrible, so far removed from reality, that at first I had no emotional reaction other than disbelief. I was at the broken window, looking into the room, and the room smelled of smoke and charred flesh.

I'd like to think I am good in an emergency, but the truth is, instinct takes over, and it doesn't always lead to intelligent action. The moment I smelled the smoke, I went completely spastic. My only thought was to get as far away as possible as fast as possible. I tumbled through the door, all flailing arms and frantic legs, and slid down five stairs before getting my footing. I was about to open the ground-floor door when there was a sound like a giant pilot light igniting. *Phunnnnf!*

I opened the stairwell door to a wall of flame and more spastic horror. I slammed the door shut and ran back up the stairs. There were no windows in the storeroom, only windows in the torched office. I scrambled over broken glass into the office, opened a window on the outside wall, and looked down. I was at least thirty feet from the ground.

So here was a choice. I could dive headfirst and splatter like Humpty Dumpty, or I could stay in the building and burn like the guy at the desk.

Randy came running from the body shop. 'Jump!' he yelled at me.

'It's too far.'

A second guy came running. 'Holy shit,' he said. 'What's she doing up there?'

'Get the truck,' Randy said to the guy. 'Hurry!'

Flames were starting to lick up the side of the building, and the floor was hot under my feet. An eighteen-wheeler rolled out of the body shop, over the grass, and idled at the front of the warehouse.

'He's going to drive it under you, and you need to jump fast before it catches fire,' Randy yelled at me.

Okay, so it was a little Hollywood. Doesn't mean it wouldn't work. And it's not like I had a lot of options.

I straddled the open window, the truck moved in, I swung my other leg over, sucked in some air, and jumped. I hit the metal roof feet first and lost my balance. I went to my hands and knees, looking for something to grip, clawing at air. I slid over the side of the trailer and grabbed a strut as the truck drove away from the building. I hung like that, flopping around and swearing, for just a couple of seconds before my fingers released and I crashed to the ground.

I was spread-eagled on my back with all the air knocked out of me. I had cobweb vision. The truck engine chugged in my ear, and Randy bent over me. His face was inches from mine, the sun framing his Wild Man of Borneo hair in a glorious corona.

I couldn't speak. The air hadn't yet returned to my lungs. 'Un,' I said.

'What should I do?' he asked. 'Should I feel for broken bones? Maybe around your ribcage. Loosen your clothes.'

'*Un!*'

'It was worth a try,' he said. 'A guy's gotta try, right?'

'I'm assuming I'm not dead.'

'No. You're just a little scratched up and . . .'

'And what?'

'And nothing.'

'You're looking at my hair. What's wrong with my hair?'

'It's a little . . . singed.'

I closed my eyes. 'Shit.'

'You're not gonna cry, are you? My girlfriend always cries if I say the wrong thing about her hair. I *hate* that.'

I made an effort to get up, but I was in pain everywhere and not making much vertical progress. Finally, Randy got me under the armpits and dragged me to my feet.

'I don't suppose you found the guy you were looking for,' Randy said.

'Hard to tell.'

'Are you waiting around for the police and the fire trucks?'

'Do you think they'll come?'

'Not unless we call them.'

'I'm not inclined to do that.'

'Me either.'

'Thanks for getting me out of there,' I said to Randy. 'That was a really big truck.'

'It's a double-decker car hauler. We use it to . . . uh, haul cars.'

The warehouse was an inferno, completely engulfed in flames, the heat stinging my skin. Black smoke billowed about a quarter mile into the sky.

'It's a decent fire,' Randy said, looking up at the smoke. 'We might get some action on this one.'

I limped to the Buick, managed to get behind the wheel, and did some slow breathing. I sat for a couple of minutes, collecting myself. A bay door to the body shop opened, and the car hauler rolled out. The shop had cleaned up for visitors.

I got the Buick started and followed the hauler to Route One. Sirens screamed in the distance, but we were traveling away from them. When we reached Route One, the hauler went north and I went south. I took the Broad Street exit and drove back to my apartment. Ranger's Porsche and my purse were still at my parents' house, but I wasn't going to retrieve them looking like this. I'd lost about an inch of hair, and the ends were scorched black and frizzed. I was cut and scraped and blistered and sore. I was going to take a shower and crawl into bed and stay there until my hair grew back.

I stepped out of the elevator and slowly propelled myself down the hall, leaving smudges of soot and blood. Before the day was over, Dillon would be working on the carpet with his rug shampooer. Mental note: Get a six-pack for Dillon.

I opened my door, trudged inside, and almost keeled over when I saw Ranger. He was sitting in my living room, in my only good chair, his elbows on the arms, his fingers steepled together in front of him. His face showed no emotion, but he was radiating anger. I could have popped corn on the invisible energy Ranger was throwing.

'Don't start,' I said to him.

'Do you need a doctor?'

'I need a shower.'

His eyebrows raised ever so slightly.

'No,' I said.

I limped into the bathroom and whimpered when I saw my reflection in the mirror. I closed the door and dropped my clothes onto the floor. Lucky for me, the weather was still cool, and I'd been wearing a heavy sweatshirt and jeans. The clothes had saved most of my skin from the broken glass. I washed away the grime and a lot of the blood. I slapped some Band-Aids over the deeper gashes, got dressed in clean clothes, and went out to face Ranger.

'You got home early,' I said.

'I had to fly charter. Couldn't get on a commercial plane with my man.'

'How did you know I wasn't visiting my mom?'

'Your visits are never that long. Hal got suspicious and called your cell and talked to your grandmother.'

'I wanted to take a look at the warehouse, and I was afraid I'd be followed by a RangeMan caravan.'

He didn't say anything to that. If you didn't know Ranger, you would think he looked relaxed in the chair, one long leg extended, one bent at the knee, arms on the upholstered armrests. If you knew him at all, you would be extremely wary.

I sat across from him, on the couch, easing myself down. I leaned my head back and closed my eyes for a moment, struggling with composure, not wanting to burst into tears in front of Ranger. I opened my eyes and blew out a sigh because he was still there, watching me.

'I assume you burned the warehouse down,' Ranger finally said.

'It wasn't my bad. I think someone set a bomb, and I got caught.'

'Anyone else in there?'

'A dead guy. He was sitting behind a desk on the second floor. Looked like he'd been toasted with a flame-thrower. I only know flamethrowers from movies and the six o'clock news, but that's what it looked like to me. The body was burned beyond recognition. It was awful. Both Dickie and Smullen are missing. I suppose it could have been one of them. No way to know for sure.

'I was leaving when the building caught. I was in the stairwell. Something went *phunnnnf* and then there was fire everywhere. I had to go back up to the office and jump out the window. That's the short version.'

'Did anyone see you there?'

'No one we need to worry about.'

'You should pass this on to Morelli so they know to look for the body.'

'I'll pass it on, but trust me, there's no body left.'

'What kind of shape are you in?' Ranger asked. 'Are you functioning? We've still got Stewart Hansen on ice at RangeMan. You can bring him in now, and no one will associate you with the cannabis farmhouse fire.'

'He won't tell anyone?'

'I don't think he'll remember,' Ranger said. 'And if

he does say something, I doubt anyone will believe him. We've been keeping him very happy.'

'Do you have him drugged?'

'Quality weed, Ella's cooking, and nonstop television on a fifty-inch plasma.' Ranger stood and pulled me to my feet. 'Would you rather do this tomorrow?'

'No. I'll be okay.'

'You don't look okay. You've got blood soaking through your jeans.'

I looked down at my leg. 'I should have used a bigger Band-Aid.'

'Do you need stitches?'

'No. It's just a cut. I had to go through a smashed window to get out of the building.'

'I'm going to ask you again. Do you need stitches?'

I didn't know. I hoped not.

'Let me see it,' Ranger said.

I bit into my lower lip. This was embarrassing.

'Babe, I've seen it all,' Ranger said.

'Yes, but you haven't seen it lately.'

'Has it changed?' he asked.

That got me smiling. 'No.'

I popped the snap to my jeans and slid them down. I was wearing a lime green lace thong, which was a lot like wearing nothing.

Ranger looked and smiled. 'Pretty,' he said. Then his attention moved to the gash in my leg. 'I know you don't want to hear this, but it'll heal faster and neater if you get some sutures in it.'

We put a washcloth against the cut and wrapped my leg with surgical tape.

'Do you have any other injuries that are this serious?' he asked.

'No,' I said. 'This was the worst.'

We went to St Francis emergency and had a minimal wait. The kids with colds and the after-lunch heart attack victims had all been cleared out. There'd been only one Sunday afternoon gang shooting, and he'd been DOA. And it was still early in the day for domestic violence.

My leg was pumped full of local anesthesia and stitched. I got salve for the burns on my neck and face, and antiseptic ointment for my other scrapes and cuts.

Louise Malinowski was working emergency. I'd gone to school with Louise. She was now divorced with two kids and back home living with her mom.

'Who's the hot guy out there?' she asked, helping me get my jeans up over my numb leg and new stitches.

'Carlos Manoso. He owns a security agency downtown.'

'Is he married?'

'He's as unmarried as a man can get.'

Ranger watched me buckle myself in. We'd left the Buick in my lot and taken his Porsche turbo. It was black and new and fast, just like all his other cars, but even more so.

'Where do all these new black cars come from?' I asked him.

'I have a deal. I provide services for cars.'

'What sort of services?'

'Whatever is required.' He put the car in gear and pulled away from the hospital. 'I'm going to take you to your parents' house so you can get your purse, and I want you to call Morelli.'

Not something I was looking forward to. This wasn't going to make Morelli happy.

'What?' Morelli said when he answered the phone. Not sounding especially mellow.

'How's it going?'

'It's going not fast enough. What's up?'

'Did you hear about the fire at the warehouse on Stark?'

'No. I don't hear about anything. I'm locked away, babysitting a moron, and I'm looking at an episode of

"*Raymond*" that I've seen forty-two times.'

'Dickie and his partners owned a warehouse on Stark and—'

'Oh, Christ,' Morelli said. 'Don't tell me.'

'It burned down . . . just now.'

'Are you okay?'

'Yeah. Ranger took me to get stitches.'

There was silence on the other end, and I imagined Morelli was staring down at his shoe with his lips pressed tightly together.

'Anyway, I'm fine,' I told him. 'I just got cut on some glass when I had to break a window to get out. Is it okay to talk on your cell phone like this? I mean, no one can listen, can they?'

'Everyone can listen,' Morelli said. 'Don't let that stop you. Is this conversation going to get worse?'

'If you're going to give me attitude about this, I'm not going to talk to you.'

I looked over at Ranger, caught him smiling, and punched him in the arm.

'No one saw me,' I said to Morelli. 'I left before the fire trucks arrived. And it wasn't my fault. I'm pretty sure someone set a bomb. The thing is, there was a guy sitting behind a desk on the second floor, and I think he'd been toasted with a flamethrower. I doubt there's much left of him after the second fire, but Ranger wanted me to tell you.'

This created a lot more silence.

'Hello?' I said.

'Give me a moment,' Morelli said. 'I've almost got myself under control.'

'How much longer are you going to be on this assignment?' I asked Morelli.

'At least two more days. Let me talk to Ranger.'

I gave Ranger my phone. 'Morelli wants to talk to you.'

'Yo,' Ranger said. He did some listening, and he cut his eyes to me. 'Understood,' he said to Morelli. 'Don't expect miracles. She's an accident waiting to happen.' Ranger disconnected and handed the phone back to me. 'I'm in charge of your well-being.'

'Morelli should mind his own business.'

'That's exactly what he's doing. You're a couple. You *are* his business.'

'I don't feel like his business. I feel like my own business.'

'No shit,' Ranger said.

What was worse, I was caught off guard by the couple status. 'Do you think Morelli and I are a couple?'

'He has his clothes in your closet.'

'Only socks and underwear.'

Ranger parked in my parents' driveway and turned to face me. 'You want to be careful what you tell me. My moral code stops short of "Do not covet someone else's woman." You've been holding me at arm's length, and I respect that, but I'll move in if I feel that barrier relax.'

I already knew this, but having it said out loud was disconcerting. I didn't want to make more of it than was necessary, so I tried being playful. 'Are you telling me socks and underwear are borderline in terms of couple qualifications?'

'I'm telling you to be careful.'

When Ranger issued a warning, he didn't do playful.

'That's just great,' I said. 'I'm so *not good* at being careful.'

'I've noticed,' Ranger said.

My grandmother opened the front door and waved.

Ranger and I waved back, and I eased myself out of the car and went to retrieve my bag.

'Is that blood on your pants leg?' my grandmother asked when I stepped into the foyer.

'Kitchen accident,' I said. 'It's fine. Gotta go. Just came in to get my bag. I'll bring the Buick back later.'

I hurried to the Porsche and angled in.

'Barnhardt is two houses down and across the street,' Ranger said. 'She was here when we drove up. She must have spotted the Cayenne.'

Ranger rolled out of the driveway and down the street. Joyce rolled with us, staying a couple car lengths back.

'I'm taking you home with me,' Ranger said. 'I have to catch up on paperwork and meet with Tank, and I don't want to worry about you. You can spend the night and turn Hansen in when the court opens in the morning.'

'I can't spend the night at RangeMan.'

'Morelli said I should keep you safe.'

'Yes, but no one's after me. I've just had some unfortunate luck.'

'Babe, you've destroyed a car, burned down two buildings, stapled a guy's nuts, and you have sixteen stitches in your leg. Take a night off. Have a glass of wine, watch some television, and go to bed early.'

# *Eleven*

anger's apartment occupies the seventh floor of the RangeMan building. It's professionally decorated in neutral earth tones and classic comfortable furniture. It's cool. It's calm. It's inviting in a mildly masculine way. The carved mahogany front door opens to a long narrow foyer. Coat closet and powder room on one side. Cherry wood credenza on the other. Ranger's housekeeper, Ella, keeps fresh flowers on the credenza, plus a silver tray for keys and mail. Modern kitchen with stainless appliances and granite countertops to the right at the end of the hall. Breakfast bar. Small dining room. Small living room. The master bedroom suite consists of a den, a bedroom with king bed and smooth, white, thousand-thread-count sheets, a dressing room with all black clothes, and a weapons cabinet, and a luxurious bathroom with walk-in shower that smells like Ranger's Bulgari Green shower gel.

Ranger electronically unlocked his apartment door and I followed him inside. He took an identical lock fob from a drawer in the credenza and gave it to me.

'If you decide to leave, take the GPS monitor with you. Hal's bringing the Cayenne back. It'll be parked downstairs with the key on the seat. It's yours for as long as you need it. I'm sure Ella has dinner in the kitchen. Help yourself. I've got a lot to do. I'm going to grab a sandwich downstairs.' He curled his fingers into my sweatshirt, dragged me to him, and kissed me. 'If you want to stay up for me, I'll make it worth the wait,' he said, his lips barely touching mine when he spoke. And he was gone.

I've lived in Ranger's apartment once before for a short time when my life was in danger. And for a short time, I worked in the RangeMan office. The building felt very safe back then, but after a while claustrophobic.

I prowled through the kitchen and found a chicken stew with rice and vegetables. I scarfed down the stew with a glass of wine, and took a second glass into the den to watch television. I sunk into Ranger's big, comfy couch and remoted the plasma.

Morelli's house was comfortable ground for me. It

was filled with hand-me-down furniture left to him by his Aunt Rose. It looked a lot like my parents' house, and in a strange, unexpected way the house fit Morelli. When Morelli had time, the house was kept neat and orderly. When Morelli was overworked, the house became cluttered with abandoned shoes and empty beer bottles.

Ranger's apartment felt exotic. The furniture was expensive and chosen for Ranger. Very comfortable but a little sterile. No family photos. No dog-eared books. This was a place where Ranger slept and worked and ate but didn't live.

Morelli's house was a destination for him. Ranger's apartment felt like part of his journey.

I probably should have gone home, but the truth is I love visiting Ranger's apartment. It smells great . . . like Ranger. His television is bigger and better than mine. He has better water pressure in his shower. His towels are softer and fluffier. And his bed is wonderful, even when he isn't in it. Ella irons his sheets and plumps his pillows. If there's a woman out there who could make me turn, it would be Ella.

I fell asleep in front of the television. I woke up at eleven and again at eleven-thirty. I forced myself away from the television and into the bedroom, shucked most of my clothes, and crawled into Ranger's fabulous bed.

The alarm jolted me awake, and I had a moment of utter confusion before realizing I was at RangeMan. The room was dark, but I could see Ranger outlined against his dressing room light. He crossed the room and stood at the bedside to turn the alarm off.

'I have an early meeting with a client this morning,' Ranger said. 'And I want to talk to you before I get involved in RangeMan business. Ella has breakfast on the table.' His cell phone rang, and he left the bedroom.

I painfully rolled out of bed, my whole body aching from the fall off the car hauler. I flipped the light on, limped across the room to Ranger's closet, and shrugged into a robe that had been bought for Ranger, but I was sure had never been worn. I couldn't imagine Ranger lounging around in a robe.

Ella was a small, slim woman with intelligent dark eyes, short black hair, and contained energy. Ella's husband managed the property, and Ella managed the men of RangeMan. She cooked and cleaned and did whatever was necessary to get Ranger out of his apartment each morning in presentable condition. She bought his shower gel, did his laundry, ironed his orgasmic sheets, and set out fresh flowers.

The breakfast tray she brought to his door was almost always the same. Coffee, fresh fruit, whole-grain bagels, lox, fat-free cream cheese. An egg-white frittata with vegetables. Very pretty. Very healthy. This morning, Ella had set the dining-room table for two.

Ranger ended his call and joined me at the table. He was in corporate attire. Black dress slacks, black shirt, black-on-black striped tie, black gun and holster. He draped a black cashmere sports coat on an empty dining-room chair, then poured coffee while still standing, and sat across from me.

'Holy cow,' I said to him. But I was thinking *Holy Cow!*

'I wasn't trying for holy cow,' Ranger said. 'I was shooting for respectable.'

'Good luck with that one,' I told him.

Ranger was strong inside and out. He was intelligent. He was brave. He was physically and emotionally agile. He was incredibly sexy. He was deceptively playful. But more than anything else, Ranger reeked of bad boy. It would take a lot more than a cashmere sports coat and an Armani tie to offset the testosterone and male pheromones that leaked out of him. I doubted Ranger would ever be entirely respectable.

'Okay,' Ranger said. 'I admit respectable was a stretch. How about successful?'

'Yes,' I said. 'You look very successful.'

He helped himself to fruit and a slice of the frittata. 'I'm going to make a deal with you. The deal is that you work with me on the Dickie thing, and you don't go off on your own.'

'That's the deal?'

'The alternative is that I lock you in my bathroom until I get this mess figured out.'

'What about you? Are you going off on your own, without me?'

'No. I'll include you in everything.'

'Deal.'

'Gorvich, Petiak, and Smullen all have legitimate addresses, but none of them spend any time at them. And they don't spend a lot of time at the office downtown. I had someone search the three residences, and he found nothing. No computers. No clothes in the closets. Nothing in the refrigerator. We've been calling their phones and only get a message service. Never a callback.'

'Lula and I went through the law firm's apartment building on Jewel Street and discovered Smullen was keeping a woman on the top floor. The woman said Smullen lived there when he was in the country. He was missing in action when we got there, and his girlfriend was angry. I should check to see if he's still missing.' I took a bagel and loaded it up with cream cheese. 'Why don't these guys live in their houses?'

'Maybe they're worried an unhappy client might come calling. I've been looking at the material you lifted from the law office. Rufus Caine paid the firm a little over a million dollars last year for legal services. I thought we might want to talk to him.'

You couldn't be associated with crime in Trenton and not have heard of Rufus Caine. Vinnie had never bonded him out, so everything I knew was second-hand. And what I knew, mostly, was that he wasn't a nice guy. 'Rufus Caine is middle-management pharmaceuticals. Will he talk to us?'

'I have a relationship with Rufus. He lives and works out of a slum apartment building behind the train station. I thought we'd pay him a visit this afternoon. In the meantime, I have your FTA, Stewart Hansen, ready to go. Call the control room when you want him brought down to the garage. I'll send one of my men with you, but you probably don't want to involve

RangeMan in the delivery.' Ranger finished his coffee and pushed back from the table. 'I have to run.'

Hansen was in the backseat of a Ford Explorer, physically ankle-chained to the floor, mentally floating in La La Land. Ranger hadn't been kidding when he said they'd been keeping Hansen happy. Hard to tell if Hansen was in this euphoric state from too many episodes of *Scooby-Doo* or too much wacky tobacky.

I parked the Explorer in the public lot across from the courthouse and unlocked Hansen's ankle shackles. His hands were still cuffed behind his back, and I had to help him out of the SUV. Ranger's guy was in the front passenger seat, looking nervous, not sure how much help he was supposed to give me and still stay politically correct.

'I'll be back,' I told the RangeMan guy. 'Don't go anywhere.'

I maneuvered Hansen into the building, stood him in front of the docket lieutenant, and Hansen started giggling.

'Shit,' the docket lieutenant said. 'Last time I was that happy, I was in charge of the evidence room and we'd just busted a gangbanger carrying a suitcase full of medicinal weed.'

I completed the paperwork, got a body receipt, and called Connie and told her Hansen was in the lockup in case someone wanted to spring him again.

Ranger had said he'd be busy until noon, and it was still early, so I jogged to the SUV, got behind the wheel, and drove to Coglin's house. Ranger had made me promise to work with him on the Dickie thing. He hadn't said anything about my FTAs.

'Small detour,' I said to the RangeMan guy. 'What's your name?'

'Brett.'

He didn't look like a Brett. Guys named Brett were supposed to have a neck. This guy looked like he should be named Grunt.

I parked at the curb and had Brett follow me to the door. Brett was wearing a full utility belt with gun, stun gun, a can of pepper spray that could take down a grizzly, and cuffs. He was dressed in RangeMan SWAT, and he was scary-looking as hell. My intent was that Coglin would see Brett with me and keel over in a dead faint before he got to fire off the shotgun.

I knew Coglin was home. I'd seen him moving in the glassed-in front porch just before I'd parked. I hadn't heard the car leave from the backyard, so I rang the bell and listened for the car. If I heard the car engine catch, I'd take off and run him down at the cross street. I rang the bell again.

Brett was close behind me at the ready. 'Should I break the door down?'

'No,' I said. 'It's probably not locked.'

Brett stepped in front of me and tried the door handle. He pushed the door open, stepped inside and *bang!* Brett was covered in funk and short mousy brown hairs.

Hard to tell what the creature had been. I was guessing sixty-pound rat.

'What the—' Brett said.

'It's getting old,' I yelled into Coglin's house. 'I'll be back.'

I led Brett to the Explorer and drove him back to RangeMan.

'What is this stuff on me?' he asked. 'What happened?'

'I think you might have been beavered, but there's no way to know without DNA testing.'

I walked him upstairs to the control room and turned him over to Hal. Down the hall, Ranger stepped out of his meeting and glanced my way.

'It wasn't my fault,' I said to Ranger.

Ranger smiled and returned to his meeting.

*

Ella brought salad and sandwiches up at noon and Ranger strolled in minutes behind her.

'How'd the meeting go?' I asked him.

'Good.'

He selected a sandwich and ate it standing up in the kitchen. I did the same.

'I notice you're dressed in RangeMan colors,' Ranger said to me.

'Turns out I have clothes in your closet.'

'More than just underwear and socks,' Ranger said. 'They were left from the last time you stayed here.'

'Does that make us a couple?'

'Spend another night with me, and I'll explain couple to you,' Ranger said.

I was tempted to ask him how we'd spent last night, but thought maybe it was best not to know. I'd gone to bed alone, and he was up and dressed when the alarm went off. I was telling myself he'd slept on the couch. That was my story and I was going to go with it.

He removed his tie and unbuttoned his dress shirt, and I managed to keep myself from dragging my tongue down his chest to his belt buckle. I conjured the image of Morelli in my kitchen and told myself it wouldn't be a good idea to spend another night here.

Ranger disappeared into his dressing room, and

when he returned, he was in cargo pants, T-shirt, and cross-trainers. His gun was clipped to his belt. He grabbed our jackets and hats from the coat closet. His hat said SEAL and mine said RANGEMAN.

'Let's roll,' Ranger said.

We were in Ranger's turbo, parked on Ellery, looking out at the pathetic apartment building where Rufus Caine conducted his business. Other buildings on the block were graffiti-decorated, but Caine's building was unscathed. It was four floors of eroded redbrick and peeling paint trim. And the front door was missing.

'Are you sure you want to leave the Porsche here?' I asked Ranger. 'What are the chances it'll be here when we come back?'

'Chances are good. Only a dealer would leave a turbo sitting out here in front of Caine's building. And no one wants to steal that car. No one wants that kind of trouble.'

We left the car and stopped at the building's stoop. The tiny foyer was littered with used condoms and syringes and what I hoped was *dog* poo.

Ranger scooped me up and carried me to the stairs. 'This way we only have one pair of shoes to throw away,' he said.

We hiked to the fourth floor and Ranger knocked on the door.

'Yeah?' came through the closed door to us. 'Who's there?'

'Ranger.'

The door opened and a toady looked out at us. 'Who's she?' he asked Ranger.

Ranger didn't say anything, and the toady backed up and opened the door.

There were four people in the room. Three goons and Rufus Caine. Easy to tell Rufus. He was the two-hundred-pound, five-foot-five guy having a midlife crisis, all decked out in jewelry and hair plugs. He was on the couch with a napkin daintily perched on his knee and a glass of champagne in his hand. There was a mound of sandwiches on a large plastic take-out platter on the coffee table in front of him.

'I was having lunch,' Rufus said to Ranger. 'Help yourself.'

'I just ate,' Ranger said. 'But thanks.'

Rufus eyeballed me like I was dessert. 'Who's your bitch?'

'This is Stephanie,' Ranger said. 'She's running relief for Tank.'

'I didn't know you and Tank had that kind of relationship,' Rufus said.

Ranger didn't smile.

'So wassup?' Rufus asked.

Ranger didn't say anything. He just stared at Rufus. Rufus made a little flick with his hand and the three idiots left the apartment.

'Sit,' Rufus said to Ranger.

Ranger sat, and I stood. I was the muscle in the room.

'I'm thinking about retaining some counsel,' Ranger said. 'I'm looking at Petiak, Smullen, Gorvich, and Orr.'

'Good firm,' Rufus said.

'Why is it good?'

'Discreet. Got a good business ethic.'

'And?'

'Understands the barter system. You sure you don't want a sandwich?'

'I want to know more about the barter system,' Ranger said.

'Why?'

Ranger didn't say anything. He didn't blink. He didn't smile. He didn't sigh. He just silently stared at Rufus.

'Good thing I like you,' Rufus said to Ranger, 'because you could improve on your social skills. You're not exactly a fun guy. Anyone ever tell you that?'

Ranger cut his eyes to me and then back to Rufus.

'The barter system is where you trade some shit for other shit,' Rufus said. 'Wait a minute. Maybe I don't mean the barter system. What is it when you say you're paying for legal advice, but you're really paying for inventory?'

'Lying,' Ranger said.

'Yeah, that's what those assholes understand . . . lying.'

Ranger reached forward and took the bottle of champagne off the coffee table and refilled Caine's glass. 'Anything else you want to tell me?'

'What's your angle?'

'No angle,' Ranger said. 'Like I told you, I'm looking to retain counsel and I like the firm. I'm just having a hard time finding someone to talk to. No one's answering the phone.'

'Do you have something to . . . barter?'

'You want to stay away from Jimmy Monster. He's wearing a wire.'

'Ow.'

'And?' Ranger said.

'I'm meeting Victor Gorvich tonight. He has a package for me. We used to make the drop at a warehouse, but the warehouse burned down, so I'm seeing him at ten at Domino's.'

'The strip club on Third Street?'

'That's the one. Just make sure my business is concluded before you move in.'

Ranger stood. 'Be careful,' he said to Rufus.

'Fuck that,' Rufus said.

We were a couple blocks away from the apartment building when my cell phone rang.

'I can't talk long,' Morelli said. 'I just wanted to pass some information on to you. The guy in the warehouse was identified by his wedding band and key ring. It was Peter Smullen.'

'Holy crap.'

'The guy in the warehouse was Peter Smullen,' I said to Ranger.

'Who are you talking to?' Morelli asked.

'Ranger.'

'You're with Ranger?'

'You told him to take care of me.'

'Yeah, but I didn't mean—'

'I'm getting static,' I said to Morelli. 'Hello? Hello?'

And I disconnected. 'He needed a moment to collect himself,' I said to Ranger.

'Understandable.'

'Let's recap,' I said to Ranger. 'First the law firm's accountant goes swimming with the fishes. Then Dickie gets dragged out of his house. And now Peter Smullen is dead.'

My cell phone rang again.

'We got cut off,' Morelli said.

'Cell phones,' I said. 'Go figure.'

'I wanted to tell you Marty Gobel might want to talk to you again. Smullen's secretary said Smullen was supposed to meet with you the night he disappeared.'

'Are you suggesting I might be under suspicion for Smullen's murder?'

'You have an alibi, right?'

I hung up and slouched in my seat. 'Smullen's secretary told the police I was supposed to meet with Smullen the night he disappeared.'

Ranger hooked a U-turn on Broad. 'Let's see what Smullen's girlfriend has to say about all this.'

We passed Joyce, who was now going in the wrong direction in her rented white Taurus.

'I used to be such a badass,' Ranger said. 'Everyone

was afraid of me. Everyone wanted to kill me. I needed Tank walking behind me to keep the paid assassins under control. And now look at me. I'm followed by a woman in a rented Taurus.' He made a vague gesture with his hand. 'And I can't remember the last time someone tried to kill me.'

'It wasn't that long ago,' I said. 'It was in my apartment, and you got shot a bunch of times, and it wasn't all that much fun.

'Not to change the subject, but if I understood the conversation back there, Victor Gorvich is supplying Rufus with drugs.'

Ranger turned off Broad and drove toward the projects. 'Not only is he supplying drugs, he's laundering the money through the firm. He's billing Rufus for legal advice when Rufus is actually paying him for inventory. If you look at the client list you lifted, it's a shopping cart filled with the World's Most Wanted. Not just drug dealers, but gunrunners and agents for dictators. One or more of the partners is shuffling drugs around and washing the money as billable hours.'

'Gorvich, for sure.'

'Looks that way.'

Ranger parked curbside at the law firm's slum

apartment building, and we both got out. Ranger took a remote gizmo, aimed it at the Porsche, and the Porsche chirped.

We hoofed it up to the top floor and rang the bell. No answer. We rang it again, and Uncle Mickey stuck his head out his door.

'She isn't there,' Uncle Mickey said. 'She went shopping.' He looked at Ranger and retreated into his apartment.

Ranger took his little tool out of a pocket on his cargo pants and opened the apartment door.

Smullen's apartment had been freshly painted and carpeted. The furniture was new. The kitchen appliances were new. The countertop was Corian. The building was a slum, but Smullen's apartment was not. Smullen's toilet worked.

Smullen's clothes were hanging in the closet and neatly folded in bureau drawers. His toiletries were still in the bathroom. I checked pants pockets for the bug, but didn't find it.

I walked out of the bedroom and caught Ranger at the living-room window, looking down. He was standing hands on hips, watching two men direct a flatbed tow truck up to the Porsche. His car alarm was wailing away, and the men were ignoring it.

Ranger unlocked and raised the window, unholstered his gun, took aim, and shot one of the men in the leg. The guy crumpled onto the pavement and rolled around, holding his leg. The flatbed driver jumped out and helped drag the wounded guy into the truck, and they drove away. Ranger aimed his gizmo at his car and silenced the alarm.

'Do you feel better now?' I asked. 'You got to shoot someone today.'

'I've still got the touch,' Ranger said.

'Smullen's clothes are here, but I didn't find the bug. Did you come up with anything interesting?'

'No. He doesn't have a home office. Not even a laptop squirreled away somewhere.'

The lock tumbled on the front door, and Smullen's girlfriend pushed into the apartment. She had a brown grocery bag in the crook of her arm, and she was out of breath from the stairs.

'What the fuck is this?' she said to Ranger and me.

'We came to visit, but you weren't home,' I said to her.

She cut her eyes to Ranger. 'Who's the hot guy? Is he a cop?'

'No. He's Ranger.'

'Why's he dressed like a cop? What is this, Halloween and no one told me?'

I glanced back at Ranger. 'You aren't going to shoot her, are you?'

'Thinking about it.'

'Was Peter involved in anything shady at work?' I asked her.

'Sure. He was a lawyer.'

'I mean *really* shady. Like illegal. Trafficking in drugs, for instance.'

She set the bag on the kitchen counter. 'I don't think so. Why would he do something like that? He was making a fortune just being a lawyer.'

'Did he have another office somewhere? I noticed he doesn't have a home office here.'

'He works at the law office. What's the deal, anyway? I'm calling the cops. You jerk-offs broke into my apartment. Hey, wait a minute. You aren't going to kidnap me, are you? Omigod, you've got Peter, right? That's why he hasn't come home. You've got Peter! Help!' she yelled. 'Help! Police!'

'Go ahead,' I said to Ranger. 'Shoot her.'

'We aren't going to kidnap you,' Ranger said. 'And we didn't kidnap Peter Smullen. In fact, we have some very bad news for you.'

'Help!' she yelled. 'Help! Help!'

Ranger looked at me. 'You have any ideas besides *shoot her*?'

'I love your boots,' I said to her. 'Vuitton, right?'

She looked down at the boots. Knee-high, black leather, stacked heel. 'Yeah,' she said. 'They cost a fortune, but I *had* to have them. I got a bag to match. You want to see the bag?'

'Sure.'

She went into the bedroom and came back with the bag. 'This is the shit, right?' she said.

'It looks great on you. You can carry a big bag like that,' I told her. 'It's a to-die-for bag. And speaking of dying . . . Peter Smullen is dead.'

'Waddaya mean, he's dead?'

'He was caught in a fire in a warehouse last night and he died. I'm so sorry,' I told her.

'How do you know?'

'It was made public this morning.'

She was deer-in-the-headlights for a moment. 'Are you sure?'

'He was identified by his wedding band and his key ring.'

'Sonovabitch. All that money and I was so close to getting my hands on it, and the jackass had to get himself toasted in a fucking warehouse. Life is so unfair.' Her eyes darted around the room. 'This apartment belongs to the law firm,' she said. 'I need a truck! Do you have a truck?'

'No.'

'We'll have to rent one.'

'Uh, actually we have to be moving along,' I said. 'Like to stay, but . . .'

Ranger was at the door.

'Uncle Mickey lives across the hall,' I told her. 'He can get you a truck.'

I followed Ranger down the stairs and out of the building. I was about to get into the Porsche when I spotted Joyce half a block away.

'Be right back,' I said to Ranger.

I jogged down to Joyce and leaned in her car window. 'Peter Smullen is dead,' I said. 'He was killed in a warehouse fire last night. His girlfriend lives in that building we just left. She's on the top floor. We couldn't get any information out of her, but you might want to try.'

'Are you shitting me?'

'No. Swear to God.' I jogged back to Ranger and slid into the passenger seat. 'I think I got rid of Joyce for a while.'

# Twelve

Ranger and I were in his den watching a basketball game.

'How's your leg?' he asked.

'It's a little sore.'

'I need to leave for Domino's. Do you want to come with me or would you rather stay here?'

'I'll go with you.'

He looked at my V-necked sweater with the RangeMan logo embroidered in purple. 'Do you have something to wear that doesn't say RangeMan?'

'No. Even my underwear has your name on it.'

'It's Ella. She got a machine that stitches the logo, and she can't control herself. She puts it on everything.' He stood. 'I'm going to change. I'll be ready to go in a minute.'

I'd been to Domino's once before. Lula and I made an apprehension there last spring. It was a typical titty bar with a raised stage and pole dancers. I was told it had a back room for lap dances, but Lula and I didn't get back there. Our man was at the bar, stuffing money into G-strings.

Ranger had changed into black jeans and a long-sleeved, collared black shirt that he wore out to hide his gun.

'Do you have money for the girls?' I asked him.

'I try not to hand money out at strip bars. It's like feeding stray cats. Once you feed them, they never go away.'

'Yes, but I'll be there to protect you this time.'

Ranger held my jacket for me. 'I usually rely on Tank, but tonight the job is yours.'

We took the elevator to the garage, and Ranger chose a black Explorer over one of his private cars. Easier to blend. Domino's was just ten minutes away from RangeMan. For that matter, everything was ten minutes from RangeMan. Ranger had placed his security company in a good location. If an alarm went off anywhere in Trenton, RangeMan was there in ten minutes or less.

On weekends, Domino's rocked. It was filled to capacity with bachelor parties and couples out for fun. On a Monday night, it was half empty, and there was no problem getting a table. Ranger steered us to a dark corner where he could put his back to the wall. Most of the men were at the bar that surrounded the dance platform. A bunch of sad regulars and some out-of-town businessmen who'd straggled in from the hotels on Route One. I was the only woman.

The music was loud. Disco. The two women onstage were in four-inch stilettos and dental floss. They looked like they wouldn't mind getting out of the shoes.

A waitress stopped by, all smiley face. 'Hey handsome,' she said to Ranger. 'What'll it be?'

'Vodka rocks,' Ranger said. 'Two of them.'

I raised an eyebrow at him when the waitress left. 'You drink vodka rocks?'

'Less to dump on the floor,' he said.

We didn't want to make an entrance and have Gorvich spot us, so we'd arrived early. The disadvantage to this soon became apparent. Ranger was a bimbo magnet.

The dancers finished their set, and one immediately strolled over to our table and straddled Ranger.

'Want a private party?' she asked.

'Not tonight,' Ranger said. He handed her a twenty, and she left.

'What about the cat-feeding theory?' I asked him.

'Out the window.'

Our drinks were delivered and a new dancer popped up in front of Ranger. 'Hey sweetie,' she said. 'How's it going?' And before Ranger had a chance to answer, she had her huge breasts in his face and her leg over his lap.

'Not tonight,' Ranger said. He handed her a twenty, and she left.

'I'm seeing a pattern here,' I said to Ranger. 'How often do you come here?'

'Too often. I thought you were going to run interference.'

'It's like they come out of nowhere. Before I know it, they're on top of you.'

A woman in rhinestone pasties and a rhinestone G-string stopped by, and Ranger handed her a twenty before she got her leg over him.

'You could go through a lot of money fast this way,' I said to Ranger.

'All for you, babe. Small price to pay to keep you out of jail.'

He dumped his vodka onto the floor behind him. The waitress swooped in, took his glass, and gave him a fresh vodka.

Rufus rolled in at five minutes to ten. He took a seat at a table by the bar and ordered a drink. One of the girls approached him and was allowed to do her thing. Guess the room in the back was closed on Monday, and the action came out front.

Ranger and I watched her gyrate and bounce and rub against Rufus.

'I know men like this sort of thing,' I said to Ranger, 'but personally I prefer a shoe sale at Macy's. On the plus side, we'll be in good shape if we have to follow him. She's shedding so much body glitter, he's going to glow in the dark.'

The dancer slithered up Rufus, and his entire face got smushed into her breasts.

'She's going to kill him,' I said to Ranger. 'He's going to suffocate. Do something.'

'He's okay. His color still looks good,' Ranger said.

'His color is terrible. He's purple.'

'It's the lights.'

'Do men have . . . you know, reactions to this rubbing and writhing stuff in public?' I asked Ranger.

'I guess, but this is the first time I've seen someone turn purple.'

At ten after ten, the big blond muscle guy with the stapled nuts came into the bar and sat across from

Rufus. He said something to the dancer, and she abruptly got up and left. Rufus called for the check and finished his drink. He paid his bill and left with the muscle guy.

'Give them time to get out of the building,' Ranger said. 'We don't want to ruin this by getting recognized.'

'Aren't you afraid of losing them?'

'Tank is in the lot, and Hal is on the street.'

Ranger took a call from Tank.

'They're moving,' Ranger said, snapping his phone closed.

He signaled the waitress and dropped a hundred dollars on the table. We left the club and followed Tank's directions through town. We turned into the projects, and I guessed where we were headed. The law firm's apartment building.

There was only on-street parking on Jewel Street, and at this time of the night, every parking place was taken.

'Rufus went in the car with the muscle,' Tank said over the speakerphone. 'He got dropped off in front of the building and the muscle kept driving. Hal followed the car to Stark Street and lost it in traffic. I'm double-parked across the street from the building. Rufus went in and hasn't come out. No one else has gone in since I've been here. Only a few minutes.'

Ranger called Hal. 'Look at the back of the building and make sure it's secure.'

'Yessir,' Hal said. 'I'm a couple blocks away. I'll get right to it.'

Ranger circled the block and found a parking place on a side street. We left the car and walked to where Tank was idling. We stood on the sidewalk and looked up at the building. Lights were on in units 1A and 3A. Curtains were drawn in 3A.

'It has to be the third floor,' I said. 'I was in every apartment, and I can't see any of the others as a possibility.'

'I told Rufus I'd wait for him to clear before I made a move, but this feels off,' Ranger said.

'What do you want to do with Gorvich when you find him?' I asked.

'I want to talk to him.'

A car careened onto Jewel half a block away and screamed past us, going in the opposite direction. Two men in the car. The passenger in shadow. The driver was the blond muscle guy.

Hal was half a block behind with his foot to the floor. Tank jerked away from the curb, hooked a U-turn, and Tank and Hal disappeared down the street in pursuit.

Ranger and I ran to the building and took the stairs two at a time to the third floor. I smelled the gasoline before we even reached the top of the stairs. It was mingled with cooked meat and forest fire.

Ranger didn't bother with the locksmith tool. He put his foot to the door and crashed it open. Smullen's girlfriend had moved fast. The apartment looked completely cleaned out, with the exception of a large upholstered couch. Probably too awkward to get down the stairs on short notice. Either end of the couch was intact. The middle of the couch was charred. And the two bodies sitting on the couch were charred. The wall behind the couch was burned black.

'This is just like the warehouse,' I said. 'Someone's doused this apartment with gasoline. There's probably a bomb in here somewhere.'

Ranger grabbed me and shoved me out of the apartment. 'Go to the second floor and get everyone out of the building.'

I flew down the stairs and started banging on doors. I had two apartments empty and was on the third when Uncle Mickey hustled down the stairs with Ranger behind him.

'Go to the first floor,' Ranger said to me. 'I'll finish up here.'

We had everyone on the street and sirens were wailing in the distance when flames shot out of the windows to 3A. The fire raced through the structure, and Ranger and I ran to the neighboring building and made sure everyone evacuated.

The police cars were the first on the scene and then the fire trucks and paramedics. I was relieved to give the disaster over to the professionals and fade away into the crowd of bystanders. I was sweating from horror and exertion and the heat of the fire, and I was shivering with nervous energy.

Ranger pulled me into a shadow and wrapped his arms around me. I held tight to his open jacket and tucked my face into him, trying to get my teeth to stop chattering. Ranger wasn't trembling, and he wasn't sweating. His breathing was measured and normal.

'Breathe,' Ranger said, his voice soft against my ear. 'Try to breathe deeper.'

His calm washed into me, the shivering and chattering stopped, and tears rolled down my cheeks and soaked into his shirt.

'I f-f-feel like an idiot,' I said to him.

'It's just a letdown from the adrenaline rush.'

'Why aren't you letting down?'

'My body is more efficient at producing and using adrenaline.'

We stood like that, locked together, for a couple more minutes, until I stopped crying.

Finally, Ranger looked down at me. 'How are you doing?'

'I'm good.'

'I want to talk to Tank,' Ranger said. 'Stay with me.'

'I'm pooped. I thought I'd go sit in one of the cars.'

Ranger took my hand. 'Not yet. I don't want you out of my sight.'

'Afraid I'll burn down another building?'

'Afraid you'll get arrested.'

Five men in RangeMan black stood shoulder-to-shoulder in front of us. Tank and Hal were among them. Ranger dismissed all but Tank.

'Hal got to the back of the building just as the car was leaving,' Tank said. 'Hal saw a rope hanging from a third-floor window. Looked like someone might have rappelled out. Hal had to turn around to follow the car, and we were both too far behind to catch him. He was really moving.'

'Did Hal get a plate?'

'He got a plate the first time he followed him. We've already traced it.'

'Stolen?' Ranger asked.

'Yes.'

'I'm taking Stephanie home. Stay here a while longer and let me know if anything weird goes down.'

Ranger opened his apartment door for me and walked me to the kitchen.

'Are you hungry?' he asked.

'Famished. And tired.'

'I can call Ella. She'll make whatever you want. Or you can prowl through the kitchen. There's still peanut butter from the last time you were here.'

'Peanut butter sounds perfect.'

I shucked my coat and assembled a peanut butter and olive sandwich while Ranger leaned against the kitchen counter and punched a number into his phone.

'Who are you calling?' I asked.

'Morelli. Do you want him on speakerphone?'

'No. I haven't the energy.'

'We need to talk,' Ranger said to Morelli. 'There was a second fire tonight. Two people toasted by a flamethrower. I saw them just before the building exploded. Same drill as the warehouse. Both times there were victims already burned, accelerant in the

241

area, and there must have been an incendiary device on a timer. I'd like to see the reports. And it would be good to get a fast ID on the bodies in the apartment building tonight.'

Morelli said something, and Ranger looked over at me.

'No, she wasn't directly involved,' Ranger said. 'She was with me the whole time. She's fine. Her hair didn't even catch fire.'

I rolled my eyes and gave Morelli and Ranger the finger. 'I wanted to bring this to you first,' Ranger said. 'If you're unavailable, I can go to your captain. This probably could benefit from a task force.'

Ranger flipped his phone closed and uncorked a bottle of red wine. He poured me a glass and ate an olive from the bottle.

'Is Morelli going to run with this?' I asked.

'He's going to make a phone call.'

I had my sandwich made, but I was so exhausted I could hardly chew. I washed a chunk down with wine and felt all my bones dissolve.

'I'm going downstairs to research flamethrowers,' Ranger said. 'I'll be up later.'

I finished the sandwich and wine and fell asleep wearing one of Ranger's T-shirts. It was big and comfy, and it was the first thing I laid hands on in the dressing room.

Sleep is very strange stuff. One minute you don't know anything, and then you're awake and life starts over. I opened my eyes to Ranger, fully dressed, standing over me, coffee cup in his hand.

'I let you sleep as long as possible,' he said. 'We have a meeting at the station in a half hour. You have ten minutes to shower and get dressed. I'm putting your coffee in the bathroom.'

'Meeting?'

'Fire marshall – that would be Ken Roiker – Morelli, Captain Targa, Marty Gobel. Don't know who else. We're going to give information, and we're going to get information.' He looked down at me. 'If I leave, you'll get up, right?'

'Yeah.'

'You won't go back to sleep?'

'No.'

'I don't believe you. You have that go-back-to-sleep look.'

He ripped the covers off and dragged me into the bathroom. He turned the shower on and shoved me in still wearing his T-shirt.

'You are such an asshole,' I yelled at him.

'Ten minutes,' he said. And he left the bathroom, closing the door behind him.

I was at the sink, wearing his robe with the hair dryer in my hand, when he rapped on the door. 'Ten minutes are up.'

'Bite me,' I said.

'I've got clothes for you.'

I stuck my head out. 'You picked out my clothes?'

'It wasn't hard. They're all the same.'

I took the clothes, closed the door, and got dressed. Only the bra didn't have RangeMan embroidered on it.

I gave up on the hair drying and skipped makeup. I'd take care of that in the car.

Ranger was waiting in the kitchen. He had coffee in a travel mug and a bagel with cream cheese in a Styrofoam box. Ranger hated being late for a meeting. Only death or dismemberment or the opportunity for morning sex were considered acceptable reasons for Ranger to be late to a meeting.

I took the coffee and bagel and trotted after Ranger out of the apartment and into the elevator.

'Do we know any more about last night?' I asked.

'Tank saw Joyce at the fire scene, and it sounded like

she had Smullen's girlfriend with her. Other than that, no.'

We got into the turbo and Ranger drove out of the garage. I had my coffee in the turbo's cup holder, the bagel in one hand and a mascara wand in the other.

'Don't jerk around,' I said to Ranger. 'I could go blind doing this.'

'Wouldn't it be safer to do without?'

'Yeah, but I hide behind it. I put it on when I need to feel brave.'

'You don't need to feel brave today. Nothing bad is going to happen at this meeting.'

'I've been sleeping in your bed, and I've got your name embroidered on my underpants, and now I'm going into a meeting where your air space is going to intersect with Morelli's.'

'Babe, nothing's been happening in my bed, and no one's going to see your underpants in this meeting unless you go goofy.'

We parked in the public lot and crossed the street to the municipal building. Ranger had meeting instructions, so we ignored the cop-in-a-cage and went directly to a conference room. There were six men already seated. Ranger and I took our seats, and that left one chair empty. Morelli. Morelli's chair was directly opposite mine. Ranger was to my right. Already I was sweating the seating arrangement.

The conference room door opened, and Morelli entered. He nodded to everyone and claimed his place at the table. He looked across at me and smiled. The smile was small and intimate, and his brown eyes softened just a little for just a moment. He was in jeans and a cream sweater with the sleeves pushed to his elbows.

I had no idea what was going on inside Morelli or Ranger. They looked perfectly at ease and in control. Both of them were good at hiding emotion. Both were good at compartmentalizing. I wasn't good at any of that stuff. I was a wreck inside.

'Sorry I'm late,' Morelli said. 'I had to wait for the babysitter.'

Everyone knew Morelli had someone locked down.

'You called this,' Targa said to Morelli. 'You want to run it?'

'Stephanie and Ranger have information they want to share with us,' Morelli said. 'And they're hoping we have information to share with them.' His eyes went first to me and then to Ranger. The eyes didn't say anything. Morelli was in cop mode.

'For reasons that are obvious, Stephanie and I have

been looking for Dickie Orr,' Ranger said. 'Stephanie was looking for him in the warehouse when the fire started. And we were in the apartment building last night when that fire occurred. We know that all three fire victims were dead before the fire. We know there was an accelerant in the apartment. I called 911 and did a fast search, but I didn't find anything that looked like a bomb. And for that matter, in both instances, there was no explosion of any significance.'

'You saw the victims before the fire?' Targa asked.

'Stephanie saw Smullen. We both saw the two bodies in the apartment building. All three had been burned beyond recognition. The scorch trail suggested flamethrower.'

'The accelerant was gasoline,' Roiker said. 'We found the cans.'

'Do you know how it was ignited?' Ranger asked.

'Both times it started in a kitchen. In the case of the warehouse, it was a corner set aside for a cooler and a microwave and a toaster. The lab guys are still working, but it looks like someone rammed something that would burn into the toaster . . . Hell, it could have been one of those breakfast tart things. The pop-up mechanism was disabled and the toaster was wired with an interior timer. We suspect the toaster was fitted

247

with a fuse to make sure the flames reached the accelerant, but there was no evidence of it.'

'The flaming toaster bomb,' Marty Gobel said. 'We see a lot of them.'

Morelli cracked a smile and Ranger nudged my knee with his.

'Have you identified the victims from the apartment fire?' Ranger asked.

'Working on it. Not a lot left of them. The explosion was set closer and the fire burned hotter.'

'We saw Rufus Caine enter the building. And we believe he was meeting Victor Gorvich,' Ranger said. 'Tank was watching, and he didn't see either man come out the front of the building. Someone rappelled out a back window.'

Ranger didn't share information on the drug connection or the missing $40 million, and no one mentioned Dickie Orr.

Five minutes before the meeting closed, Morelli's phone buzzed and he went outside to take the call and never returned. At eleven o'clock, Ranger and I left the building and buckled ourselves into the Porsche.

'Do you think he was pulling our leg on the toaster?' I asked Ranger.

'No. He's not that clever. I did a fast run through the

apartment, looking for an incendiary, and didn't see anything. Smullen's girlfriend had taken everything except the couch and the toaster. I saw the toaster and didn't give it a second look.'

'Next time we enter a building soaked in gasoline, we'll think to unplug the toaster.'

Ranger glanced in his rearview mirror when we were a block from RangeMan. 'It looks like Joyce got her Mercedes running.'

I turned and looked out the back window. Joyce was a car length behind us.

'I have to give her credit,' I said. 'She's good.'

'She's too good,' Ranger said. 'She's finding us on the road.'

He keyed himself into the underground garage and parked in his space in front of the elevator.

'Do you have plans for today?' he asked me. 'I can give you paperwork if you haven't anything better to do.'

'I have two skips I'm working on. I thought I'd check on them.'

'If you're going to leave your bag anywhere, please take the monitor with you. Put it in your pocket.'

'Is it okay if I only take one?'

'How many do you have?'

'Three.'

Ranger sat there for a beat. 'I only planted one.'

'Shit.'

We rode the elevator to Ranger's apartment, went inside, and I emptied my bag onto the kitchen counter.

Ranger picked a pen out of the mess. 'This is mine.'

I took it from him and put it into my pocket. 'This lipstick is another one,' I said, handing him the tube.

'I'm guessing this is from Joyce,' Ranger said. 'You can buy these in The Spy Store.'

'And the third.' I gave him what looked like a menthol cough drop in a paper wrapper.

'This is good,' Ranger said, examining the cough drop. 'Super small. Well disguised. How did you discover it?'

'I tried to eat it.'

'That's the flaw. You can write with my pen.'

'This is so creepy. Three people planted a transmitter on me, and I never knew they were doing it. What else am I missing? We know one of the transmitters belongs to you, and you planted it on me to protect me. We suspect the second belongs to Joyce, and she wanted me to lead her to Dickie. So what does this third one represent?'

'It could be as simple as one more person with the

same agenda as Joyce. One of the partners who thought you might lead him to Dickie and the money. Maybe someone was casting a wide net. Maybe Joyce is walking around with a transmitter in her bag too.'

'You don't want me to freak over this.'

'I don't want you to get bogged down in negative emotion. And the truth is, we aren't sure what these toys do. I'm going to take them downstairs and give them to one of my tech guys.'

'Omigod, I just had a thought. I killed Rufus Caine! If the cough drop is a transmitter, the owner would have known we visited Rufus. He would have known we were at the club. And he would have known we followed Rufus to the apartment.'

'You didn't kill Rufus. And even if you did, it wouldn't be much of a loss.'

'Death by flamethrower is gruesome.'

'That's the appeal. The threat is demoralizing. It instills fear. And fear can be a controlling, paralyzing emotion. There are paramilitary groups that make good use of flamethrowers. It's not an especially effective way to kill a man, but it sends a message.'

'You think someone is sending a message here?'

'No. I think this killer is a freak. He has a reason for

killing these people, but he's also getting off on the experience. He torches them, and then he sets a fire to hide his thrill kill. Problem is, both times you screwed things up. You saw the torched bodies before the fire. His secret is out.'

'He might not know that.'

'If he's the owner of the cough drop, he knows.'

'What about not wanting to scare me?'

'You asked,' Ranger said. 'Are you scared?'

'Big time.'

'You're safe here.'

'Yes, but I can't stay here forever. In fact, I can't stay here tonight. I think my free pass has expired.'

'I don't want to force you to leave and put you in harm's way,' Ranger said, 'but I have limits.'

'You need a larger apartment,' I told him. 'You need a guest room.'

'I don't know why I put up with you,' Ranger said. 'You're a real pain in the ass.'

'You put up with me because I'm amusing, and you love me, and I pose no threat to your lifestyle because I'm involved with Morelli.'

'That's all true,' Ranger said. 'But it doesn't make you any less of a pain in the ass.'

I shoved my stuff back into my bag. 'I'm heading

out. I need to check on Rex, and then I'm going to the office.'

'I need to stay here, but I can give you one of my men.'

'Not necessary. I'm okay.'

'I thought you were scared.'

'It's a way of life.'

---

'What the heck is this?' Lula asked when I walked into the office. 'You're all in RangeMan black. Are you working for RangeMan again?'

'I ran out of clean clothes, and this was available. I'm going to try to talk to Coglin. Want to ride along?'

'Sure. Maybe we could stop at the video store. Tank's coming over tonight, and I'm gonna rent a movie. I need something to put him in the mood. I was thinking one of them *Lethal Weapon* movies. Or maybe *Transporter*.'

'What kind of mood were you aiming for?'

'Man mood. In all my years of being a 'ho, I learned blood is better than sex if you want to get a man stirred up for action. You let a man watch someone getting his face mashed in, and you got a horny guy. It's the beast thing.'

Something to keep in mind if I ever want to do it with a beast.

'We have all the *Lethal Weapon* movies at Morelli's house. You can borrow them if you want.'

'You sure he won't mind?'

'He isn't home. He's locked down with a witness. And even if he was home, he wouldn't mind.'

'That'd be great since I was going to have to kite a check to get movie money.'

# Thirteen

**M**orelli's house is officially outside the Burg, but not by much. It was a five-minute drive from the bonds office. I parked the Cayenne and fished Morelli's house key out of my bag.

'I'll be right out,' I said to Lula. 'Stay here.'

Morelli lives in a narrow two-story house configured a lot like my parents'. Rooms are shotgunned with living room going to dining room going to kitchen. Front door. Back door. Downstairs powder room. Small, barren backyard leading to an alley. Three small bedrooms and old-fashioned bath upstairs. Morelli inherited the house from his Aunt Rose and little by little has been making it his own.

I unlocked the front door and stepped into the short hallway that serves as foyer and also leads to the stairs. I'd expected the house would be silent and empty, but the television was on in the living room. My first reaction was confusion, fast followed by a rush of embarrassment. Someone was living here in Morelli's absence. Maybe an out-of-town relative or a down-on-his-luck cop. And I'd barged in unannounced.

I was about to quietly sneak out when Dickie Orr walked in from the kitchen. He was eating ice cream out of the tub, his hair was a mess, as if he'd just rolled out of bed, and he was in his underwear – a white undershirt with a chocolate ice cream stain dribbling down the front and baggy striped boxers.

Time stood still. The earth stopped rotating. My heart stuttered in my chest.

'Wha . . .' I said. 'Wha . . .'

Dickie rolled his eyes and shoved his spoon into the ice cream. 'Joe!' he yelled. 'You've got company.'

I could hear Morelli's sneakered feet on the stairs and then he was in the room.

'Oh, shit,' Morelli said when he saw me.

I gave him a little finger wave. 'Hi.'

I was feeling awkward. Embarrassed that I had stumbled into this, and angry that it had been kept from me.

'I can explain,' Morelli said.

'Uh-hunh.'

'Good luck on that one,' Dickie said. 'There's no explaining to her. You make one slip up and that's it. Sayonara.'

'Shut up, Dick breath,' I said. 'And anyway, it wasn't one slip up. In the fifteen minutes we were married, you screwed half the women in Trenton.'

'I have a high libido,' Dickie said to Morelli.

'It had nothing to do with your libido. It had to do with the fact that you're a pathological liar and a worm.'

'You have control issues,' Dickie said. 'Men aren't designed for monogamy, and you can't handle that.'

I narrowed my eyes at Morelli. 'Hit him.'

'I can't hit him,' Morelli said. 'He's in my protective custody.'

'And you!' I said to Morelli.

'I had no choice,' Morelli said. 'He had to get squirreled away somewhere, and I had the house, so he got dropped in my lap.'

'You could have told me!'

'I couldn't tell you. You would have acted differently.'

'I thought I was going to jail for murder!'

'I told you not to worry,' Morelli said.

'How was I supposed to know that actually meant something? People say that all the time.'

'What about me?' Morelli said. 'Where's the

sympathy for me? I've been trapped in my house with this idiot.'

'Boy that hurts,' Dickie said. 'I thought we were bonding.'

'What about the shooting at your house the night you disappeared?' I asked Dickie. 'And what about the blood on your floor?'

Morelli was hands in pockets, rocked back on his heels. 'Dickie shot one of the hired help in the knee. And then he ran like hell out his back door, right Dickie?'

'I ran like the wind.'

'And why is Dickie here in protective custody?'

'They wanted him on ice while they investigated the law firm's client list. The original thought was we needed him to testify against his partners, but his partners have disappeared in one way or another. One is confirmed dead and another presumed dead. And the third dropped off the face of the earth when Dickie went missing.'

'You can't find Petiak?'

'Vanished. We know he's still around because from time to time one of his goon squad surfaces.'

'So I'm off the hook.'

'Yep,' Morelli said.

258

'What about Gorvich? I thought I was a suspect there.'

'I wanted you to dredge up an alibi in case the press came to you.' His attention fixed on my RangeMan jacket. 'What are you doing in RangeMan clothes? You were head-to-toe RangeMan this morning.'

'I ran out of clean clothes and these were available.'

'Available? Where were they available?'

'In Ranger's closet.'

'Are you fucking kidding me? I'm holed up here with the witness from hell and you've moved in with Ranger?'

'You told him to take care of me.'

'Not *that* way!'

'There's no *that* way going on. It's no different from what you've got here. You've got Dick-head in protective custody. Does that mean you're sleeping with him?'

The color was rising in Morelli's face. 'I'll kill him.'

'You will *not* kill him. Read my lips . . . nothing has happened between us.' At least, not the main event. I chose to believe the prelims didn't count in this case. 'And I'm not moved in with him. I'm going home and I'm going to get on with my life now that I know I'm not a murder suspect.'

'Maybe you should move in here,' Morelli said. 'There's a lunatic out there with a flamethrower, and you're mixed up in it somehow.'

'No thanks. I already did time with Dickie. I'll take my chances with the flamethrower.' I went to the television and looked through the DVDs stacked alongside. 'I just stopped around to borrow the *Lethal Weapon* collection.' I found the boxed set and looked over at Morelli. 'You don't mind?'

'What's mine is yours,' Morelli said.

I let myself out and jogged to the Porsche.

'I thought you decided to take a nap in there,' Lula said.

I handed the DVDs over to her and pulled the car out of Morelli's driveway. 'It took a while to find them.'

In a half hour, we were in front of Coglin's house. I paged through his file, found his phone number, and called him.

'I'm in front of your house,' I said. 'I want to talk to you, and I don't want to end up with squirrel guts in my hair. Can we call a truce for ten minutes?'

'Yeah, I guess that would be okay,' Coglin said. 'If you promise you won't try to take me in now.'

'Promise.'

Lula followed me to the door. 'He better not go back on his word. I don't want to smell like rodent when Tank comes over tonight.'

I opened the door and took a step back. 'Is it okay to come in?' I yelled into the house.

Coglin appeared in the hall. 'I disconnected the booby trap. It's safe to come in.'

'Someday you're gonna hurt someone with those beaver bombs,' Lula said.

'I only use stuffing that's soft,' Coglin said.

'Yeah, but what about them button eyes? Suppose you got hit with one of them eyes? That would leave a bruise.'

Coglin had an apron on. 'I'm kind of busy,' he said. 'What did you want?'

'Are you stuffing up some roadkill?' Lula asked.

'No. I'm making a meatloaf for supper.'

'I wanted to talk to you about your court appearance,' I said to Coglin. 'When you didn't show up, you became a felon. And the original charge didn't look that bad. Destruction of property. The details aren't on the bond application. What sort of property did you destroy?'

'I went nuts and exploded an opossum in a cable company truck.'

'Uh-oh,' Lula said. 'The cable police will get you for that one.'

Coglin turned white. 'Omigod, there are cable police?'

'She's kidding,' I told him. 'You're kidding, right?' I said to Lula.

'Probably,' Lula said.

'It all started when the city put in new water pipes,' Coglin said. 'They cut through my cable line when they dug a trench through my front yard to lay the new pipe. So I called the cable company and left my name, but they never called me back.'

'Those fuckers,' Lula said. 'They never call anyone back.'

'I called them and left my name every day for three weeks, and no one ever called me back. Then after three weeks someone actually answered a phone at the cable company. A real person.'

'Get out,' Lula said. 'They don't have real people working there. Everyone knows that.'

'No. I swear, it's true. Someone answered the phone. So after they had me on hold for an hour, I explained the problem and they said they would send someone out in two weeks, and they gave me the day. So I stayed home all that day, and the next day, and the next day. And on the third day, someone came to fix my cable problem. Except they were told the problem was inside my house, and it was really outside, so they couldn't fix it.

'It's not like I just have television, you know. I sell my animals on the Internet, and I didn't have any Internet connection all this time. So I gave the guy twenty dollars, and he ran a line from the junction box across the street to my house. Only it's like a plastic cable kind of thing, so right away, with all the cars rolling over it, the cable started breaking. So I wrapped it in electrician's tape. And I do that twice a day to hold the cable together.'

'How long you been doing this?' Lula asked.

'Three months. I keep calling them back and telling them, and they keep saying they're going to send the first available crew out to me, but I have to be home or I'll get put at the end of the line. So that's why I can't go downtown with you. I never leave for more than five minutes unless it's real late at night. Even when it looks like my car is gone and I'm not in the house, I'm watching from somewhere. I can't take a chance on missing the cable repairman.'

'And the opossum in the truck?'

'The cable repairman stopped at my neighbor's

house three weeks ago and swapped out his broken box, and I went postal and threw a performance piece through the driver's side window.'

'And you think they're still gonna give you cable service after you bombed their truck?'

'They send me a bill every month, and I always pay on time. I figure that means something. And twice I got an automated message that said a crew was scheduled, but they never showed up.'

'Well, I can understand why you can't go to the police station and get rebonded,' Lula said. 'There's extenuating circumstances.'

'They might *never* show up,' I told Coglin.

'My friend Marty lives on the next block, and he had the exact same thing happen, and they showed up one day and fixed his cable.'

'How long did he wait?'

'It was almost five months.'

'And he stayed home for five months?' I asked Coglin.

'Yes, you have to. It's the rule. He lost his job, but he got his cable fixed.'

'I hate those fuckers,' Lula said.

'So as soon as the cable guy shows up and fixes your cable, you'll call me?'

'Yes.'

Lula and I walked back to the Cayenne and stopped to look at the cable running across the road. It was thick with electrician's tape, and in places had been wrapped in foam and then overwrapped with the tape.

'So what's going on with you and Tank?' I asked Lula. 'Is it serious?'

'Yeah, but only for about twelve minutes at a time.'

'Twelve minutes is good.'

'We've been working up to it. And then, if you add all the twelve minutes together, you get a whole hour. You want an hour with Morelli, you just get him watching one of them *Lethal Weapon* movies.'

I wasn't sure I wanted an hour. My egg timer was set on twenty-two minutes. Eighteen, if Morelli was on his game. An hour sounded like a lot of work. And if it was divided up into five twelve-minute sessions, I suspected I'd need mechanical devices. Although there was no doubt in my mind Morelli could manage it.

I drove Lula back to the office and dropped her at her car. 'Looks like Joyce is parked across the street,' Lula said. 'And she's got Smullen's girlfriend with her.'

I waved at them. 'Hi,' I said.

'Fuck you,' Joyce yelled.

'She's in a mood,' Lula said.

Most likely because it was a lot harder to pick up my trail now that I wasn't broadcasting.

'Have fun tonight,' I said to Lula. 'See you tomorrow.'

I drove to my apartment with Joyce tagging along. No threat there. I wasn't going to lead her to anything. It was late afternoon, and I was going to have a peaceful evening at home. I'd call Ranger and tell him I was home with Rex and that everything was right with my world. Then I'd shove something frozen into the microwave, crack open a beer, and watch television. And Joyce could sit in my lot until her ass fell asleep. The 40 million dollars was out there somewhere, but I didn't care anymore. Joyce's problem, not mine. I was off the hook. I wasn't wanted for murder. Hooray.

I parked, ran upstairs, and waltzed into my apartment. Nice and quiet. Not as luxurious as Ranger's apartment, but it was mine, and it felt like home. I gave Rex fresh water and dropped a small chunk of cheese into his cage.

Something banged against my front door. I went to the peephole to look out but before I reached the door, there was a wrenching noise and another loud thud, and the door flew open and crashed against the wall.

It was the big bleached-blond muscle-bound moron with the stapled balls. He rushed inside and grabbed me. I shrieked, and he clamped a hand to my mouth.

'Shut up,' he said, 'or I'll hit you. I'd like to do that anyway, except my boss wants you in one piece.'

'Why?'

'I don't know. That's just his way.'

'No, I mean why does he want me?'

'My boss doesn't like people who get too nosy. And you've got a knack for being in places you don't belong. My boss thinks you know something.'

'Who, me? No way. I don't know anything. You could fill a room with what I don't know.'

'You can tell it to my boss. He wants to talk to you. You can cooperate and walk out with me. Or I can stun-gun you and carry you out. Which is it?'

One more stun gun and I was going to permanently forget half the alphabet.

'I'll walk out.'

He turned and Joyce was standing there with a gun in her hand.

'No way, José,' Joyce said. '*I'm* following her. I saw her first. You want the money? Find it yourself.'

'Fuck off. And my name isn't José. It's Dave.'

'I'm counting to three, Dave. If you aren't hauling

ass by three, I'm going to shoot you in the nuts.'

'What is it with my nuts? Why's everybody picking on my nuts?'

'One,' Joyce said.

'You're getting on my nerves.'

'Two.'

'Screw this,' Dave said.

He grabbed the barrel of the gun, the gun discharged, and Joyce shot off the top of his pinkie finger.

Dead silence. We were all surprised.

Dave looked at his shortened pinkie, his eyes rolled back in his head, and he crashed face-first to the floor.

'Shit, Joyce,' I said to her. 'There's blood all over the hall and Dillon just did the floors.'

Joyce put her boot to Dave and rolled him onto his back. 'Was his nose always flat like that?'

'No. And he didn't used to have blood coming out of it either. He broke it when he fell on his face.'

Joyce took his hand and shoved it into his pants so he wouldn't get any more blood on the floor. 'What do you want to do with him? We could call 911. Or we can put him in the elevator and push the button.'

'Was he alone?'

'No. He has a partner waiting in a black BMW.'

'We'll turn him over to the partner.'

We dragged him to the elevator and rode him down to the ground level. Then we dragged him out to the parking lot, and Joyce whistled through her teeth to get the partner's attention.

The BMW drove up and the partner got out and squinted down at Dave. Dave still had his hand rammed into his pants, and his crotch had a big bloodstain.

'Jesus, lady,' Dave's partner said. 'Goddamn.'

'It's not as bad as it looks. Joyce wanted to shoot him in the nuts, but the gun discharged prematurely. Probably that happens a lot with you guys, right?'

'What?'

'Anyway, she just shot his pinkie finger off. We put his hand in his pants so he wouldn't bleed on the carpet.'

'Man, that's cold.'

'Do you need help getting him into the car?'

Dave's partner reached inside and popped the trunk.

'He's not dead,' I said to the partner.

'This is a new BMW with real leather seats. I don't want him bleeding all over everything. He'll be fine in the trunk.'

Joyce had her gun drawn, presumably protecting

269

her investment, which was me. Go figure, saved by Joyce Barnhardt.

'Don't try anything stupid,' Joyce said to Dave's partner. 'It was disappointing to have to settle for a pinkie finger. I wouldn't mind getting a second chance to shoot someone's nuts off.'

I grabbed Dave's leg and helped wrangle him into the trunk. We closed the lid, and the BMW sped out of the lot.

'So what's the deal for the rest of the day?' Joyce said. 'Are you staying here?'

That was the original plan, but I had a feeling Dave might come back after he got his nose straightened and his finger stitched up.

'I'm going to spend the night at RangeMan,' I told Joyce.

'Give him a tug for me,' Joyce said. And she walked to her car and took off.

I ran upstairs, hung my bag on my shoulder, and wrapped my arms around Rex's aquarium. I carted Rex out to the Porsche. Then I ran down to the basement and told Dillon about the door and the carpet. Dillon didn't look all that surprised. It wasn't the first time he'd had to fix my door.

# Fourteen

At seven o'clock, I heard the keys get tossed onto the silver tray in the hall, and seconds later, Ranger walked into the kitchen.

'I thought you were staying in your apartment tonight,' Ranger said.

'Change of plans.'

He glanced at Rex on the kitchen counter. 'This looks serious.'

'Remember the guy who got his boys stapled? He came visiting. He wanted me to go for a ride with him, but I declined.'

Ranger took two wineglasses out of the cabinet and un-corked a bottle of red. He poured two glasses and gave one to me. 'What did it take to discourage him?'

'Joyce Barnhardt with a gun. She tailed me to my apartment and saw Dave follow me into the building.

That's the guy's name, Dave. She came up to check things out and decided Dave was a threat to her future earnings. So she shot the top of his pinkie finger clear off his hand. Then Dave's partner came and loaded him into the trunk of their Beemer and drove him away. That's the short version.'

'Go figure,' Ranger said.

'Exactly.'

We both sipped some wine.

'That's not even the best part of the day,' I said to Ranger. 'I stopped at Morelli's house to get a DVD for Lula, and I walked in on Dickie.'

'Dickie Orr?'

'Yep. It wasn't Dickie's blood in his house. The goon squad was sent to roust him, and he shot one of them in the knee and fled. Morelli has him in protective custody. He's locked away so he can live to testify against his partners, but his partners are disappearing. Smullen is confirmed dead. The police are presuming Gorvich is dead. And they can't find Petiak.'

The doorbell buzzed and Ranger opened the door to Ella and dinner. He took the tray from her and carried it into the kitchen.

'Have you eaten?' he asked.

'A peanut butter sandwich at five.'

Ella had sent grilled vegetables, pork tenderloin, and saffron rice for two.

'Ella knew I was here?'

'Everyone knows you're here. There aren't a lot of secrets in this building. Only the private apartments and the lavatories aren't monitored.'

'Do they know anything about our relationship?'

'No. And they won't ask.'

'Not even Tank?'

'Not even Tank.'

'So they think we're sleeping together.'

'Probably.' Ranger set two place settings at the breakfast bar. 'Did Morelli or Dickie say anything about the money?'

'No. Morelli said the police were investigating the law firm's client list, but he didn't say more than that. It wasn't a long visit. Lula was outside, waiting in the car.'

We both dug into the food.

'Did Dave say anything interesting?'

'He said I was nosy, that I had a knack for being in places I didn't belong, and his boss didn't like it.'

'So they were going to do what to you?'

'Dave didn't say, but I don't think it was anything good.'

I cleaned my plate and looked over at the tray. No

dessert. Ranger never ate dessert. Another reason I couldn't marry Ranger. That and the fact he didn't see marriage as an option.

We loaded the dishwasher, put the leftover food in the fridge, and migrated into the den to watch television.

'Do you watch television a lot?' I asked him.

'Almost never.' He remoted his way through the guide. 'No games on tonight. Only boxing.'

I thought about Lula's theory on bringing out the beast in a man. So far, Ranger had the beast under control. Best not to disturb that balance.

'No boxing,' I said.

'Okay, let's roll through the movies. *The Terminator*, *Pulp Fiction*, *Braveheart*, *The Transporter*, *Deliverance*. Any of those turn you on?'

Where was *Terms of Endearment* when you needed it? 'They're all sort of violent,' I said.

'And?'

'There must be other movies.'

Ranger clicked through more of the guide. 'Bruce Lee?'

'Keep going.'

'I'm not watching *Jane Eyre*.'

'Okay, great, go with Bruce Lee.'

'Maybe you'll learn something,' Ranger said.

'Just don't get any ideas.'

'About what?'

'About anything.'

Ten minutes into Bruce Lee, I sucked in some air. 'Uh-oh,' I said.

The *uh-oh* had been an inadvertent exclamation. Nature had struck at an inopportune time, placing me in an awkward position.

Ranger looked over at me. 'What?'

'Nothing.' At least nothing I wanted to share with Ranger.

'It's something. What is it?'

'Cramps.'

'Babe.'

'I need . . . you know,' I said to him.

'You don't have anything with you?'

'I was planning on staying in my apartment. And then I left in a hurry. And I forgot until just now.'

'Do you want me to send one of my men out for something?'

'Would they do that?'

'I'd have to pay him extra.'

'Maybe Ella can help me.'

I ran downstairs to see Ella, and ten minutes later, I was back on the couch.

'Everything okay?' Ranger asked.

'Yes. Ella had some.'

Bruce Lee was kicking ass on the screen, and God knows what this was doing to Ranger's libido, but I now realized nature had come through for me. What had at first seemed like an embarrassing disaster was in actuality a blessing. This was my lucky week. First Joyce, and now nature.

Ranger slid an arm around me and nuzzled my neck. Bruce Lee was getting to him.

'Lula has a theory that violent movies put a man in the mood,' I said to Ranger.

'Everything puts a man in the mood,' Ranger said.

'Good thing I got cramps, eh? I'm safe.'

'Not from me,' Ranger said.

Eek. 'Guess again,' I told him.

Ranger changed channels to *Jane Eyre*. 'The two toys we found in your bag were simple transmitters. With the exception of my device, you're supposed to be clean. How did Joyce find you this afternoon?'

'She picked me up at the bonds office.'


I opened my eyes and looked at the clock. Almost eight a.m. No Ranger. I checked under the covers. I was still wearing all the clothes I'd started with when I went to bed. Another night of successfully dodging the bullet. I scrambled out of bed and into the shower.

I'd had a brilliant idea halfway through *Jane Eyre*. I knew how I was going to get Coglin to court to re-register. I'd have Grandma babysit his house. I got dressed in more RangeMan black and went to the kitchen to forage for breakfast. I called Ranger with a fast message while I finished my coffee.

'I'm heading out,' I said. 'I'm going to get Grandma and take her to Coglin's house. I've got the pen transmitter with me. See you later.'

Morelli was up next.

'What's new?' I said.

'Unfortunately, nothing. What's new with you?'

I told him about Dave and Joyce.

'So I'm back at RangeMan,' I said.

'I'm going to try to put a positive spin on this,' Morelli said. 'At least I know you're safe.'

'This morning I'm doing bounty hunter stuff,' I said. 'I'm going to get Grandma to help me.'

'So much for safe.'

Connie was last on the list. 'If I can get Coglin to the courthouse, can you get him rebonded right away?' I asked her. I can catch people, but I can't write bond. Only Connie and Vinnie can do that.

'As long as the judge will grant bond. Lula is here. She can answer the phones. How are you going to get Coglin to the courthouse? I thought he was beaver-bombing everyone.'

'It turns out he can't leave his house because he's waiting for the cable company.'

'Those fuckers,' Connie said.

'Yeah, well I'm going to have Grandma house-sit for him.'

I took the elevator to the garage and powered up the Cayenne. As I rolled out, I kept my eyes open. I was pretty sure Dave and his partner would surface at some point in the day. Without the help of a transmitter, they were going to have to make a pickup choice based on my history as they knew it. They knew I'd spent nights at RangeMan, but I was thinking between the broken nose, the stapled nuts, and the amputated pinkie finger, Dave wasn't moving so fast this morning. I probably had time to get Grandma and drop her off at Coglin's house before the bad guys were on the hunt.

I drove three blocks, adjusted my rearview mirror, and saw the black SUV two cars back. I called Ranger.

'Who's with me today?' I asked him.

'Hang on. I have to talk to control.' A couple

minutes later, he returned. 'It's Binkie. He's new. And he's riding solo. I'm short today. Don't give him a hard time. And if you go back to your apartment, don't get undressed in your foyer or living room. I've installed monitored security cameras.'

'Roger and out.'

Truth is, I didn't want to give Binkie a hard time. I was grateful to have someone watching my back. I circled my parents' block before parking. I didn't see anything out of the ordinary, so I pulled into the driveway behind my dad's Buick.

Grandma was watching morning television when I walked in. 'Look at you,' she said. 'You look like Ranger. And look at the shirt with RangeMan written on it. Ain't that a pip.'

'I have to take someone downtown to get rebonded, and he needs someone to house-sit. He's expecting the cable company.'

'Those fuckers,' Grandma said. 'Excuse the language. Just let me get my purse.'

I went to the kitchen to tell my mom.

'It'll be good for her to get out and do something,' my mother said. 'She's been feeling down because Elmer got shipped off to an assisted-living complex in Lakewood.'

Grandma was wearing her favorite lavender-and-white running suit. Her hair had faded to orange, and she had her big black patent leather purse in the crook of her arm. I wasn't going to ask what she had in the purse.

'I'm all ready,' she said, getting her coat out of the hall closet. 'Where are we going?'

'North Trenton. Hopefully this won't take long.'

Binkie stuck close to me all the way to Coglin's. When I parked in front of Coglin's house, Binkie parked half a block away. I got out and waved to him, and he waved back.

Grandma followed me up the sidewalk and waited while I rang the doorbell.

Coglin stuck his head out. 'I'm still waiting,' he said.

'I brought you a house-sitter,' I told him. 'This is my Grandma Mazur. She's going to stay here while you go with me to get bonded out again. She'll wait for the cable company.'

'I guess that would be okay,' Coglin said. He looked Grandma over. 'Are you up to the cable company?'

'Bring 'em on,' Grandma said.

'Don't let them leave without fixing my cable.'

Grandma patted her purse. 'Don't worry about it.' She stepped inside and looked around. 'What the heck's going on here?'

'Carl is a taxidermist,' I told Grandma.

'The best in the city,' Coglin said. 'I'm an artiste.'

'I never seen anything like this,' Grandma said. 'You should go on the shopping channel. I bet you could clean up.'

'I've thought of that,' Coglin said. 'I even wrote a letter to Suzanne Somers once. I think my performance pieces would be especially popular.'

'Everything's real lifelike. You expect them to just start walking around.'

'Sometimes when pets die, people bring them here to get restored, so they can take them home and put them on display,' Coglin said.

Grandma was standing wide-eyed in front of a dog with big glass eyes and a tooth missing. 'Isn't that something. That's a pip of an idea. I'm surprised they haven't thought to do that with people.' Grandma looked to me. 'I could have brought your grandfather home and set him in his favorite chair.' She slid her dentures around and gave it more thought. 'Would have been hard when I moved into your mother's house. It's already jammed full of furniture. I would have had to get rid of Harry.'

'Sometimes my pieces get sold on eBay,' Coglin said.

'I love eBay,' Grandma said. 'Harry probably wouldn't have fetched much, but the chair was worth something.'

I put a call in to Connie and told her I was leaving for the courthouse with Coglin in tow.

'Just be careful not to touch any of the performance pieces,' Coglin told Grandma.

'Don't worry about me. I won't break anything,' Grandma said.

'And don't shoot anyone,' I said to Grandma. 'Especially the cable people.'

'Those fuckers,' Grandma said.

'That wasn't so bad,' Coglin said when we turned onto his street. 'I didn't have to wait in jail or anything.' He was sitting forward, straining against his seatbelt. 'I don't see a cable truck.'

'It's still early,' I told him.

I parked in front of his house and Binkie parked behind me. Coglin got out and checked the cable stretching across his street for breaks. It looked intact, so we went to the house to spring Grandma.

Grandma had the door open before we reached the porch. 'Good thing I was here,' she said. 'The cable man showed up almost as soon as you left. He ran a

282

new cable under the road, and I stood out there and watched him to make sure he wasn't fibbing about the new cable. And then I wouldn't let him leave until he came in and tried the television. And it looks to me like everything's good now. And he's sending someone to remove the old cable that's running across the road. Probably won't happen for another six months, but it don't really matter.'

'Oh gosh,' Coglin said. 'I can't believe it. The nightmare is over. I can leave the house during the day. I can fill e-mail orders and pay my online accounts.' He swiped at a tear. 'I feel real stupid getting all emotional like this, but it's been terrible. Just terrible.'

'That's okay,' Grandma said. 'We all get like that over the cable company.'

'I can't thank you enough. This was so nice of you to stay here.'

'I've been having a good time looking at all the animals,' Grandma said. 'It's like being in a museum or something. My favorite is this big groundhog because he has three eyes. Imagine that, a groundhog with three eyes.'

Grandma reached out and touched an eye and *bang!* Grandma was head-to-toe groundhog. There was groundhog hair stuck everywhere.

'Son of a bee's wax,' Grandma said.

'That's okay,' Coglin said. 'I've got a bunch of groundhogs.'

I led Grandma down the sidewalk to the car and got her strapped in.

'He must have overstuffed it,' Grandma said.

'It happens all the time,' I said to Grandma. 'Don't worry about it. I'm going to take you home, and we'll get you cleaned up and you'll be good as new.'

I called my mother from the road to warn her.

'Grandma had a little accident,' I said to my mother, 'but she's fine. She's just got some groundhog stuck to her. I think if you scrub her down with Goo Gone, she'll be okay. And maybe you could call Dolly and see if she's got an opening at the hair salon for a wash and set . . . maybe a cut.'

There was a silent pause and I could imagine my mother making the sign of the cross and looking over at the liquor cabinet. I disconnected and turned into the Burg.

'I hear Elmer got shipped off to Lakewood,' I said to Grandma.

'Yeah, he was a dud anyway. I'm thinking about taking up bowling. Lucy Grabek joined one of them leagues, and she got a pink bowling ball with her name on it. I wouldn't mind having one of those.'

I parked in front of my parents' house and my mother came out to collect Grandma.

'Is this really groundhog?' my mother asked.

'The little brown hairs and patches of hide are groundhog. I don't know about the white stuff. I think it's some kind of synthetic foam.'

Binkie and I waved good-bye to Grandma and my mom, and then we drove to the bonds office.

Connie had reached the office ahead of me and was writing out my capture check. 'Good work,' she said. 'That was clever of you to have Grandma babysit. How'd she do?'

'She got woodchucked.'

'I bet it was the third eye that got her,' Lula said. 'You can't hardly resist the third eye.'

'How'd last night go?' I asked Lula. 'Did the movies work?'

'We never got to the movies. Turns out he don't need no mood enhancement. I'm telling you, I think I'm in love. I might even learn to cook for him.'

Connie and I did raised eyebrows.

'Okay,' Lula said. 'Learning to cook probably isn't gonna happen, but I could learn something.'

My phone buzzed and I picked up to Morelli.

'He's gone,' Morelli said.

'Who?'

'Dickie.'

'Where'd he go?'

'I don't know. I was working upstairs, and when I came down, he was gone. Television on. Back door unlocked.'

'Is anything missing?'

'Not that I can tell. My car is still here. His clothes are all here. No signs of struggle. No blood on the floor.'

'Maybe he went for a walk.'

'He's not supposed to go for a walk. He's not supposed to leave the house. That was the deal. I've been out driving around, and I don't see him.'

'Do you think someone took him?'

'I don't know.'

'Maybe he went to find Joyce for a nooner.'

'Joyce. That's a good idea. Is she still following you?'

I looked out the big plate-glass window in the front of the office. 'Yeah. She's sitting across the street. Do you want me to talk to her?'

'Yes, but you can't let her know anything about Dickie.'

'What was that about?' Lula wanted to know.

'Morelli thought Bob was missing, but he found him. I'll be right back. I want to say hello to Joyce.'

I crossed the street, the Mercedes's driver's side window slid down, and Joyce looked out at me.

'Hey,' I said. 'How's it going?'

'It's not. Why don't you get off your ass and do something. You think I have nothing better to do than follow you around?'

Smullen's girlfriend was in the seat next to Joyce.

'I never caught your name,' I said to her.

'Rita.'

'Going tag team?' I asked Joyce.

'If I keep her next to me, I don't have to worry about her sneaking up and stabbing me in the back.'

'Fuck you,' Rita said to Joyce.

'All right then,' I said. 'Guess I'll be moving along.'

Joyce glanced at the black SUV parked behind Ranger's Cayenne. 'Do you have a permit for a parade?'

'That's Binkie. He's practicing surveillance techniques.'

I went back to the office and dialed Morelli. 'Nothing there,' I said.

'I can't believe this happened. I lost my witness. I'll probably get busted back to uniform patrol.'

'He was a witness, not a prisoner. It's not like you could chain him to the toilet.'

'I don't suppose you'd want to come over and cheer me up,' Morelli said.

'You lost a witness and that's the first activity that comes to mind?'

'That's *always* the first activity that comes to mind.'

'Sorry, but here's the second bad news of the day. It's that time.'

'So?'

'Yeesh.'

'Okay, let's table my love life for a couple hours. I need to find either Dickie or Petiak,' Morelli said.

'Petiak is easy. We just set me out on the curb and wait for him to kidnap me.'

'I'm not excited about that plan.'

'Just for giggles, let's suppose Dickie didn't get snatched. Let's suppose he went after the money.'

'What money?' Morelli asked.

'The forty million dollars.'

'I don't know anything about forty million dollars.'

'The forty million Dickie withdrew from the firm's Smith Barney account. The forty million everyone wants, including Joyce and Rita, Smullen's girlfriend. Didn't Dickie tell you about the forty million?'

'That little prick better hope I don't find him because I'm going to kill him.'

'You're going to have to take a ticket on that one.'

'How do you know about this?'

'Joyce left her front door open one day and I happened to wander in and sit down at her kitchen desk and the drawer sort of opened and I found a bunch of numbers—'

'Stop. I don't want to know,' Morelli said.

'I just got a capture check. Suppose I treat to lunch.'

'That would be great, but I'm afraid to leave the house in case our boy returns.'

'You're in luck. I deliver.'

I left the bonds office and was about to plug the key into the Porsche's ignition when Ranger called.

'I'm looking at a monitor, and I'm not believing what I'm seeing,' Ranger said. 'Dickie Orr just broke into your apartment. Isn't he supposed to be holding hands with Morelli?'

'Morelli just called and said Dickie disappeared.'

'Looks like we found him. Tank's on his way. Stay away from the area until I give you an all clear.'

Yeah, right. Douche bag Dickie just broke into my apartment, and I'm going to stay clear. Not. I put the car in gear and wheeled around into the Burg.

First thing, I had to lose Joyce. I cut through the alley behind Angie Kroeger's house, hung a fast right, ripped through the parking lot for the Colonial Bar and Grill, and came out on Broad. I drove Broad for two blocks, hit Hamilton, and zipped past the bonds office. Joyce was nowhere in sight. Neither was Binkie. I was pretty sure Binkie had his Bluetooth working, calling the control room to see where the devil I was. The control room would be tuned to the GPS transmitter in the Cayenne and my purse, but I'd be in my lot by the time Binkie caught up with me.

I came up on my building and saw the black RangeMan SUV parked close to the back door. Tank was inside, doing his thing, so I hung back by the Dumpster, sitting at idle, trying to keep as low a profile as possible. Not easy in a Porsche Cayenne.

After a few minutes, the door to the building opened and Tank and Dickie emerged. A shot was fired and Tank went down. A black BMW whipped out of a parking space and slid to a stop in front of Dickie. Two men in the car. Dave was one. And his partner was driving. Dave jumped out of the car, grabbed Dickie, and shoved him into the backseat. Dave had two black eyes, a Band-Aid across his nose, and a huge bandage on his pinkie finger. He turned and drew his gun on Tank and fired.

I mashed my foot down hard on the gas and put my hand to the horn. Dave looked up in surprise but didn't move fast enough. Possibly the result of having had his nuts stapled. I bounced him off my left fender and took the side door off the BMW. I stopped and put the Cayenne into reverse. I wasn't entirely rational at that point, but I'm pretty sure my intent was to run over Dave a second time and finish the job. Fortunately for Dave, he was able to drag his ass into the Beemer before I got to him. The Beemer took off, laying rubber on the asphalt, squealing out of the lot as it passed Binkie on the way in.

Binkie and I ran to Tank. He was hit in the chest and leg. He was conscious and swearing and bleeding a lot, so we didn't wait for help. We loaded Tank into the back of the Explorer and took off for Saint Francis Hospital. I was driving and Binkie was in back, applying pressure, trying to slow the bleeding. I called 911 so emergency would be waiting for us. Then I called RangeMan and Morelli.

We off-loaded Tank at emergency, and he was whisked away. We were still in the drop zone when Ranger arrived in his turbo, followed by a RangeMan

SUV. Morelli was behind the SUV with his Kojak roof light flashing.

We all got out and stood in a clump, five guys and me. If adrenaline was electricity, we were turning out enough to light up Manhattan.

'How bad is it?' Ranger asked.

'He should be okay,' Binkie said. 'He was hit in the thigh and right side of the chest. Didn't sound like he had a lung problem. Maybe cracked a rib.'

'Dave shot him once from a distance and then again at pretty close range,' I told Ranger. 'Fortunately, his aim wasn't great with the big bandage wrapped around his pinkie finger.'

Ranger went inside to complete the paperwork. When he was done, he joined Morelli and me in the ER waiting room. Binkie waited outside.

'I don't think Dickie was with Dave,' I said. 'Dickie seemed surprised to see Dave. I think Dave and his partner were waiting for me, and they hit the jackpot.'

We all looked over when the waiting-room door slid open and Lula burst in and stormed across the floor, arms waving, hair standing on end.

'What the heck happened here?' Lula shouted.

'Tank was investigating a break-in and he got shot,' I told her.

Lula turned on Ranger. She was in his face, hands on hips, eyes looking like a raging bull's. 'Did you send that man out all by hisself? What the Sam Hill were you thinking? You got him shot. And I'm here telling you, he better be okay with all his parts in working order, or you're gonna answer to me. I don't fucking believe this.' She looked around, searching the room for someone who looked official. 'What's happening here? I want to see the doctor. I want to get some answers. He better not be fucking dead is all I'm saying. I'm holding all you accountable.'

Ranger was showing nothing. He was in his zone, listening and thinking. Only his eyes moved and focused on Lula. She finished her tirade and Ranger redirected his attention to Morelli and me.

'Hey!' Lula yelled, back in Ranger's face. 'You look at me when I'm having a breakdown. And don't you pull that mysterio silent shit on me. I don't take that bus, you see what I'm saying? You're just a little pipsqueak compared to that man you got shot. And nobody even called me. I had to hear it on the police band. What's with that? Holy shit. Holy fuck. Goddamn.'

And then it was like she was a big balloon and someone let all the air out. Lula sat down hard on the floor, eyes unfocused.

Jean Newman was the nurse working the desk. She came over and eyeballed Lula. 'Looks to me like she hyperventilated,' Jean said, getting Lula on her feet. 'I'll take her in the back and put a pressure cuff on her and give her some juice.'

We sat there for a moment, absorbing the silence that filled the void left by Lula.

Ranger's mouth wasn't smiling much, but his eyes were flat-out laughing. 'It's been a long time since I was called a pipsqueak,' he said.

Morelli grinned. 'That wasn't even the best part. She called you on the mysterio silent shit. You're hanging out there naked.'

'Not the first time,' Ranger said.

'Where do we go from here?' I asked.

'Maybe not far,' Morelli said. 'You told me the guy who grabbed Dickie had a broken nose and heavily bandaged finger. He might have come here to get patched. And if he did, he would leave a paper trail. Medical insurance, address, whatever. Plus, you just bounced him off your fender. If he was hurt, he'd have to go somewhere for an X-ray. If not here, Helen Fuld.'

'You are so smart,' I said to Morelli. 'I guess that's why they pay you the big bucks.'

Morelli stood. 'You two stay here and worry about Tank, and I'll go do my cop thing.'

He didn't have to badge Jean. She was from the neighborhood. She knew Morelli and his entire family. She knew he was a cop. And even if Morelli hadn't been a cop, she probably would have answered his questions because the Burg doesn't have a sense of secret. The Burg is gossip central. And more important, women seldom said no to Morelli . . . for anything.

'Do you have any idea why Dickie went to your apartment?' Ranger asked me.

'No. It's not like we're friends.'

'He was looking for something.'

'Money? A gun?'

'If I was Dickie, I'd be looking for the forty million,' Ranger said.

'I can guarantee you, I haven't got it in my apartment.'

'Still, someone broke into your apartment right after Dickie went missing. And now Dickie walked out of his safe house and went straight to your apartment. It feels like there should be a connection. Maybe Dickie was the first intruder, and maybe he wasn't looking for something. Maybe he was hiding something. And maybe he came back to get it.'

'Why would he hide something in *my* apartment?'

'You'd just had a confrontation. You would be on his mind. And you weren't someone anyone would think he'd go to with his treasure. You would feel safe.'

'If he hid something, wouldn't he know exactly where it was? Wouldn't he have gone directly to that spot when he broke into my apartment?'

'Maybe it was originally in plain sight, and it got moved. I don't know. I'm just thinking out loud. I'm sure there are other possibilities.'

Morelli returned with his notepad in hand. 'His full name is Dave Mueller. He didn't use insurance. Paid in cash. He came in on Jean's shift for his pinkie, and she copied his address from his driver's license. According to his license, he's living in the same apartment complex where Smullen and Gorvich kept apartments.'

'I'll check it out,' Ranger said.

Morelli tore a page out of his notepad and handed it to Ranger. 'This is the address. Jean called around. None of the clinics have a record for Mueller, so I'm guessing either Stephanie killed him, or else he has no broken bones or internal bleeding.'

'I almost never kill people,' I said to no one in

particular. We sat for another half hour in our own thoughts, until an aide came to find us.

'Pierre is out of surgery and awake,' she said. 'You can see him now.'

I looked at Ranger. 'Pierre?'

'If you want to live, you'll forget you heard that,' Ranger said. 'Tank isn't overly fond of being named Pierre.'

Lula was already in the room when we got there.

'How's it going?' I asked her.

'I'm better now,' she said. 'I just had a moment, but I had a glass of juice and a pill, and now I'm back to my old self.'

'I thought that *was* your old self,' I said to Lula.

'Hunh,' Lula said.

Tank had his eyes open, but there wasn't much going on behind them, and he looked like he was down a quart of blood.

'I talked to the doctor, and he said Tank's in good shape,' Lula said. 'He's just still dopey from the anesthetic. He might even be able to go home tomorrow.'

'Yo,' Tank said.

'Yo,' we all answered.

'I'm gonna stay with him awhile,' Lula said. 'Make

sure he don't rip no tubes out chasing nurses down the hall.'

Ranger and Tank did one of those male bonding hand things, and Ranger and Morelli and I filed out of the room and into the hall.

'I'm going back to my apartment,' I said. 'Maybe I can find whatever it was Dickie was looking for.'

'If you'll take over my Stephanie watch, I can visit Dave,' Ranger said to Morelli.

'Done,' Morelli said.

I felt my blood pressure raise just a tic. 'Excuse me. Time out. Nice to know you're concerned about my welfare, but I'm not excited about getting passed around like luggage.'

Morelli and Ranger looked at each other.

'The ball's in your court,' Ranger said to Morelli.

'I have nothing,' Morelli said.

'Terrific,' I told him. 'You have exactly one minute to come up with something. And while you're at it, you can explain this buddy-buddy routine. What happened to the rivalry, the animosity? You used to think Ranger was a nut. What about that?'

They stood hands on hips, counting down.

'It's her time of the month,' Morelli finally said.

'Dude,' Ranger said.

I huffed out of the hospital to the parking garage and realized I had no car. The Porsche was still in my lot.

Morelli was behind me, smiling. 'Need a ride?'

# Fifteen

I plugged the key into my front door lock, and Morelli drew his gun.

'The apartment is monitored,' I told Morelli. 'RangeMan would call if someone entered.'

'Humor me,' Morelli said. 'Ranger handed you over to me, remember? It'd be embarrassing if you got kidnapped on my watch.'

'Admit it. This is weird.'

'Beyond weird, but if Ranger and I draw a line in the sand that can't be crossed right now, everyone will lose.'

Forty minutes later, there was nothing left to be searched. We'd covered every square inch and found nothing.

'Let's run through this one more time,' Morelli said. 'Dickie's got forty million dollars stashed somewhere, and everyone but the Easter Bunny is looking for it.

Dickie leaves the safe house and comes straight here and starts searching. He thinks something is here, but it looks like he doesn't know where. The conclusion we've reached is that he hid something out in the open, and it got moved.'

'Except I don't remember moving anything. And nothing seems to be missing.'

We went to the kitchen and hauled out cold cuts and bread and made sandwiches.

Morelli looked over at the small security camera in my foyer. 'Sharing you with Ranger doesn't even rate high on my "hate this" list compared to being beamed into his control room while I make a sandwich.'

'Did you report Dickie's kidnapping?'

'Yes. There's a bulletin out on him.'

My kitchen phone rang and I answered it on speaker.

'Stephanie?' the voice said. 'I'm surprised you returned home.'

'Who is this?'

'I've been wanting to speak to you, but you've been very uncooperative.'

'Well, here I am. What did you want to speak to me about?'

'You have something I need. You have the key.'

'I have a bunch of keys. Which one are you interested in?'

'I'm not amused. You know which key.'

'The key to the forty million dollars?'

'Yes. Now listen closely. If you give me the key, I'll allow you to live. If you choose to be difficult, I'll make sure you have a horrific death. You've already seen some of my work. The next victim will be your ex-husband. He's served his purpose. And as you know, I like to keep things tidy.'

'How am I supposed to get the key to you?'

'I think it would be nice if you brought it in person.'

'Not going to happen,' I told him.

'Do you think I'm scary?'

'Yes.'

'You have no idea. You haven't even seen my best work.'

'Back to the key . . .'

'I'll think of something. Do you like surprises?'

And he hung up.

Morelli didn't look happy. 'You're getting too good at this,' he said. 'You've been scared and threatened so many times, you're starting to think it's normal. You were so cool with that guy. And he was insane.

Genuine psychopath. And you played him.'

'Isn't that what I was supposed to do?'

'Yes, but that isn't what I want the woman I love to do. You should have freaked. You should be shaking and crying. Look at you. You're smiling.'

'I did a good job.'

Morelli pulled me into him and wrapped his arms around me. 'You did a great job. I'm proud of you, but I wish your life was different. I don't want you involved in this garbage.'

'He thinks I have a key.'

'We looked everywhere, and we didn't see a key.'

'A key might be easy to miss.'

'I didn't miss a key. It's not here,' Morelli said.

'Then what the heck's he talking about?'

'The more disturbing question is why would he think you have a key?'

'Dickie.'

'That's my best guess,' Morelli said. 'Dickie told him you have the key.'

Morelli's hand had managed to get under my shirt and was starting to head north.

'We're on television,' I said to him.

'Shit,' Morelli said, removing his hand, stepping back from me. 'I forgot.'

My cell phone buzzed, and I tuned in to Grandma Mazur.

'I'm at the beauty parlor, and I'm all done,' she said. 'I was hoping you could give me a ride. Your mother's car is still on the blink.'

'Sure,' I said. 'I need to go to the office anyway.'

Ten minutes later, I picked Grandma up at the salon. 'I didn't expect to see Joseph,' Grandma said, getting into Morelli's SUV.

'I can't get rid of him,' I told her.

Grandma looked pretty good, considering she'd just been groundhogged. As far as I could see, she didn't have any gunk clinging to her. And her hair was newly washed and curled and had faded to apricot.

'I even got my nails done,' Grandma said. 'I got them to match my hair, and I got a new lipstick too. Dolly said I couldn't wear red with my hair this color, so I got a lipstick named Orgasm. It's gotta be good with a name like that.'

Morelli almost ran up on the curb at the thought of Grandma wearing a lipstick named Orgasm.

'Are you still looking for Diggery?' Grandma wanted to know.

'Yes.'

'They buried Stanley Berg today, and I heard at the

beauty parlor that he went in the ground wearing a diamond pinkie ring and a new Brooks Brothers suit that would fit Simon Diggery. And the weather is nice and mild. We're supposed to get some rain later, but I don't think a little rain would stop Diggery if he needed a new suit.'

We dropped Grandma off, then went to Morelli's house to get Bob. Morelli parked in the alley behind his house, took the key out of the ignition, and dropped it into his pocket.

'Wait here,' Morelli said. 'I'll be right out.'

I gave him a raised eyebrow. 'You took the key?'

'You wouldn't be here when I came out if I left the key.'

'I still might not be here.'

'Yeah, but at least I'd have my car.'

Morelli jogged to his back door, disappeared inside the house for a few seconds, and reappeared with Bob. Bob bounded out of the house, tethered to his leash, doing his happy dance. He tinkled on a small patch of dead grass, then rushed to the back of the SUV, anxious to go for a ride. Morelli loaded Bob into the car and got behind the wheel.

'Now what?' he asked.

'I was going to stop in at the office.'

'Okay,' he said, putting the SUV in gear. 'To the office.'

'This is ridiculous. Are you going to stick with me all day?'

'Like stink on a monkey, Cupcake.'

Connie was putting together files when I walked in.

'I have some new guys for you,' she said. 'Nothing big. Possession, domestic violence, and grand theft auto. All FTA.' She put the paperwork in a folder and handed it to me. 'How's Tank? I understand he was shot.'

'He's going to be okay. I saw him when he came out of surgery.'

'Lula flew out of here when she heard.'

'We met her at the hospital. She decided to stay with Tank for a while. Make sure he behaves himself.'

The front door banged open and Lula swung in. 'They wouldn't let me stay. They said I was a disruptive influence. Do you believe that? Hell, I wasn't disrupting nothing.'

'Imagine, someone thinking you're disruptive,' Connie said.

'Yeah, they got a bunch of stick-up-their-ass nurses in that place,' Lula said. 'It was okay, anyways, because they gave Tank some happy juice in his IV and he fell asleep.' She looked through the front window. 'What's Morelli doing out there?'

'Waiting for me,' I said.

'Why?'

'I don't want to talk about it.'

'He's babysitting you, isn't he?' Lula said. 'It's got something to do with Tank getting shot, right?'

'Do you want the long version or the short version?' I asked them.

'I want the long version,' Connie said. 'I want all the details.'

'Yeah,' Lula said. 'I don't want to miss nothing. I gotta feeling this is gonna be good.'

It took a little over ten minutes for me to get through the long version, mostly because Lula went on a rant that Morelli didn't tell me about Dickie.

'What do you mean he didn't tell you?' Lula said. 'After all you do for him?'

'Yeah,' Connie said. She looked over at Lula. 'What do you mean?'

'I'm talking about the nasty,' Lula said.

We all thought about that for a moment.

'Okay, maybe that's not a good example,' Lula said. 'Everybody wants to do the nasty with Morelli.'

'There must be other things you do,' Connie said.

Connie and Lula waited to hear what I did for Morelli.

'Sometimes I babysit Bob,' I said.

'See that,' Lula said. 'She babysits Bob. Right there he should have told her. He didn't tell me, and I'd slap him a good one.'

'You'd slap Morelli?' Connie said. 'Joe Morelli?'

'Okay, maybe not Morelli,' Lula said. 'But most men.'

'Seems to me he was just doing his job,' Connie said.

'Yeah, and it don't look like Stephanie does a whole lot for him,' Lula said. 'Maybe you should do more for Morelli,' she said to me.

'Like what?'

'Well, we wouldn't expect you to cook or clean or anything, but you could pick his undies up off the floor and fold them. I bet he'd like that.'

'I'll keep that in mind,' I told Lula.

'Boy, you get into a lot of trouble,' Lula said to me. 'Trouble finds you. Good thing you got Morelli riding shotgun for you, even if it is sort of humiliating and demeaning.'

'Yeah,' I said. 'Good thing.'

I took the FTA folder from Connie, left the office, and got into Morelli's SUV.

'What's new?' he asked.

'I have some new FTAs. And Lula said I should pick your undies up off the floor and fold them. She said you'd like that.'

'I'd hate that. I leave them on the floor so I can find them if I have to leave in a hurry.'

Grandma Mazur called on my cell phone.

'You'll never guess,' she said. 'That nice Mr Coglin just called to thank me again. And we got to talking, and one thing led to another, and he's coming for dinner.'

'Get out.'

'Good thing I got my hair and my nails done. I guess he's a little young for me, but I'm pretty sure I can handle it. I thought you and Joseph might want to come to dinner too.'

I'd sooner poke myself in the eye with a sharp stick.

'Gee,' I said. 'I think we have plans.'

'That's a shame. Your mother made lasagna. And she's got chocolate cake for dessert. And I was sort of hoping you could come in case your father don't like taxidermists. It's always good to have a police officer at the table in case things get cranky.'

I looked at my watch. Almost five o'clock. Dinner would be at six. Morelli and I would have an hour to take Bob to the park for a walk.

# Sixteen

Grandma was waiting at the door when we got to the house.

'Mr Coglin isn't here yet,' she said.

Morelli let Bob off the leash, and Bob ran into the kitchen to say hello to my mother. I heard my mother shriek and then all was quiet.

'He must have eaten something,' Grandma said. 'I hope it wasn't the cake.'

The house smelled good, like Italian spices in marinara sauce and garlic bread in the oven. The dining room was set for six. Two bottles of red wine on the table, a bowl of grated Parmigiano-Reggiano. My father was asleep in front of the television, and I could hear my mother working in the kitchen, talking to Bob.

'Be a good boy, and I'll give you a little lasagna,' she said to Bob.

311

I followed Grandma into the kitchen and looked around for Bob damage. 'What did he eat?' I asked my mother.

'It was almost the cake, but I caught him in time.'

I went to the stove and stirred the extra sauce cooking in the pan. I loved being in my mother's kitchen. It is always warm and steamy and filled with activity. In my mind, I have a kitchen like this. The cabinets are filled with dishes that actually get used. The pots sit out on the stove, waiting for the day's sauces and soups and stews. The cookbook on the counter is dog-eared and splattered with grease and gravy and icing smudges.

This is a fantasy kitchen, of course. My actual kitchen has dishes, but I eat standing over the sink, paper towel in hand. I have a single pot that is only used to boil water for tea when I have a cold. And I don't own a cookbook.

Sometimes, I wanted to marry Morelli so I'd have a kitchen like my mom's. Then, other times, I worried that I couldn't pull it off, and I'd have a husband and three kids, and we'd all be eating take-out standing over the sink. I guess there are worse things in the world than take-out, but in my mother's kitchen, take-out feels a little like failure.

The doorbell chimed and Grandma took off like a shot.

'I've got it!' she yelled. 'I've got the door.'

My mother had the hot lasagna resting on the counter. The bread was still in the oven. It was three minutes to six. If the food wasn't on the table in eight minutes, my mother would consider everything to be ruined. My mother operates on a tight schedule. There is a small window of opportunity for perfection in my mother's kitchen.

We all went into the living room to greet Carl Coglin.

'This here's Carl Coglin,' Grandma announced. 'He's a taxidermist, and he got the best of the cable company.'

'Those fuckers,' my father said.

'I brought you a present for being so nice and watching my house,' Coglin said to Grandma. And he handed her a big box.

Grandma opened the box and hauled out a stuffed cat. It was standing on four stiff legs, and its tail looked like a bottlebrush. Like maybe the cat had been electrocuted while standing in the rain.

'Ain't that a pip!' Grandma said. 'I always wanted a cat.'

My mother turned white and clapped a hand over her mouth.

'Holy crap,' my father said. 'Is that son of a bitch dead?'

'His name is Blackie,' Coglin said.

'He won't explode, will he?' Grandma asked.

'No,' Coglin said. 'He's a pet.'

'Isn't this something,' Grandma said. 'This is about the best present I ever got.'

Bob came in, took one look at Blackie, and ran off to hide under the dining-room table.

'Goodness,' my mother said, 'look at the time. Let's eat. Everyone take a seat. Here, let me pour the wine.' My mother poured herself a tumbler and chugged it down. It took a couple beats to hit her stomach, and then the color started to come back into her face.

Grandma dragged an extra chair to the table so Blackie could eat with us. Blackie had close-set eyes, one higher in his head than the other, giving him a pissed-off, slightly deranged expression. He peered over the edge of the table, one eye focused on Morelli and one eye on his water glass.

Morelli burst out laughing, I gave him an elbow, and he bowed his head and sunk his teeth into his lower lip to gain some self-control. His face turned red, and he started to sweat with the effort.

Bob growled low in his throat and pressed himself against my leg.

'I'm not eating with a dead cat at the table,' my father said.

Grandma put her hands over Blackie's ears. 'You'll hurt his feelings,' she said to my father.

'Just shoot me,' my father said. 'Morelli, give me your gun.'

My mother was on her third glass of wine. 'Honestly, Frank,' she said. 'You're such a drama queen.'

Morelli's phone buzzed, and he excused himself to take the call.

I grabbed his shirt when he stood. 'If you don't come back, I'll find you, and it won't be pretty.'

Minutes later, he returned, leaning close to me. 'That was Ranger. He has Dickie, and he's drugged but okay. He was being held in Dave's apartment. I don't know any more details. Ranger's taking Dickie to RangeMan. I said we'd be over when we were done here.'

'Carl said he would teach me taxidermy,' Grandma said. 'I was gonna take up bowling, but now I'm thinking taxidermy might be the way to go. Carl said I could do my taxidermy right here in the kitchen.'

My mother's fork fell out of her hand and clattered onto her plate.

✤

Dickie was in a holding cell at RangeMan. He was stretched out on a cot with an ice bag on his face. We were looking at him through a one-way window in the door.

'I didn't know you had holding cells,' I said to Ranger.

'We like to think of them as private rooms,' Ranger said.

'Why's he got the ice bag?'

'To keep the swelling down on his broken nose. It's not a bad break. We put a Band-Aid on it and gave him some Advil. Apparently they had to encourage him to talk.'

'Anything else wrong with him?'

'Yeah, lots of things,' Ranger said, 'but not from the time spent with Dave. They gave him something to keep him quiet. We won't get much information out of him until it works its way through his system. We can keep him here until he comes around, but we can't keep him against his will beyond that.'

'You might as well unload him on me now,' Morelli said. 'I'm going to get stuck with him eventually anyway.'

'I'll have him brought to your house. We'll bring him in through the back.'

'What about Dave?' I asked Ranger.

'Never saw Dave. Dickie was alone in the apartment. They had him chained up in the bathroom. We set an alarm off when we went in, so it's likely Dave won't return. I left a man in the area just in case. I did a fast search of the apartment, but didn't find anything that would tell us where Petiak is hiding. We didn't wait for the police.'

Ranger walked us down to the parking garage.

'What do you want to do about Stephanie?' Ranger asked Morelli. 'She can't go back to her apartment. Do you want to leave her here, or do you want her with you?'

'I don't see her living in the same house as Dickie,' Morelli said to Ranger. 'Can you be trusted with her?'

'No,' Ranger said. 'Not for a second.'

'Good grief,' I said. 'I won't stay with either of you. I'll stay with Lula or my parents. I need to go after Diggery tonight anyway.'

'So tell me again what's going on,' Lula said.

We were in her Firebird in front of RangeMan, and Binkie was at idle behind us.

'We're going after Diggery,' I said. 'Stanley Berg was buried this morning in a nice new suit and a diamond pinkie ring.'

'I'll drive you to the cemetery, but I'm not walking around with you. I'm staying in my car. There's a full moon out tonight. That cemetery is probably full of werewolves and all kinds of shit.'

I looked out the windshield. 'I don't see a moon.'

'It's behind the clouds. Just 'cause you can't see it don't mean it isn't there. The werewolves know it's there.'

'Okay, fine. Wait in the car. Leave the window cracked so you can call the police if you hear me screaming.'

'Sounds like a plan to me,' Lula said. 'I swear, you're a crazy person. You go around up to your eyeballs in snakes and dead people and exploding beavers. It's just not normal. Even when I was a 'ho, my life wasn't that freaky. Only thing normal about you is your hot boyfriend, and you don't know what the heck to do with him. To make matters worse, you got that spook Ranger sniffing after you. Not that anyone wouldn't want him sniffing after them. I mean, he is finer than fine. But he's not normal.'

'Sometimes he seems normal.'

'Girl, you aren't paying attention. He is way better than normal.'

Lula pulled up to the gate leading in to the

cemetery and stopped. 'I can't go no further,' Lula said. 'This sucker's closed to traffic at night.'

'I'll go the rest of the way on foot,' I told her.

'You got a flashlight?'

'I can't use a flashlight. I can't take a chance on Diggery seeing me.'

'This is nuts,' Lula said. 'I can't let you go out there by yourself. You don't even got a gun.'

'Binkie will go with me.'

'Binkie don't look like the sharpest tack on the cork-board. I can't turn you over to Binkie. Honest to goodness, we should all be at home watching television, working our way through a bag of chips, but no, we're out in a bone-yard. The way things are going, we probably find Diggery, and he got his snake with him.'

I got out of the Firebird and walked back to Binkie.

'I'm after an FTA who sidelines as a grave robber,' I said to Binkie. 'I have reason to believe he'll be here tonight.'

Binkie looked at the pitch-black cemetery. 'Oh jeez.'

I understood Binkie's reluctance to traipse through the cemetery. At first glance, it was kind of creepy, but I'd chased Diggery through this cemetery before at night and lived to tell about it. What I've discovered with my job is that there's a difference between being brave and being stupid. In my mind, bungee jumping is stupid. Stalking an FTA in a cemetery at night doesn't seem to me to be all that stupid, but the creep factor is moderate to high, so it requires some bravery. And I've found I can sometimes force myself to be brave. Usually, the bravery is accompanied by nausea, but hell, it's not a perfect world, right?

'You can wait here,' I said to Binkie.

Binkie opened his door and stepped out. 'No way. Ranger'll kill me if anything happens to you. I'm not supposed to let you out of my sight.'

Lula came over and checked Binkie out. He was in RangeMan SWAT black with a loaded utility belt, and he stood a full foot taller than Lula.

'You got silver bullets in that Glock you're carrying?' Lula asked.

'No, ma'am.'

'Too bad, on account of this place is probably full of werewolves tonight, and you need silver bullets to get rid of those bad boys. And we should probably have garlic and crosses and shit. You got any of those?'

'No, ma'am.'

'Hunh,' Lula said.

I set out, walking down the private road that led into

the cemetery. It was an old cemetery that sprawled over maybe fifty acres of low, rolling hills. It was laced with paths leading to family plots that held generations of hardworking people laid to rest. Some of the headstones were elaborately carved and worn by time and weather, and some were flat pieces of recently polished granite.

'Where are we going?' Lula wanted to know. 'I can't hardly see anything.'

'The Bergs are just ahead on the left. They're halfway up the hill.'

'How far on the left? It all looks the same.'

'They're behind the Kellners. Myra Kellner has an angel carved at the top of her marker.'

'I don't know how you remember these things,' Lula said. 'Half the time, you get lost in Quakerbridge parking lot, but you know where the Kellners and Bergs live in this graveyard.'

'When I was little, I used to come here with my mother and grandmother. My relatives are buried here.'

I used to love the cemetery excursions. The family plot, like my mother's kitchen, is tended by women.

'This is your Great-Aunt Ethel,' Grandma Mazur would say to my sister, Valerie, and me. 'Ethel was ninety-eight years old when she died. She was a pip. She loved a good cigar after dinner. And Ethel played the accordion. She could play "Lady of Spain" by heart. Her sister Baby Jane is buried next to her. Baby Jane died young. She was only seventy-six when she died. She choked on a kielbasa. She didn't have no teeth. Used to gum all her food, but I guess you can't gum kielbasa so good. They didn't know the Heimlich in those days. And here's your Uncle Andy. He was the smart one. He could have gone to college, but there was no money for it. He died a bachelor. His brother Christian is next to him. Nobody really knows how Christian died. He just woke up dead one day. Probably, it was his heart.'

Valerie and I had every square inch of our plot committed to memory, but it was part of the experience to have Grandma point out Great-Aunt Ethel. Just as it was part of the experience to go exploring in the tombstone forest while my mother and grandmother planted the flowers. Val and I visited the Hansens and the Krizinskis and the Andersons on the top of the hill. We knew them almost as well as Great-Aunt Ethel and Baby Jane. We planted lilies for Easter and geraniums for the Fourth of July. In the fall, we'd visit just to clean things up and make sure all was right with the family.

I stopped going to the cemetery when I was in junior high. Now I only go for a funeral or to chase down Simon Diggery. My mother and grandmother still go to plant the lilies and geraniums. And now that my sister has moved back to the Burg with her three girls, I'm sure they'll help plant the lilies this year and listen to Grandma talk about Ethel.

'Here's an angel,' Lula said, stepping off the path, heading uphill. 'Excuse me,' she said, walking on graves. 'Sorry. Excuse me.'

Binkie was silent behind me. I turned and looked at him, and he had his hand on his gun. I wasn't sure what he thought he might have to shoot.

'Simon Diggery isn't usually armed with anything other than a shovel,' I told Binkie. 'Lula and I have done this before. We'll get to the grave site and find a place to hide. Then we'll let Simon dig himself into a hole. It makes the apprehension easier.'

'Yes, ma'am,' Binkie said.

'I hate being ma'am,' I told him. 'Call me Stephanie.'

'Yes, ma'am, Stephanie.'

'I'm at the top of the hill, and I don't see no fresh-dug grave,' Lula said.

'Are you sure you turned at Kellner?'

'I turned at the angel. I don't know about Kellner.'

I squinted into the darkness. Nothing looked familiar.

'Is that rain I feel?' Lula asked. 'It wasn't supposed to rain, was it?'

'Chance of showers,' I told her.

'That's it,' she said. 'I'm going home. I'm not being out here in the rain. I'm wearing suede.' Lula looked around. 'Which way's home?'

I didn't know. It was pitch black, and I was all turned around.

'We can't go wrong if we go downhill,' Lula said, taking off. 'Oops, excuse me. So sorry. Excuse me.'

It was raining harder and the ground was getting slick underfoot.

'Slow down,' I said to Lula. 'You can't see where you're going.'

'I got X-ray vision. I'm like a cat. Don't worry about me. I just gotta get this coat out of the rain. I can see there's a tent ahead.'

A tent? And then I saw it. The grounds crew had erected a tarp over a hole dug for a morning burial.

'I'm just waiting under this tent until the rain lets up,' Lula said, rushing forward.

'No!'

Too late.

'Whoops,' Lula said, disappearing from view, landing with a loud *whump*.

'Help!' she yelled. 'The mummy got me.'

I looked down at her. 'Are you okay?'

'I think I broke my ass.'

She was about six feet down in a coffin-sized hole. The sides were steep and the surrounding dirt was fast turning into mud.

'We have to get her out of here,' I said to Binkie.

'Yes, ma'am. How?'

'Do you have anything in the car? Rope?'

Binkie looked around. 'Where's the car?'

I had no idea.

I flipped my cell phone open and called Ranger.

'We're in the cemetery and we're lost,' I said to him. 'It's raining and it's dark and I'm cramping. I've got the transmitter thingy in my pocket. Can you get a bead on us?' There were a couple beats of silence. 'Are you laughing?' I asked him. 'You'd better not be laughing.'

'I'll be right there,' Ranger said.

'Bring a ladder.'

We were a ragtag group, standing in the rain at the cemetery gates. Ranger and two of his men fading into the night in their black rain gear, Lula head-to-toe mud, and Binkie and me soaked to the skin.

'I feel funky,' Lula said. 'I got graveyard mud on me.' She had her car keys in her hand. 'Do you need a ride somewhere?' she asked me.

'I'm good,' I said to her.

Lula got into her car and drove off. Binkie left and Ranger's men got into their SUV and left.

'Just you and me,' Ranger said. 'What's the plan?'

'I want to go to Morelli's house. I want to be there when Dickie starts talking.'

Thirty minutes later, Ranger walked me to Morelli's back door and handed me over.

'Good luck,' Ranger said to Morelli. 'You might want to hide your gun.'

And Ranger left.

Morelli brought me into the kitchen. 'Diggery?' he asked.

'Never saw him. We got lost in the cemetery and had to get Ranger to track us down. I need a shower.'

I slogged upstairs to the bathroom, locked myself in, and stripped. I stood in the shower until I was all warmed up and squeaky clean. I ran a comb through my hair, wrapped a towel around myself, and shuffled into Morelli's bedroom.

Morelli was in the middle of the room looking like he wanted to do something but wasn't sure where to begin. Bed linens and clothes were in a crumpled mess on the floor, and there were empty beer bottles, plates, and silverware on all surfaces.

'This isn't good,' I said to him.

'You have no idea what this has been like. I hate this guy. I hide in my room. I'd like to hit him, but it isn't allowed. He eats all my food. He controls the television. And he's always talking, talking, talking. He's everywhere. If I don't lock my door, he just walks in.'

'Is he still drugged?'

'Yeah. I'd like to keep him that way.'

'Do I have any clothes here?'

'Some underwear. I think it's mixed in with mine.'

I found the underwear and borrowed a T-shirt. I located some clean sheets and made the bed.

'This is nice,' Morelli said. 'I knew the room needed something, but I couldn't figure out what. It was sheets.'

'Stick a fork in me,' I said, crawling into bed.

# Seventeen

I woke up to someone banging on the bedroom door and Morelli in bed next to me with the pillow over his face. I took the pillow off Morelli. 'What's going on?'

'If I go out there, I'll kill him,' Morelli said.

I crawled out of bed, toed through the clothes on the floor, and located a pair of sweatpants that looked fairly clean. I stepped into the sweats and rolled them at the waist. I was still in Morelli's T-shirt. Didn't bother to brush my hair. I opened the door and looked out at Dickie. He had two black eyes and a Band-Aid on his nose.

'Yeah?' I said.

'Jesus,' he said. 'What are you doing here? The nightmare never ends.'

Good thing for him I didn't have a staple gun.

'How did I get here? Last thing I remember I was

kidnapped,' Dickie said.

'Go downstairs and look for breakfast. We'll be right down.'

I turned and bumped into Morelli, who was standing behind me, naked. What is it with men that they can walk around like that? I could barely get naked to take a shower.

'No clothes?' I asked him.

'You're wearing my last almost-clean sweats.'

'Underwear?'

'None. I need to do laundry. Dickie's been wearing my clothes.'

'I'm not going downstairs with you naked.'

Morelli kicked through the clothes and came up with a pair of jeans. I watched him put the jeans on commando, and my nipples got hard.

'I could have these pants off in record time,' Morelli said, eyes on my T-shirt.

'No way. Dickie might hear.'

'We could be quiet.'

'I couldn't concentrate. I'd be imagining Dickie with his ear to the door.'

'You have to concentrate?' Morelli asked.

'Hey!' Dickie yelled from the foot of the stairs. 'There's no milk.'

I followed Morelli down the stairs to the kitchen, where Dickie was eating cereal out of the box.

'There's no milk,' Dickie said. 'And there's no more orange juice.'

'There was orange juice last night,' Morelli said.

'Yeah, but I drank it.'

Morelli fed Bob and got the coffee going. I looked for something to eat that might not be contaminated with Dickie cooties. I didn't mind sharing a cereal box with Morelli, but I wasn't going to eat from something Dickie had just stuck his hand in. God knows where that hand was last.

'Tell me about the key,' I said to Dickie.

'What key?'

I glanced at Morelli. 'I'm going to hit him.'

'I'll close my eyes,' Morelli said. 'Tell me when it's over.'

'You can't do that,' Dickie said. 'You're supposed to protect me. Especially from her. You do one little thing wrong with her and the Italian temper comes out. And God forbid you come home late for dinner.'

'Four hours!' I said. 'You'd come home four hours late for dinner, and you'd have grass stains on your knees and your shirt caught in your zipper.'

'I don't remember that part,' Dickie said. 'Did I used to do that?'

'Yes.'

Dickie started laughing. 'I wasn't making a lot of money back then. I couldn't afford a hotel room.'

'It's not funny!' I said.

'Sure it is. Grass stains and rug burns are always funny.' He looked over at Morelli. 'She didn't like to do doggy.'

Morelli slid a look at me and smiled. There wasn't much I didn't like to do with Morelli. Okay, a few things, but they involved animals and other women and body parts that weren't designed for fun.

'What?' Dickie said. 'What's that smile? Oh man, are you telling me she does doggy with you?'

'Leave it alone,' Morelli said.

'Is it good? Does she bark? Do you make her bark like a dog?'

'You need to stop,' Morelli said. 'If you don't stop, I'm going to *make* you stop.'

'Arf, arf, arf !' Dickie said.

Morelli gave his head a small shake, like he didn't fucking believe he had Dickie in his kitchen. And then he grabbed Dickie by his T-shirt and threw him halfway across the room. Dickie hit the wall spread-eagle like Wile E. Coyote in a Road Runner cartoon, and the cereal flew out of the box. Bob came running from the living room and snarfed up the cereal.

'What's that about?' Dickie asked, struggling to get to his feet.

'Trying to get your attention.'

I handed Morelli a cup of coffee. 'Ask him about the key.'

'I'm telling you I don't know anything about a key,' Dickie said.

'Let me refresh your memory,' I said to him. 'You left the safety of this house and went straight to my apartment, where you were caught on camera breaking in and searching for something. Later that day, I got a call from a guy who wanted the key.'

'So?'

'So I know there's forty million dollars out there. I know everyone wants it. And I know someone thinks I have the key. And unless I can figure this out, I'm going to get barbecued like Smullen and Gorvich.'

'Let's start from the beginning and build up to the key,' Morelli said. 'How did you meet Smullen and Gorvich and Petiak?'

'I met Petiak at a financial-planning conference. We got to be friends, and he introduced me to Smullen and Gorvich. I'd just been passed over for partnership, and I could see the handwriting on the wall. Office politics weren't in my favor. So I was looking at options. Petiak had money and clients but no ability to litigate if the need should arise. He suggested we go into business together, and I agreed. I knew his client list was questionable, but I thought I could live with it.'

'Smullen and Gorvich?'

'We needed more money to buy the building, and Petiak knew Smullen and Gorvich from a previous life, and he knew they were looking for a place to practice. It was all a con, of course. They were always the unholy triad. At some level, I suspected this, but I had no idea how unholy they actually were. I was desperate to be a partner somewhere and get my own business established, so I didn't look at anything too closely.'

Dickie shook the cereal box and turned it upside down. Empty. The cereal was all on the floor. 'I'm hungry,' he said. 'This was the last of the cereal. And I want coffee.'

'Help yourself to the coffee,' Morelli said.

'I need cream. I can't drink black coffee.'

Morelli looked like he was going to throw him against the wall again.

'I'll go to the store,' I said.

Not so much as a favor to Dickie. More because I needed cream for my coffee too.

'I want to go with you,' Dickie said. 'I'm tired of being cooped up in this house.'

'I can't take a chance on having you recognized,' Morelli said. 'If Petiak or one of his idiots spots you in my car, we'll blow our cover.'

'I can wear a hat,' Dickie said.

'Put him in a hooded sweatshirt,' I told Morelli. 'He can put the hood up and slouch down. I need food.'

Morelli got a hooded sweatshirt off the living-room floor and tossed it to Dickie. 'I'm going with you,' Morelli said. 'Give me a minute to find clothes.'

My socks had dried, but my shoes were still wet. I grabbed a jacket from Morelli's hall closet and put a ball cap on my head.

We all skulked out to the SUV parked in the back of the house. Dickie rode shotgun, and I got in behind him. Morelli walked Bob down the alley until Bob did everything he had to do, and then Morelli ran Bob back and put him in the cargo area.

Morelli went south to Liberty Street and pulled into a strip mall that was anchored by a 7-Eleven. I took everyone's order, Morelli gave me a wad of cash, and I went shopping. I was on my way out with a bag of food when I spotted Diggery at the other end of the mall, doing taxes out of the back of a beat-up Pontiac Bonneville. He had the trunk lid up, and he had a little folding table and two stools set out. There were seven people in line. I handed the bag over to Morelli and walked down to Diggery.

'Oh jeez,' he said when he saw me.

'You're up early,' I said to him, checking out his fingernails for signs of fresh dirt.

'This here's convenience taxes,' Diggery said. 'You can pull your pickup in and get your fresh coffee and then come get your taxes done and go off to work.'

'I was next,' a woman said to me. 'You gotta get to the rear of the line.'

'Chill,' I told her. 'I'm wanted for murder, and I'm not in a good mood.'

'Here's the thing,' Diggery said to me. 'I know it's not a big deal to go get bonded out again, but it's gonna cost me more money, and I don't have it. I had to buy winter coats for the kids and rats for the snake. If you let me finish my tax business, I'll come with you. I'll have money from the taxes. Tell you what, you cut me some slack here, and I'll do your taxes. No charge.'

'How much longer do you need?'

'Two weeks.'

'I really could use some help with my taxes.'

'Just put your pertinent information in a shoe box and bring it all to me. I'll be able to fit you in next Monday. I'll be at Cluck-in-a-Bucket on Hamilton Avenue between ten and twelve at night.'

'What was that about?' Morelli asked when I got back to the SUV.

'Simon Diggery doing taxes. He said he needed the money to buy rats for the snake, so I let him go.'

'That's my girl,' Morelli said. He flipped a bagel back to Bob and took us home.

I'd gotten bagels, doughnuts, cream cheese, milk, orange juice, bread, and a jar of peanut butter. Dickie chose a bagel and loaded it up with cream cheese. Morelli and I ate doughnuts.

'Talk while you eat,' Morelli said to Dickie. 'You went into business with Smullen, Gorvich, and Petiak. Then what?'

'It was all looking good. We bought the building, and then we were doing well, so we made some other real estate investments. Petiak and Gorvich both had home offices and I only saw them at the off-site Monday meetings. Fine by me. I always thought Petiak was a little creepy. He has this quiet way of talking, choosing his words as if English is his second language. And there's something about his eyes. Like light goes in but doesn't come out. And Smullen had ties to South America, so I saw him sporadically. It was a little like having my own firm. I had my own clients and my own staff. There were four names on the stationery, but I was usually the only partner in the building.'

Morelli refilled his coffee and topped off my coffee and Dickie's. 'What went wrong?'

'It was Ziggy Zabar, the accountant. He figured out what was really going on, and he wanted to get paid off.'

'And what was really going on?' Morelli asked.

'It's actually very clever,' Dickie said. 'They were using the law firm to launder money. Petiak was a military guy until he got booted out for something . . . probably insanity. Anyway, he was a supply officer. Worked in a depot and had access to all the munitions. And he saw a way to tap into these depots all across the country and move munitions out of the depots into his private warehouse.'

'The warehouse on Stark Street?'

'Yes. Next comes Peter Smullen. Smullen is married to a woman from a cartel family. Smullen has contacts all over South America. These contacts have dope but need guns, so Smullen takes the dope, and Petiak delivers the guns. The last piece to the puzzle is Gorvich. Gorvich is the drug dealer. He gets the stuff from Smullen and packages it up and distributes it. Now comes the good part. The money Gorvich takes in for drug sales is recorded as payment for legal services. It gets deposited in the firm's account and is sanitized.'

Morelli took another doughnut. 'So Petiak smuggles guns off government property, stores them in your warehouse, and then ships them off to South America. The cartel pays for the guns with drugs. The drugs gets shipped to Trenton, probably to the warehouse, where they're packaged and sold to local dealers. And the dealers pay for the dope in billable hours.'

'Yep,' Dickie said. 'Genius, right?'

'Not exactly. Zabar figured it out.'

'Well, it was good in theory,' Dickie said. 'It would make a good movie.'

'Where do you fit in all this?'

'I was the token real lawyer in the firm. I was supposed to give them some legitimacy. The only reason I know anything is because Smullen made a phone call from his office and I happened to be in the hall. He was on speakerphone talking to Petiak, and they were making plans to pull all the money out of the firm and disappear. Petiak said there was no rush. He said Zabar was taken care of and wasn't going to make any more problems. This was Tuesday morning, after the Monday partners' meeting that Zabar was supposed to attend. Smullen said if Zabar could figure it out, there were others in the accounting firm that could do the same thing. Petiak agreed but said they had to give Gorvich two weeks to transact business.'

Bob came in and sat at Morelli's feet.

'You ate your bagel in the car,' Morelli said to Bob. 'You'll get fat if you eat another bagel.'

Bob heaved himself to his feet and padded back to the living room.

'Was this when you cleaned out the Smith Barney account?' Morelli asked.

'Not right away. I didn't know what to make of it. My worst fear had always been that one of Gorvich's drug dealers would walk in and shoot up the office. I knew our client list was scary. A conspiracy never occurred to me.'

'You must have known they were all from Sheepshead.'

'Everyone has a circle of professionals they tap into when the need arises.'

'They bought their degrees on the Internet,' I said to Dickie.

'At the time, I didn't care. I didn't have the resources to make a success on my own, so I was willing to do some denial to get a partnership.'

'Why didn't you go to the police when they killed Ziggy Zabar?'

'I didn't know they killed Zabar. Petiak said he took care of him. That could have meant anything. Later in the week, the police came asking if Zabar had attended the meeting, but even then I still thought he was just missing. Petiak could have paid him off, and Zabar could have gone to Rio. Anyway, have you seen Petiak? He's not a guy you could walk up to and ask if he killed your accountant.' Dickie pushed back in his chair. 'You need a television in here. How can you have a kitchen without a television?'

'I manage,' Morelli said. 'So what I'm supposed to believe is that you heard a phone conversation suggesting your partners were going to take your money and run and you didn't do anything?'

'I didn't confront them, if that's what you mean. These are guys who have professional hit men on their client list. I represent Norman Wolecky. I backed out of the hall without making a sound, and when the building emptied out for the night, I went through all the financial records, and I found out how much money we had at Smith Barney. I knew from the phone conversation that something illegal had gone down, but I couldn't figure out what it was. I thought it was probably something like tax evasion. If it was tax evasion, I knew I was fucked. I signed the returns just like everybody else. What was pissing me off was that they were going to take the money and leave me behind to take the fall. I was sitting on this information, waiting for someone to come to me, and no one did. So Friday afternoon, I went to Joyce's house so no one would hear me, and I cleaned out the Smith Barney account. It was easy. All four of us have our own password to access the account. My plan was to wait for the Monday meeting. If they didn't say anything to me at the Monday meeting, I was going to leave the country and enjoy my forty million. Screw Smullen, Gorvich, and Petiak. My mistake was that I didn't leave soon enough. Smullen found out about the withdrawal and sent the goon patrol to my house Monday night.'

'You still could have fled,' I said to him. 'Why did you hang around?'

'To begin with, I didn't have a passport. It was in my

house, and my house was filled with cops. And then when I went back to my house, my passport was missing. I know there are ways to get a fake passport, but I'm not James Bond. I don't know how to go about getting a fake passport, and the thought of using one scares the crap out of me. I get nervous when I have to take my shoes off at the airport. I'm innocent and I feel guilty. What am I going to do when I'm actually guilty?

'So I put myself in a cheap motel in Bordentown until I could come up with a plan. I'm not talking to anyone. Not even Joyce. Okay, maybe phone sex, but that was it. And then I'm watching television, and the local news comes on, and they're talking about how Zabar, the accountant, washed up on the banks of the Delaware. Now I know Petiak killed Zabar. This is serious shit. This isn't just income tax evasion, this is also murder.

'Time to get out of Dodge, I tell myself. If I can't go to an island and lose myself, I can at least go to Scottsdale. Unfortunately, it turns out I can't get to the money. Now I'm really in a bind. I have no more cash in my pocket, and I'm afraid to use a credit card and have it traced. I get to thinking about the warehouse and the apartment building the firm owns, and I wonder if I can hang out there for just a couple days until I can locate the money. I go to the apartment building, and it's in use. Full. No empty apartments. Then I go to the warehouse, and I see Gorvich in the parking lot talking to Eddie Aurelio. Two of Aurelio's soldiers are standing watch at parade rest by Aurelio's Lincoln. It's like a scene out of *The Godfather*. I don't know a whole lot about the Trenton drug scene, but I know Aurelio is big-time mob.

'I drove past the warehouse and got on Route One and kept going until Princeton. I stopped at a Starbucks and tried to get my heart rate down over a latté. Decaf. I didn't know what the hell was going on, but I was running out of options until I could get the money. So I called the police and told them about Gorvich and Aurelio and Gorvich's client list, and about Smullen and Petiak taking care of Zabar the accountant. I told them I'd testify to all this, but they had to put me someplace safe. And I told them I only trusted Morelli. So here I am.'

'Why Morelli?'

'Because you have the key,' Morelli said to me. 'He needed to be close to the key. He knew we were seeing each other, and he thought he might catch some stray information. He's been sitting here waiting for another

344

opportunity to retrieve the key. What he didn't realize was that Petiak was staking out your apartment for entirely different reasons.'

'Petiak is doing cleanup,' Dickie said. 'He's getting rid of anyone who looks like a threat. At least, that's the way he tells it. After spending some very scary time with him, my feeling is he's gone gonzo. I think Stephanie popped up on his radar screen and he just wanted to enjoy the experience of taking his flamethrower to her.'

'And you gave him more reason, didn't you?' Morelli said.

'He hit me! First that RangeMan gorilla attacked me in the apartment, and then I got kidnapped on the way out of the building. It was traumatic. I was handcuffed, and they rammed me down onto the floor of the car so I couldn't see anything. And then when they dragged me out, I still didn't know where we were. I only knew I was in a two-car garage. No windows. No other cars. There was just the light from the garage-door opener.

'Petiak was there with his spooky eyes. He didn't say anything to me. I still had my hands locked behind my back, and he hit me in the face. Just like that . . . *bam!* "What the fuck was that?" I said to him. "That was to let you know I'm serious," he said. Then he asked me where the forty million was and I said I didn't know. So he hit me again, except that time it wasn't in the face, and I decided to tell him whatever he wanted to know.'

'You told him Stephanie had the key.'

'I told you. He *hit* me!'

I saw Morelli's eyes turn black, and I felt the air pressure change in the room. I stepped between Morelli and Dickie and put a hand to Morelli's chest.

'You don't want to kill him,' I said to Morelli.

'Get out of my way.'

'This is complicated enough. And we might need him for something. And you'd have to go before a review board if you kill him.'

'I don't get it,' Dickie said to Morelli. 'What's the big deal here? He already wanted to kill her. It's not like he could kill her twice. Man, you two are a pair. You have anger-management issues. I hope you're not planning on reproducing. Hate to see a kid with her hair anyway.'

I turned to Dickie. 'What's wrong with my hair?'

'It's always a mess. You should get Joyce to help you with it. She has great hair. If you'd been more like Joyce, things might have worked out differently.'

After that, things happened pretty fast, and when

Morelli pulled me off Dickie, his nose was bleeding again. Someone had knocked Dickie off his chair and gone after him like Wild Woman. I guess that was me. Morelli had me at the waist with my feet two inches off the floor.

'I don't know why I always feel like I have to take care of you,' Morelli said to me. 'You do such a good job of it all by yourself.'

There was blood splattered across the floor, soaking into Dickie's shirt.

'Crap,' I said. 'Am I responsible for all that blood?'

'No, he cracked his nose on the table when he panicked and tried to get away from you. If I put you down, do you promise not to go after him again?'

'Forever?'

'No. Just in the next ten minutes.'

'Sure.'

Morelli got some ice out of the freezer, wrapped it in a towel, and handed it to Dickie. 'Do you suppose you could try being a little less obnoxious?' he asked him.

'What'd I do? I'm sitting here minding my own business, trying to be cooperative. Talk to Bitchzilla over there.'

I looked at my watch. 'Nine minutes,' I said to Morelli.

347

'I've got blood all over my shirt,' Dickie said.

Morelli mopped the blood up off the floor with some wadded paper towels. 'First of all, it's *my* shirt. And second, it's still the cleanest shirt we've got until we do laundry.'

'Well, for cripes sakes, do the laundry,' Dickie said.

'I don't have a washer or dryer, and I can't leave you in the house alone.'

'I can take the laundry to my mom's house,' I said. 'Gather it up for me.'

'I want to know the rest of the story first,' Morelli said.

Dickie had his head tipped back with the ice pack over his nose. 'I'm not talking anymore. I have a headache.'

Morelli went to the powder room and got a bottle of Advil. 'From what I've heard so far, you didn't know a whole lot about the drugs-for-arms business. How did you find out about all that?'

'Petiak told me after he hit me. He's on a big nutso ego trip. Had to tell me all the details of his master plan. Even demonstrated his flamethrower. Almost burned the fucking garage down. I gotta admit, the flamethrower is pretty cool. He says he sells a lot of them to the South American drug lords. Apparently scares the bejeezus out of the locals. And I have to tell

348

you, I almost messed myself at the thought of getting it turned on me.'

'Why didn't he turn it on you?'

'I imagine he wanted to make sure I was telling the truth about the key. I got stun-gunned, and I guess injected with something, and next thing I knew, I was back here.'

'And the key?' Morelli asked.

'It's actually a key card. It allows the cardholder to access a high-security account in Holland from a satellite location here in the States. I have the account numbers memorized and a second set in a safety deposit box, but they aren't any good without the card. Without the card, I have to go to Holland to appear in person and pass a retinal and fingerprint scan. Not an option without a passport.'

'Stephanie seems like an odd choice for the key keeper.'

'I didn't choose her. She took the key with her when she left my office. The key's in the clock. I wasn't too worried about it because I knew she'd take care of the clock. I figured in some ways it was probably safer than if I'd left it at the office.'

'What clock?' Morelli asked.

'Her Aunt Tootsie gave us a desk clock as a wedding

present. I was using it in my office, and Sticky Fingers took it on her way out. I went to her apartment twice to look for it and couldn't find it. It's not here either, so I'm assuming it's at her parents' house.'

I'd entirely forgotten about the clock. I was mentally scrambling, tracing backward. When did I last see the clock? It was in my bag. Then I stopped at the food store. Put the bags in the back of the car. Put the clock with the bags. Took the bags into the house. Could I have left the clock in the car? I couldn't remember bringing the clock into my apartment.

'You're looking pale,' Morelli said. 'Like all the blood just drained out of your face. You're not going to faint, are you?'

'I think I left the clock in the car.'

'What car?'

'The Crown Vic.'

'Where is it now?' Morelli asked.

'I don't know. It broke down on Route 206 and Ranger had one of his men take care of it.'

Dickie took the ice pack off his face. 'You lost Aunt Tootsie's clock?'

'It's not your money anyway,' Morelli said to Dickie. 'It's drug money. It belongs to the government. It'll be confiscated.'

I called Ranger and asked him about the Crown Vic. He called back three minutes later.

'Binkie had it towed to the salvage yard,' Ranger said.

'Which one?'

'Rosolli's off Stark.'

'How's Tank?'

'Tank's good. He was discharged this morning. Anything I need to know?'

'Yes, but it's too complicated to tell you on the phone. I'll be around later. Did you feed Rex breakfast and give him fresh water?'

'That's part of Ella's job description.'

I flipped my phone closed. 'It's at Rosolli's.'

Dickie's eyes got wide. 'The junkyard? My God, they'll compress it to the size of a lunchbox.'

'I'll call it in,' Morelli said. 'They'll send someone out to locate the car.'

'What about me?' Dickie said. 'Do I stay here?'

'Your status hasn't changed,' Morelli said. 'Until I hear otherwise, you're in protective custody.'

'Get me your laundry basket,' I said to Morelli. 'I need clean clothes. I think I'm starting to mold.'

# Eighteen

Grandma Mazur had Blackie under her arm when she opened the door.

'What are you doing with Blackie?' I asked her.

'I've been trying to find just the right place to set him out. I want him to look natural.'

At the risk of being unkind, Blackie would need to be in Frankenstein's lab to look natural.

'I have Morelli's laundry. I thought I'd throw it in the washer, and then I have to get back to Morelli,' I told Grandma.

'Blackie and me will take care of it for you. We haven't got anything better to do.'

I left the laundry with Grandma and ran back to Morelli's SUV. I thought maybe Lula was right and I didn't do much for Morelli. It wouldn't kill me to pitch in and clean his house today. It was only a matter of time before my life would be back to normal, although I was beginning to think weird might be normal for me. The police would get the car and the clock and the money. They'd find Petiak and lock him up. And I wasn't sure what would happen to Dickie.

Morelli's house was less than a quarter of a mile from my parents' house. I drove two blocks and was T-boned by a Hummer coming out of an alley that ran behind a row of houses. The impact rammed me into a parked car and left me breathless. Before I had a chance to collect myself, my door was wrenched open, and I was yanked from behind the wheel. It was Dave with a broken nose, bandaged finger, and brace on his knee.

'Haw,' Dave said, jamming the barrel of a gun into my ribs. 'We figured you'd come to see your mom. We've been waiting for you.'

I recognized the garage from Dickie's description. No windows. Room for two cars. Large charred area where Petiak had demonstrated the flamethrower.

'We finally meet,' Petiak said. 'I hope you brought the key.'

'Here's the thing about the key. I don't have it.'

'Wrong answer. That's not at all what I wanted to hear. That answer's making me angry.'

'Yes, but I know where it is.'

'Why can nothing ever be simple?' Petiak asked, sounding a lot like my mother.

'As Dickie probably told you, I didn't realize I had the key. He hid the key in a clock. I took the clock. I didn't know there was a key in it. I left the clock in the trunk of a car. And the car was towed to a salvage yard.'

'Dickie didn't tell me any of this.'

'What did he tell you?'

'He told me you had the key.'

'Yes. I *had* the key. But technically I don't have the key anymore.'

'Well, at least I can have the pleasure of killing you,' Petiak said.

'You're not listening to me. I know where the key is. We just have to go get it. But here's the thing . . .'

'I knew there would be another thing,' Petiak said.

'You have to promise not to kill me. And I want a reward. A finder's fee.'

'And if I don't agree?'

'I won't help you find the key. I mean, what's the incentive to finding the key if you're going to kill me no matter what?'

'How much of a reward do you want?'

'Ten thousand dollars.'

'Five.'

'Okay, five.'

I didn't for a minute think Petiak wouldn't kill me. I was trying to make him feel more comfortable, maybe not keep me on such a short leash. I had the transmitter pen in my pocket. Ranger would wonder why I was at the salvage yard. He'd call Morelli. Morelli or Ranger would discover the car. If I stalled a little, there was a good chance I might not die a hideous flamethrower death. Plus, Morelli had called the Vic into the station. If I was lucky, the police would also show up. And if I kept thinking like this, I might not pass out and throw up from terror. Just focus, I kept saying to myself. Don't panic. Too late. Inside there was panic. A lot of it.

'Where is this salvage yard?' Petiak wanted to know.

'It's at the far end of Stark Street. Rosolli's Salvage.'

We all piled into a black Beemer. Probably not the same one that was in my parking lot because this one had four doors. Dave's partner and Petiak were in front and I was in back with Dave. The flamethrower was in the trunk.

Dave didn't look happy to be sitting next to me.

'So how's it going?' I said to him.

'Shut up,' Dave said.

'What's with the knee brace?'

'You fucking ran over me with your fucking car.'

'Nothing personal,' I said to him.

'Yeah,' Dave said, 'and it's not gonna be personal when we barbecue you.'

The salvage yard was surrounded by nine-foot-high steel-mesh fencing. The entrance was gated and locked. I was guessing this was necessary because so many people wanted to steal cars that were squashed until they were only two feet high and had no working parts.

The Beemer pulled up to the gate and stopped.

'How do we get in?' Petiak asked.

'I don't know,' I said to him. 'I've never tried to get into a salvage yard before.'

'Rudy,' Petiak said to Dave's partner, 'take a look.'

Dave's partner was named Rudy. Grade school must have been hell with a name like that.

Rudy got out and looked through the gate to the other side. 'Hey!' he yelled. He turned back to us and shrugged. 'Don't see anyone.'

'It's pretty big,' I said. 'Maybe there's another entrance.'

Rudy got back behind the wheel and drove down

Stark. He followed a side road that curved around the salvage yard and did a complete loop. We didn't see any other entrances.

'This is perplexing,' Petiak said.

'Maybe you don't need the key,' I said. I knew he needed the key. He'd gotten the codes off Dickie and now he needed the key to electronically transfer the $40 million. If he went to Holland to make a personal pickup, he couldn't pass the retinal and hand scan.

'Are you sure the key is in there?' he asked.

'Yep. This is where they took the car.'

'Can you climb the fence?' Petiak asked Rudy.

'Yeah, but there's three feet of razor wire at the top. I'll get torn to shreds. I'll never get over the razor wire.'

'Go back and try the gate. Maybe it's open. Maybe there's a call box.'

Rudy went back and rattled the gate and looked around. He returned to the car. 'I don't see anything. It's locked up tight with a padlock. I could get in if I had bolt cutters.'

'Home Depot,' I said.

Petiak cut his eyes to me. 'You know where there's a Home Depot?'

Thirty-five minutes later, we were in the Home Depot parking lot, and I was imagining an elaborate rescue scenario, Ranger had tracked us down at Home Depot, and he was organizing an army to storm the salvage yard once we returned to break in with our newly purchased bolt cutters. Petiak and Dave and I were in the car, waiting for Rudy. No one was saying anything.

Finally, Rudy appeared, striding back to the car. No bolt cutters.

'Now what?' Petiak said.

'They didn't have any bolt cutters,' Rudy told him, angling himself behind the wheel.

'I know where there's a Lowe's,' I said.

Twenty minutes later, we were at Lowe's. I was loving this. More setup time for Ranger and Morelli. Probably the entire police department and the National Guard were at the salvage yard by now.

Rudy ran into Lowe's and fifteen minutes later came out. No bolt cutters.

'I'm losing patience,' Petiak said. 'Go back to the salvage yard.'

We were now forty minutes away from the salvage yard, and I was thinking it would be good if we could resolve this hostage thing soon because before long I was going to need a bathroom. I'd had a lot of coffee with the doughnuts.

I concentrated on sending Rudy mental messages. *Drive faster. Drive faster.* Unfortunately, Rudy was having none of it. Rudy wasn't taking a chance on getting stopped by a cop. Rudy was obeying all the rules. After what seemed like hours, we eased up to the salvage yard gate. Still locked. Still no one in sight.

'Ram it,' Petiak said.

'Excuse me?' Rudy said.

'Ram the fucker,' Petiak said. 'Back up and floor it and ram the gate open.'

'It's pretty sturdy,' Rudy said.

Dave was stoic beside me, but I could smell him sweating. Dave was nervous.

'Maybe we should all get out and let Rudy ram the gate by himself,' I said. 'Then we can walk in if it works.'

'We're in this together,' Petiak said. 'Rudy, ram the gate.'

Rudy backed up and idled for a moment. We all sucked in air and held our breath. And Rudy floored it and rammed the gate.

*Bang!* The gate flew off its hinges, and the front-seat air bags exploded. Dave hadn't been buckled in and was thrown forward, hitting the front seat with a good solid thud. Rudy and Petiak were fighting the air bags. I unbuckled my seat belt, opened my door, and took off.

I ran into the salvage yard, where I imagined the Marines were waiting. I didn't see any Marines, so I ran as far and as fast as I could. I passed the crusher machine and took the stairs to a grid of catwalks that led to what looked like a boxcar on stilts. I forced the door and went inside and locked the door behind me. I was in the control room for the crusher machine. I looked out, and I could see Petiak and Dave and Rudy walking my way. Petiak was holding the flamethrower and Rudy and Dave had guns drawn.

My heart was beating so hard, it was knocking against my ribcage. No one was here. There weren't even distant sirens. Somehow, the system didn't work. The pen wasn't sending a signal. Someone was asleep at the switch at RangeMan. Whatever. I was on my own. I frantically looked for a phone, but I was in the throes of blind fear, and I wasn't seeing much of anything. I was trapped in a box. No way to escape. It was only a matter of time.

They were on the stairs – Petiak first, then Rudy, and Dave bringing up the rear. I was pushing buttons and flipping switches, looking for something that would make noise, call the fire department, jettison me out of harm's way.

I was so scared, my nose was running and my eyes were brimming with tears. It was the flamethrower. I'd seen its work. I could still recall the smell of burned flesh. I could see the horrible charred cadavers.

Petiak was on a catwalk, maybe thirty feet off the ground and level with my boxcar control room. I hit a red button and the hydraulics began moving the crusher walls below me. Rudy and Dave were on the stairs approaching the catwalk, and they stopped dead in their tracks, but Petiak was relentless in his mission. I could see him coming. He reached the control room door and tried the knob. The lock held. He stepped back and gave it a blast from the flamethrower. Nothing. It was a steel fire door. For that matter, the entire control room was steel. I was looking at Petiak through a small window in the door, and I could see the rage in his face. He leveled the flamethrower at me and pumped it. Flames shot toward me, flattened on the steel door, and curled back. Black smoke clouded the window. The door wasn't sealed tight and heat and smoke crept into the room.

I stepped back and looked out the large window

facing the crusher. Dave and Rudy were off the stairs and on the ground, running to the salvage yard entrance. I couldn't see Petiak. He wasn't on the stairs. I went back to the door. Smoke was no longer seeping in. There was no more heat. I squinted through the sooty pane of glass. I didn't see Petiak. I went back to the window over the crusher and saw him.

He'd inadvertently set himself on fire, and in his confusion and horror he'd fallen off the catwalk into the crusher. I hit the red button and the crusher stopped. Not that it mattered. Petiak was clearly dead. And I suspected the crusher would have stopped before it compacted him. It was designed for cars and not maniacs.

I took a moment to get myself under control and then I looked for a phone again. I found the phone and called Morelli.

'I'm in the salvage yard,' I told him.

'I thought you were doing laundry,' he said.

'Just c-c-come get me, okay?'

'Where's the car?'

'Forget the car. Find some other way to get here.'

Then I called Ranger.

'Where the heck are you?' I asked him.

'I'm at RangeMan. What are you doing at your mother's?'

'I'm not at my mother's. I'm at the salvage yard.'

I glanced down. I was wearing Morelli's sweats. The pen was in my jeans pocket, and the jeans were getting washed. Good thing I was so dumb. If I'd thought I'd been kidnapped without the pen, I would have died of fright an hour ago.

'Babe,' Ranger said.

'You'll want to see this,' I told him.

I called Connie.

'I'm at your cousin Manny's salvage yard,' I told her. 'Where is everybody? The gate was locked and no one's here.'

'Manny's mother-in-law died. They had the funeral today. I didn't go. I only knew her in passing.'

'The short version is that Roland Petiak set himself on fire and fell into your cousin's squashing machine. I thought your cousin would want to know. And also, I'm looking for my Crown Vic. It's somewhere in the salvage yard.'

There was a stool in the control room where the operator sat when he was working the compactor. I sat on the stool and looked out the window, eager for someone to come rescue me. I didn't want to leave the safety of the little room until Morelli or Ranger was at my door. I avoided looking down into the squashing machine. I didn't want to see Roland Petiak.

I sat there for ten minutes and everyone arrived at once. Morelli and Dickie, Ranger, Connie and Lula and Connie's cousin Manny. And Joyce and Smullen's girlfriend. I couldn't remember her name.

I called Morelli's cell.

'I'm in the control room by the squasher machine,' I said. 'I'm not coming out until someone comes up here to get me.'

Everyone looked up at me, and I waved down to them and wiped my nose on my sleeve.

Morelli took the stairs two at a time and crossed the grate to get to me. I opened the door and almost collapsed. My teeth were chattering, and my legs were rubber.

'I was afraid I'd fall off the catwalk if I didn't have someone to hang on to,' I told Morelli.

Morelli wrapped an arm around me and peered into the compactor at what was left of Petiak. 'That's not good.'

'It's Petiak.'

'Are you okay?'

'So far as I can tell.' And I went down on one knee. 'Whoops,' I said. 'Guess I'm a little wobbly.'

Ranger was on the catwalk too, and between Ranger

and Morelli, they were able to get me down the stairs.

'What the heck's going on here?' Lula wanted to know when I set my feet on the ground. 'Nobody tells me anything.'

'Yeah,' Joyce said. 'What the heck's going on?'

Dickie was still in the hooded sweatshirt, standing to one side, ogling Joyce and Smullen's girlfriend. 'Hey Sex Monkey,' Dickie said to Joyce.

'Do you have it?' Joyce said.

'What?'

'You know . . . *it*.'

'Do you mean the forty million? Nope. Government's going to confiscate it.'

'You are such a turd,' Joyce said. 'I can't believe I wasted my time with you. How could you have lost that money?'

'It was all Stephanie's fault,' Dickie said.

'Asshole,' Joyce said. And she turned on her heel and stormed off with Smullen's girlfriend, matching her stride for stride.

Morelli called the dispatcher and reported the death and gave a description of Dave and Rudy.

'I forgot to take the pen,' I told Ranger.

'Sometimes it's better to be lucky than good,' Ranger said.

366

'You were right about the drugs and guns and money laundering,' I told Ranger. 'The law firm was stealing guns, trading them for drugs, and then selling the drugs. Then they billed the drug dealers for legal services and washed the money through a legitimate business ... Dickie's law firm. Dickie found out, cleaned out the firm's bank account and transferred the money to his own account. The key to Dickie's account was in the clock.'

'Aunt Tootsie's clock?' Lula asked. 'What are the chances?'

'I forgot about the clock and left it in the Crown Vic's trunk. The Vic broke down, and it got towed here.'

'When was this?' Connie's cousin Manny asked.

'Last week. It was an old cop car with "Pig" written on the side and it had a couple bullet holes in it and rodent fur on the inside,' I told him.

'I know just where that is,' Manny said. 'I remember it coming in. A couple SWAT guys, right?'

'Right.'

Ranger's cell phone buzzed, and he took a short call. 'I'm heading out,' he said to Morelli. 'She's on your watch. Next week she's mine.'

I was pretty sure he was kidding, but then, maybe not.

'Come on,' Manny said. 'I'll take you to the Vic.'

There were mountains of wheel covers and acres of scrap metal stacked together like lasagna in the salvage yard. We wound our way through a maze of cars in various stages of mutilation and finally Manny stopped at a seven-foot-tall block of multicolored metal and pointed about a third of the way up.

'See that burgundy layer? That's the Vic.'

It was twelve inches thick. 'Your Aunt Tootsie's not gonna be happy about this,' Lula said.

We retraced our steps, and watched the emergency vehicles pour into the salvage yard. EMS trucks, fire trucks, cop cars. A couple uniforms secured the area around the compactor with tape and the medical examiner and a crime scene photographer climbed the stairs to the catwalk. Marty Gobel followed.

'This is going to take a while to sort out,' Morelli said to me. 'What would you like to do? I can have someone take you to your mother's or to my house.'

I didn't want to do either of those things. I was still rattled, and I wanted to be near Morelli.

'I'd rather stay here,' I said. 'I'll find a place to hang out until you're done, and we can go home together.'

❖

It was dark when we rolled into Morelli's house. We'd stopped for a take-out pizza, and we'd picked up the laundry. I was still in Morelli's sweats and he was still commando in his recycled jeans. I clipped Bob to the long leash in the backyard, and Morelli and I leaned against the kitchen counter and ate pizza.

'This has been a very strange day,' I said.

'Yeah, but it's over and Dickie is out of my house.' Morelli helped himself to another piece of pizza. 'Why on earth did you marry him?'

'In the beginning, before we were married, he was charming. He was probably fooling around, but I didn't see it. I was impressed with the law degree. I thought it showed intelligence and ambition. My parents loved him. They were ecstatic I wasn't marrying *you*.'

'Those were my wild oats-sowing days.'

'Dickie looked like a saint compared to you.'

Bob scratched at the door, and we let him in and gave him some Bob food and a couple pieces of pizza.

'What do you suppose will happen to Dickie?' I asked Morelli.

'There's the irony. Dickie could end up being a very rich guy. As far as I can tell, he's guilty of being stupid and devious, but I'm not sure he ever got around to committing a crime.'

'What about the drug sales?'

'Word at the station is that the books were kept clean. Everyone knows the firm's dirty, but no one's been able to prove anything. Now that Petiak, Smullen, and Gorvich are dead, Dickie might end up being the sole owner of the real estate and the forty million. At the very least, he'll keep his fourth. I guess that's the bad news. But the good news is Joyce blew Dickie off big-time at the salvage yard. At least Joyce won't see any of the money.'

'I hate to see Dickie get that money. It's so wrong.'

'Justice has a way of prevailing,' Morelli said. 'Dickie hasn't got the money yet.'

I fed Bob the last chunk of my pizza. 'I'm stuffed. I want to take a hot shower and get into some clean clothes.'

Morelli locked the back door and tucked the laundry basket under his arm. 'I have a better idea. Let's take a hot shower and get into *no* clothes.' He looked at the neatly folded clothes in the basket. 'Although I am looking forward to test-driving my underwear. Your mother ironed everything. My boxers have a crease.'

And somewhere under those boxers I had a single pair of little black panties embroidered with Ranger's name that had all the potential of the toaster bomb.

'You can test-drive them tomorrow,' I said to Morelli. 'I like the no clothes idea for tonight.'

# JANET EVANOVICH

# Seven Up

'Pithy, witty and fast-paced' *The Sunday Times*

In her most explosive adventure yet, bombshell bounty hunter Stephanie Plum is dropped into a smorgasbord of murder, kidnapping and extortion – a magnificent buffet of mud wrestling, motorcycles, fast cars, fast food and fast men.

Stephanie Plum thinks she's going after an easy FTA: a senior citizen charged with smuggling contraband cigarettes. But when she and Lula show up at his house, they get more than they bargained for – a corpse in the woodshed and an old man who's learned a lot of tricks during his years in the mob, and isn't afraid to use his gun. Then there's his involvement with Walter 'MoonMan' Dunphy and Dougie 'The Dealer' Kruper (Stephanie's former high-school classmates). They've been sucked into an operation which is much more than simple smuggling, one that holds risks far greater than anyone could have imagined. And when they disappear, Stephanie goes into high-octane search mode.

But Stephanie's mind is on other matters as well, because she has two proposals to consider: vice cop Joe Morelli is proposing marriage, and fellow bounty hunter Ranger is proposing a single perfect night . . .

All in all, a typical dilemma in the world of Plum.

'Hilarious reading, with a gorgeous fistful of believable and only occasionally murderous eccentrics' *Mail on Sunday*

'Hooray for Janet Evanovich, who continues to enliven the literary crime scene' *Sunday Telegraph*

'The funniest, sassiest crime writer going' *Good Book Guide*

978 0 7553 2906 6

headline
review

# JANET EVANOVICH

# Hard Eight

'Hooray for Janet, who continues to enliven the literary crime scene'
*Sunday Telegraph*

'That girl has some class' *New York Times*

The stakes get higher, the chases get faster, and the men get hotter.

Bounty hunter Stephanie Plum has a big problem. Seven-year-old
Annie Soder and her mother Evelyn have disappeared – and
estranged husband, Steven, shady owner of a seedy bar, is not at all
happy. Finding a missing child is an unusual assignment, but as a
favour to her parents' neighbour, Evelyn's grandmother, Stephanie
agrees to follow the trail – and finds a lot more than she bargained for.

The case is somehow linked to the very scary Eddie Abruzzi. Both
cop Joe Morelli, Stephanie's on-again, off-again fiancé, and Ranger,
her mentor and tormentor, have warned her about Abruzzi – but it's
Abruzzi's soulless eyes and mannerisms that frighten her most.
Stephanie needs Ranger's expertise, and she's willing to accept his
help to find Annie even though it might mean getting too involved
with him. Also with her are Lula (who's not going to miss the
action) and Albert, Evelyn's almost-qualified lawyer (and Laundro-
mat manager). The search turns out to be a race between
Stephanie's posse, the True Blue Bonds' agent – a Rangerette known
as Jeanne Ellen Burrows – and the Abruzzi crew. Not to mention the
killer rabbit on the loose!

Get ready for the ride of your life with Stephanie's funniest, most
riotous misadventure yet. The world of Plum has never been wilder.

Praise for Janet Evanovich:

'Pithy, witty and fast-paced' *The Sunday Times*

'Razor-sharp' *Sunday Express*

'A screwball comedy that is also a genuinely taut thriller' *Daily Mail*

'As smart and sassy as high-gloss wet paint' *Time Out*

978 0 7553 2907 4

headline
review

# JANET EVANOVICH

# To The Nines

*Stephanie Plum's got rent to pay, people shooting at her, and psychos wanting her dead every day of the week (much to the dismay of her mother, her family, the men in her life, the guy who slices meat at the deli . . . the list goes on). An ordinary person would cave under the pressure.*

*But hey, she's from Jersey.*

Stephanie Plum may not be the best bounty hunter in beautiful downtown Trenton, but she's pretty damn good at turning situations her way . . . and she always gets her man.

Her cousin Vinnie (who's also her boss) has posted bail on Samuel Singh, who mysteriously disappears just as his work visa is running out. And Stephanie is on the case to ensure the elusive Mr Singh doesn't make his disappearance more permanent. But what she uncovers is far more sinister than anyone imagines and leads to a group of killers who give a whole new meaning to the word 'hunter'. In a race against time that takes her from the Jersey Turnpike to the Vegas Strip, Stephanie Plum is on the chase of her life.

The unforgettable characters, non-stop action, high-stakes suspense, and sheer entertainment of TO THE NINES define Janet Evanovich as unique among today's writers.

Praise for Number One bestseller Janet Evanovich:

'That girl has some class' *New York Times*

'Pithy, witty and fast-paced' *The Sunday Times*

'Hilarious reading, with a gorgeous fistful of believable and only occasionally murderous eccentrics' *Mail on Sunday*

'Punchy, saucy and stacks of fun. I'm hooked' *Mirror*

978 0 7553 2908 3

**headline**
**review**

# JANET EVANOVICH
# Ten Big Ones

So your car has been blown up (again).

A local gang has put a contract out on you.

And there's a psycho on the loose.

When did going out for nachos get so complicated?

When you're Stephanie Plum, kick-ass bounty hunter.

Life is never easy for this super-sassy Jersey girl and when Stephanie witnesses a robbery on her lunch break things start to get a whole lot tougher. She must not only keep the local bail-jumpers in line but also find a ruthless killer, known as the Junkman, before he finds her. And then there's the mother of all challenges – staying faithful to her cute cop boyfriend, Joe Morelli, by resisting the charms of her seriously sexy mentor Ranger.

Sounds like a tall order but this is Stephanie Plum. And when your partner's an ex-hooker with a penchant for lurid Spandex and your grandma likes to pack heat, you take it all in your stride.

Praise for Janet Evanovich:

'Punchy, saucy and stacks of fun. I'm hooked' *Mirror*

'Crime writing at its funniest . . . classic black comedy' *The Big Issue*

'All the easy class and wit that you expect to find in the best American TV comedy, but too rarely find in modern fiction' *GQ*

'Pithy, witty and fast-paced' *The Sunday Times*

978 0 7553 0250 5

**headline**
review

Now you can buy any of these other bestselling books by **Janet Evanovich** from your bookshop or *direct from her publisher*.

*Stephanie Plum Novels*

| | |
|---|---|
| Seven Up | £7.99 |
| Hard Eight | £7.99 |
| To The Nines | £7.99 |
| Ten Big Ones | £7.99 |
| Eleven On Top | £7.99 |
| Twelve Sharp | £7.99 |

*written with Charlotte Hughes*

| | |
|---|---|
| Full House | £6.99 |
| Full Tilt | £6.99 |
| Full Speed | £7.99 |
| Full Blast | £7.99 |